BIRD, BATH & BEYOND

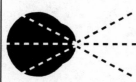

This Large Print Book carries the
Seal of Approval of N.A.V.H.

AN AGENT TO THE PAWS MYSTERY

BIRD, BATH & BEYOND

E. J. COPPERMAN

WHEELER PUBLISHING
A part of Gale, a Cengage Company

A Cengage Company

Farmington Hills, Mich • San Francisco • New York • Waterville, Maine
Meriden, Conn • Mason, Ohio • Chicago

Copyright © 2018 by E. J. Copperman.
An Agent to the Paws Mystery.
Wheeler Publishing, a part of Gale, a Cengage Company.

Wheeler Publishing Large Print Cozy Mystery.
The text of this Large Print edition is unabridged.
Other aspects of the book may vary from the original edition.
Set in 16 pt. Plantin.

LIBRARY OF CONGRESS CIP DATA ON FILE.
CATALOGUING IN PUBLICATION FOR THIS BOOK
IS AVAILABLE FROM THE LIBRARY OF CONGRESS

ISBN-13: 978-1-4328-5701-1 (softcover)

Published in 2019 by arrangement with Macmillan Publishing Group, LLC/St. Martin's Press

Printed in Mexico
1 2 3 4 5 6 7 23 22 21 20 19

For Jessica, Josh, and Eve,
because no one else is as good

CHAPTER ONE

"Polly want a cracker?"

The question was stupid for any number of reasons, and the bird to whom it was addressed stared at the interrogator blankly. First of all, his name was Barney, not Polly. Second, he probably didn't care if he had a cracker or not. Third, and most important, parrots don't actually converse with people; they just occasionally repeat what they've heard, assuming the bird has been taught diligently and patiently for a long time.

So no, Polly did not want a cracker. Or maybe she did, but she wasn't here.

We were standing, Barney and I, on the set of a television show called *Dead City,* a program whose conceit was that zombie detectives would investigate crimes against their own as well as against the living in a gritty post-apocalyptic New York, specifically in Tribeca. Because it costs too much to shoot in Midtown.

This particular set was a mock-up of the medical examiner's office, where intrepid Dr. Banacek, played by Dray Mattone, was examining the latest victim of the anti-zombie racists (are zombies a race?), who being a zombie herself could help by pointing out exactly where it hurt and describe her attackers if she'd seen them.

Barney was in a cage over the examination table, a symbol of the quirky Dr. Banacek's eccentricities. He was playing the role of Babs, the doctor's pet parrot, whose catchphrase "Can't kill a zombie!" had spawned bumper stickers, T-shirts, and countless Internet memes. Barney had stepped in when the original Babs (real name Cecilia) had passed away, luckily of natural causes and not a zombie attack.

The cameras were not currently rolling, so Barney was hanging back, biding his time. He's a professional, well thought of in parrot circles, and did not require any wing-holding or special treatment between takes. I was very proud of his behavior, particularly now that Harve Lembeck, the first assistant director, was pulling out the cliché manual on how to deal with a parrot, calling him "Polly" and requiring about his possible desire for a saltine.

"Barney's fine, Harve," I said. "But thanks

anyway."

Harve looked oddly at me, perhaps wondering who I was or why I might address him by name. It wasn't like we had met six or seven times in the past three hours — because we had — but I was just the bird's agent and therefore unlikely to help anybody get any work after this show wrapped, so I was invisible.

"What do you mean?" he asked. Nice of him not to inquire as to who I was, but you could see the confusion in his eyes.

"He doesn't need a cracker," I explained.

Harve looked at me like I was a dangerous crazy lady. "I don't have a cracker," he said, and walked behind the set, undoubtedly to tell someone else in the crew what a nut that woman with the bird must be.

It was true, I decided — I must be crazy. Not that many people choose to be a theatrical agent, and the vast majority of those who do go out of their way to attract and represent clients who are, at the very least, human. I go in the other direction.

All my clients are animals, and they are much easier to deal with than the people with whom they work.

I started Powell and Associates because I loved animals and I knew show business from literally the time I was born. My parents, Jay and Ellie Powell, raised me on-stage, mostly at the Nevele Grand Hotel in the Catskill Mountains. By the time the hotel closed, I had firmly resolved to get the hell out of show business as fast as I could and went to college with the ambition of attending veterinary school, which (once science classes were introduced) became law school. I got my law degree, passed the bar in the states of New Jersey and New York, and began representing animals with the help of a kind mentor who has since passed away.

So standing on a sound stage tending to a parrot wasn't just an acceptable way for me to pass a workday; it was the norm for me. I have represented dogs, cats, birds, the occasional horse, one chimpanzee who turned out to be a diva, and very briefly a boa constrictor. If you own an animal and think he or she might have some talent, I'm the person to talk to. Because as I said, not that many agents do what I do.

I checked on Barney, but he didn't need anything. His cage had fresh newspaper on the bottom and Heather Alizondo, the director of this week's *Dead City* episode, was back on the set, checking with Dray Mattone about the scene. The actress playing the victim, whose name I believed was

Mandy, walked over to lie down on the examination table, and makeup people surrounded her to make sure the slightly purple makeup on her face was not fading. They touched up her hair — on TV, you don't want your zombies to look unattractive, after all — and she lay down, arms at her side.

We were about to start another take. I looked at Barney's water supply, which was sufficient, and at Barney, who looked straight at me with his right eye. He did not wink to indicate he had this one with no problem. He was too much a pro.

"Quiet!" Harve, who had emerged from the bowels of the set, yelled. A bell rang. Dray walked over to the examination table as I scurried off the set and retreated to my little corner, where I could more easily be the least noticed person in the production.

"Okay," Heather said. "Let's try for a master on this one, please." She meant that if possible, the actors would work all the way through the scene without stopping, and that all three cameras in the room would be rolling while they were acting. If it went well, there would be time for pickup shots later.

"Settle down, people." That was the stage manager, Bonnie Prestoni. She had the most impressive clipboard of the bunch, one with *Dead City* emblazoned on its top and not just on a sticker like some of the others. It was *embossed.* That's power.

The second assistant director (originally known as a clapper loader, as if that helped), Tom Hedison, held up the slate, which showed the scene and take numbers along with other information, and made the clapping sound necessary before each take to help sync the sound and image in postproduction. A second or two went by.

"Action," Heather said.

Dray, playing Dr. Banacek, immediately stopped opening and closing his mouth to get it ready and set his face in "concerned" position. His hand went to his goateed chin. His eyes took on intensity. His lips narrowed.

Dr. Banacek was not pleased about something. I hadn't actually read the script other than for Barney's lines, which Heather had decided he should recite on cue even though they could easily have been added after shooting was completed. It was fairly well known that in Cecilia's last months, a human actor pretending to be a parrot had dubbed her lines in a recording studio.

Mandy lay flat on the table, convincingly purple and still enough that it was somewhat startling when she sat up, eyes wide. She had not flustered Dr. Banacek, though. Dray Mattone just folded his arms and looked at his latest patient.

"I was wondering how long that would take," he said with a slight air of impatience. Dr. Banacek had a wit so dry you could light a match on it.

"What is this place?" Mandy asked, looking around and not acknowledging the small army of technicians, the cameras, the director, and me. Actors are amazing: They can convince you of the illusion even when you can see the lights and the stagehands.

I used to work onstage. I know what I'm talking about because I was never that good an actress.

"You're in the morgue," Dray told her as she swung her legs — demurely, as this was network television — around and let them dangle off the examination table. "I'd think you'd be used to that sort of thing." You see what I mean about that dry wit.

"What happened?" Mandy said, not doubling over in laughter at his hilarious comment.

"That's what I was hoping you could tell me," Dr. Banacek told her. "They found you in a butcher shop on Thirty-Fourth Street. Now the Board of Health is worried the ground chuck is no good."

"I didn't go to a butcher shop," Mandy answered him.

I knew Barney's line was coming up, but he seemed relaxed. He wasn't distracted by the situation on set and he wasn't simply sitting back and watching; he was acting as Babs. He watched intently and moved his head back and forth, watching the actors as they delivered their lines.

"I didn't think so," Dray said, pointing at her lower legs, which I saw one camera move in to capture. Even so, there would be coverage later on to insert into the scene. Heather nodded, satisfied. "The scrapes on your legs indicate you were dragged there, maybe with a rope. Do you remember any of that?"

Mandy scratched at her arm and a piece of "skin" fell off. That was in the script, apparently, because nobody seemed the least bit worried about it. "I don't remember it. But I can tell you I have a very strong urge to eat your brain."

Dr. Banacek didn't even flinch; he was incredibly intrepid and unflappable. You couldn't flap this guy with a ten-foot fly-swatter. "I think it'll do you more good if it stays in my head for the time being," he said. "Someone shot you in the back of the skull. That wasn't an accident. Even in your condition, you can't want to be murdered again."

"Can't kill a zombie!" Barney piped up, and I saw the crew relax a little. It was his second day and he was impressing.

But Dr. Banacek didn't even acknowledge his beloved parrot's outburst. He looked at Mandy with the practiced intensity that had spawned a thousand fan clubs and millions of tweets. "Why don't you tell me what you *do* remember?" he asked Mandy, and then they both held the pose. They knew the scene was fading out.

"And . . . cut!" Heather shouted, and the crew all started moving around. "Let's print that one!" There was no applause because it was just another shot completed, and it was only eleven in the morning. There would be plenty more filmed today. Television series require long hours and lots of hard work.

I saw Heather walk to Dray first and talk to him quietly, no doubt giving notes on the previous scene. Because she'd said they would print it and did not announce another take of the same scene, the crew would now move on to the coverage — the same scene filmed separately with a camera on each actor, then shots like the leg insert they'd need of Mandy — so they were setting the scene to look the same when they started again. But the lighting crew would reset some of the key lights to highlight other areas of the set. It would be a while before the cameras rolled again.

I walked to the cage where Barney was leaning back on his perch, chilling after a job well done. "How you doin', Barney?" I asked.

"Can't kill a zombie!" he observed. He'd been carefully coached for the scene and he wasn't going to be denied.

"That's very true," I noted. I added a little seed to his feeding bowl and Barney pecked at it a bit.

"He does good work." I looked up and saw Dray Mattone, all six-foot-two of him, looking down at me with less of Dr. Banacek's intense obsession and more of the actor's own talk-show-ready charm. You never know if he's faking it, but it completely doesn't matter.

I nodded in Barney's direction. "He's a professional, just like you," I said. I extended a hand. "I'm Kay Powell. I'm Barney's agent."

Dray took my hand and held it a moment, which probably worked with a lot of women, because it was coming close to working on me. "Wow. I wish my agent showed that kind of interest. I can't get the woman on the phone."

"Well, you don't need your paper changed every few hours." Luckily that was not the case now.

"You'd be surprised." Dray grinned. I took for granted he wasn't flirting with me, since he had his pick of virtually any drop-dead gorgeous woman in Hollywood, so his interest in me was baffling. I considered that he might just be trying to be nice and then I remembered he was a successful television actor. So that wasn't it either.

"Well, I bet your agent is up for it," I said. That was sort of keeping things professional, wasn't it? "You're really successful and your agent is part of that."

He sighed theatrically — what other way is there, really? — and cocked his head. "You would think."

I checked on Barney again. He required remarkably little care at the moment, and not that much the rest of the time. This was not his usual cage, which was much larger, but the one that had been designed for Babs, especially to look good on camera. It had a couple of toys in it because Barney was not happy when not engaged, and he hopped down to chew on a piece of wood, his favorite thing to do besides act. He loved acting.

I decided not to follow up on Dray's comment about his agent. I wasn't looking for human clients, and even if I was, meddling with someone else's while the actor was still under contract would be considered highly unethical. I could have referred him to a few agents I knew who handled human clients, but he'd have to show me he was no longer with another agency, and besides, I really didn't care.

"Was it hard to bring in a new bird after the old Babs died?" he asked me. "She knew the routine around here pretty well. How did this one learn the lines so fast?"

I wished I could have let Barney fly around a little, but that probably would have caused some consternation on set and there wouldn't be time to round him up before another take was ready to go. "Well, I'm not the trainer, but you repeat it enough times and use a clicker and this kind of parrot will usually pick up the sounds pretty easily, they tell me." Actually, Patty Basilico, who owned and trained Barney, was the typical on-set handler for shooting days, but she was sick with the flu and had asked me to fill in. Patty is a sweetheart, and even though I'd known her only a few weeks, she was

18

probably my favorite of the humans who owned my clients, so I'd taken a crash course in parrot and headed for the set.

"It's amazing. I've known actors who couldn't learn their lines so fast." Dray started to stick his finger into the cage, then stopped and looked at me. "Okay?" he asked.

"Sure. Barney likes people."

Dray smiled, a lethal half-grin that had graced many a tabloid, and put his index finger into the cage to smooth back the parrot's feathers. "Hello, Babs," he said.

"He doesn't know he's Babs," I pointed out. "He's Barney."

The actor nodded, absorbing this. "Hi, Barney. What's shakin', dude?"

Barney responded as he usually did, by luxuriating in the touch and making a contented noise that sounded a lot like gargling. Then he looked Dray right in the eye and said, "What's shakin', dude?"

I thought Dray Mattone would fall over laughing. He loved that moment so dearly — or was pretending to, since it's always hard to tell when an actor is being genuine — that his eyes watered and he actually held his well-toned abs as he shook with laughter.

"Oh . . . that's great," he managed after a moment. "How did he do that after only one time?"

The fact of the matter was that I had no idea how many repetitions were necessary for Barney to learn a line, if that was simply an aberration or if he'd heard someone say, "What's shakin', dude?" fifteen thousand times before. But the key here was to appear like the woman who knows all about the parrot, so I nodded wisely and said, "He's a pro."

Dray got control of himself again. He put his hands up to his face, covering his nose and mouth, and shook his head slowly. "He sure is," he said, the sound muffled. He put down his hands. "So is Barney the only reason you're here?"

That was a weird question. Why else would I have shown up on the set of *Dead City* with a bird? But before I could answer, Heather walked over, quietly putting her hand on Dray's shoulder and steering him, once he noticed her, to a corner where she could give him more notes on the scene. I guessed. I couldn't hear a word she was saying.

Harve appeared from behind one of the flats that looked like a wall and glanced at Barney. "Can you get the bird back up on its perch?" he came close to demanding. "We're going to need it there for the take."

"Barney will be ready," I said. "Don't worry."

"Your ass if it's not," he grumbled as he walked away.

Of course Barney was ready for the next take and the one after that. In another two hours his scene — the only one he'd be required for today — was shot. I packed him up to take him to Sunnyside, Queens, where Patty lived.

But Heather stopped me on the way to the door. "Can Barney stay for another hour or so?" she asked. "I have just one tag for the end of the show and he wouldn't have to say anything, but I'd like him in the background where he could be seen."

I'd told Patty I would have Barney back by three, and it was a little before two o'clock now, but she understood this was a job and he'd have to stay as long as the work required. "How long do I have to leave him?" I asked. "I need to check in with my office." There was a schnauzer in need of grooming for an audition in a *Thin Man* revival, and I was supposed to oversee head shots for a Siamese cat named Martha.

"It'll just be an hour, hour and a half at most," Heather said. "I'll tell you what. You go ahead and do what you have to do. I'll take Barney into Dray's trailer until the moment he's needed and I'll do my best to get him out and ready to go home by the time you get back. How's that?"

I didn't want to leave a client alone, but Dray's trailer? Had to be luxurious. "Dray won't mind?" I asked.

"No. He's bonded with Barney, just told me he likes the bird."

"He'll need some stimulation," I said.

Heather looked at me strangely. "Stimulation? Dray?"

"No, Barney. He can't just sit. He needs his toys and he needs his pellets to eat. It'd be great if we could let him out to fly a bit, but I wouldn't recommend that in Dray's trailer."

She chuckled. "No, I don't think I can let Barney fly. But we'll see to it he has all his toys. Did you bring more than are in the cage?"

I gave her what I had for Barney and Heather agreed to have one of the production assistants — who probably had been longing to get into Dray's trailer under any pretense — stay with Barney for a while when I was gone. I was a little reluctant, but hadn't been planning to do much more than put the cage in my car and drive to Sunnyside, not far from where *Dead City* was filming in Astoria. Barney wouldn't have gotten much stimulation anyway.

It was a way of rationalizing the move, I know, but I'd budgeted the time and Heather was asking for more. This way Barney was in more of the show and I got to do my other work.

I took him into Dray's trailer, which was indeed quite lovely and spacious, and told the bird I'd be back soon, which I would. Then I called Patty, got her voice mail — she was probably asleep — and left a message. I put the cover over Barney's cage in the hope he would chill out, but could hear him knocking around and squawking, so I took it off again.

"I'll be right back, Barney," I told him. "Play with the wood." There was a small dowel in his cage he liked to pick up and move around. I raised it to show him and he put it in his beak. "That's a boy."

"Can't kill a zombie!" Barney responded.

I couldn't have agreed more. I left the trailer, walked to my car, and called Consuelo, my assistant back at the office in East Harlem.

"I'm glad you called," she said. "There's a movie shooting in the same studio you're at now and the production company called. They need a dog, and I thought Bruno . . ."

I'd adopted an enormous Tibetan mastiff

23

named Bruno because . . . it's a long story. "Bruno has quit the business," I said. "He's retired."

"Well, they want a big shaggy dog and we represent a few," Consuelo reminded me. "Do you have pictures on your phone?"

"Always."

She gave me the address of the production company, Giant Productions, on the lot. I drove (these places are huge) to the trailer that was serving as its headquarters while preproduction was going on.

It was a five-minute meeting. Unfortunately, it took place after forty minutes of waiting for the casting director, a harried-looking woman aptly named Harriet, to appear. I showed her some photos of my clients and she asked me to send her two, one of a bearded collie named Herbert and one of an English sheepdog called Bagels. She wanted to give the director a choice.

So by the time I got back to the *Dead City* set, I had again called Consuelo to arrange for bigger pictures to be sent to Giant Productions and for the Siamese to be beautified. The schnauzer's audition was pushed to the next day at the producer's request.

I'd gotten all that done in less than an hour, and still when I arrived back at the set, Dray Mattone had been shot dead in his trailer.

CHAPTER TWO

I'll say it: My first concern was for Barney.

Hey, that's my job, and besides, Barney was the one I knew best at the studio. We'd spent the most time together, we'd shared a few laughs (mostly me; Barney doesn't have a great sense of humor), I'd fed and cleaned up after him, and we'd bonded. Besides, I'd barely interacted with any of the humans in the place, since they all knew I was incapable of advancing their careers.

So when I got to the set again, after having been less than a mile away for less than an hour, and found the place besieged with police cars and ambulances, my first thought was that Barney had somehow gotten out and hurt himself.

Then I wondered why they'd send four police cruisers and a human ambulance for a yellow Amazon parrot, and my heart started beating a little less rapidly. Still, it wasn't a good sign that all this official activity was going on around the set where my client was working.

A uniformed cop at the door to the sound stage held up a hand as I approached practically at a run. "Nobody goes in," he said. "Crime scene."

Crime scene? Did someone *steal* Barney? "I'm a member of the company," I told him. "I'm the parrot's agent."

Maybe that wasn't the best tactic to use, but my mother always says that lying only gets you into more trouble and frequently brings up Richard Nixon when making that argument. The cop glared at me, perhaps wondering if he needed to call another ambulance, this one with padded walls. "The parrot's . . . what parrot?"

"You watch the show?" I asked. *"Dead City?"*

He shook his head. "Cop show? I never watch them. They're too unrealistic."

This wasn't going to be easy. "Well, this one has a medical examiner who has a parrot in his . . . office, and I'm the parrot's agent."

The cop, whose name tag indicated he was called Anderson, nodded as one does to a dangerous psychotic one is trying to contain without any loss of life. "You're the parrot's agent," he, well, parroted back to me.

"Don't you think I'd come up with a better story if I was lying?" I said. "My client is in there and I need to see if he's all right. Now, are you going to let me in?"

"No, I'm not. Orders are nobody goes in and nobody goes out. You're not going in and the parrot . . . the parrot? Isn't coming out. Okay, lady? So go —"

I never got to find out what he thought I should go do because a man in a relatively ordinary blue suit came through the doorway and looked at him. The guy was a little under six feet tall, I'd say, and was clean-shaven, not in the way actors are clean-shaven but always manage to have one day's growth of beard. No pocket square. Scuffed black shoes.

A detective in the New York City Police Department if ever I saw one. And I saw one.

"What's the problem, Officer?" he asked. He pulled a pack of chewing gum out of his pocket and put a stick in his mouth. Cops don't smoke anymore, I guess.

"This lady wants to go in and you told me not to let anybody do that, Sergeant. So I'm explaining to her that she can't."

The detective, who hadn't even offered the uniformed cop or me a stick of gum, looked me over, not in a sexist way. He was gathering information. "Why do you need to get inside, miss?" he said.

"I was explaining to Officer Anderson that I'm the agent for a . . . cast member on this show, and I need to see that my client is all right. What's been going on in there, Sergeant?"

"She's the parrot's agent," said Anderson, who I immediately decided did not deserve a stick of gum.

"The parrot?" the detective asked. "Babs?"

Everyone can be starstruck. Even New York cops. "That's right," I told him. "Babs is my client. Can I go in and see that he's okay?"

"Babs is a he?" The detective seemed either confused or disappointed.

"It's all showbiz magic," I told him. "Now, may I?"

The detective extended a hand. "Joe Bostwick," he said. "And you are?"

"I'm Kay Powell. What happened here, Sergeant Bostwick?"

He waved a hand. "Joe." He looked at Anderson, whose expression indicated he had become bored with us and wished he could go inside and solve a crime instead of stopping crazy ladies from walking in to confer with birds. "It's okay, Officer," he said. "I'll take responsibility for Ms. Powell."

29

Bostwick led me into the sound stage. "What happened?" I asked again. "Is everybody all right?"

He looked sad, in a professional way. "I'm afraid not," he answered. "One of the cast members has been shot."

I stopped walking. The stage — they're huge, mostly distinguished by the incredibly high ceilings, from which cinematographers hang lights and directors can suspend cameras when they want to get arty — was always a bustling place, but now it was not being used to film anything. All the crew members I recognized were present, but there were also police officers, EMS personnel, other detectives, and some studio cops walking around talking to the crew.

"Shot?" I echoed. "Who got shot?"

Bostwick, who clearly was a fan of *Dead City,* shook his head. "I'm afraid it was Dr. Banacek," he said.

"Dray Mattone? Dray got shot?" I looked around, and sure enough, Dray was not visible when virtually everyone else I'd seen here was still in attendance. "Is he okay?" That's a stupid question. How many people get shot and they're okay? The real question was one I didn't really want to ask, but Bostwick answered it anyway.

"He's dead," he told me.

I had a moment during which I honestly didn't know how to react. I hadn't really known Dray at all, but we had engaged in conversation that one time. He'd been at least professionally nice to me. For a star actor, he hadn't been a real beast, and that's what you get used to, so by comparison Dray had been a saint.

"Oh my" was the best I could do.

"I'm sorry for your loss," Bostwick said in the way cops do because that's what they've been told to say. It truly wasn't *my* loss at all, but even so, the words came across as sort of flat and studied. Bostwick could have used an acting coach.

Then it occurred to me where Barney had been stashed between scenes. "Where did it happen?" I asked with a little more edge in my voice than I'd intended.

"That's why I let you in here," Bostwick said. "I really was supposed to be keeping out anyone who wasn't physically on the premises to begin with."

"Sergeant, my client was in Dray Mattone's trailer. Are you saying that's where he was murdered?" How do you say something like that and not sound melodramatic?

"I'm afraid so," Bostwick answered. "And the parrot is the only known witness to the crime."

Well, that was crazy in so many different ways that I really had no response to draw upon. I just looked up at Bostwick and said nothing. For a while. A fairly long while. He didn't say much of anything either; I guess he was gauging my reaction, but that was mostly in the area of dumbfoundedness, accent on the *dumb.*

Finally I got myself together enough to say, "May I see my client?" And I would like it noted that I said "may I" and not "can I," despite operating under a considerable amount of stress.

He thought it over for a moment, apparently expecting me to say something else, perhaps "It was me! I did it! Arrest me, please!" and not getting what he'd wanted. Then he moved his lips back and forth, no doubt chewing on the piece of gum that I'd not been offered, and said, "I suppose so. Follow me."

It wasn't like I didn't know where Dray Mattone's trailer was situated on the lot. I'd brought Barney there and seen to it that he was settled, after all. But now I was most concerned to find out if I had to call Patty and tell her my client, whom I'd left alone for less than an hour, was spattered with blood or traumatized beyond repair.

Still, following Bostwick was the fastest

way to accomplish my goal. There were cops at every door and in every hallway, none of whom would have let me by without my official escort. We made it to the door to the outside, where the trailers were parked behind the sound stage so that civilians visiting the lot would not — heaven forbid — catch a glimpse of their idols at an unguarded moment, like walking to the set or berating an assistant.

We made it to the trailer with Bostwick flashing his badge seventy or eighty times and got inside after only one more checkpoint. I had tunnel vision for Barney's cage, but I had to sidestep a seeming army of forensic geniuses and regular cops to get there. I didn't really pay attention to anyone else until I reached Barney and held my breath getting there.

For all my worrying, my client seemed perfectly unharmed by whatever experience he'd had or seen. He was a little antsy, hopping from the floor of his cage to his perch and back again, but I'd seen him considerably more hysterical, flying around the cage and bumping unthinkingly into its bars. And that was just because his food was a few minutes late. Barney could be a diva too, if something *really* serious happened.

There was no evidence of any mayhem on

the cage itself either, so I guessed whatever happened — and this conjecture was also based on the positioning of the technicians and the videographer in the trailer and the marks made on the floor — had not been directly in front of Barney at all. He'd been in the area, certainly, but was not what you'd call an active participant.

"You okay, buddy?" I asked him. I fished in my pocket for his favorite treat, a pretzel goldfish, and extended it to the parrot, who took it and ate it immediately. "Everything okay in there?"

"Don't know much about history," Barney said. Patty had trained him to speak partially using old song recordings. It's not supposed to work because singing is different from talking, but Barney had been a remarkable pupil.

"I guess you don't," I told him. I gave him another pretzel even though I wasn't sup- posed to. "I was worried about you."

"He saw what happened." Bostwick was behind me now, so I turned to look at him when he spoke and saw the activity in the rest of the room.

It wasn't pretty. There were stains on the floor that I preferred to avoid with my eyes. There were some on the walls too, but they weren't quite as vivid or large. Bits of wood had sprayed from where the bullet had hit a windowsill. It was a large trailer, a double-wide befitting a star actor. Even so, it was crowded with people, all of whom worked for some law enforcement agency or other. And each one of them had a vital job that was being done earnestly and with intensity.

It was like being on the set of *Dead City.* Only with real blood. And, I trusted, no zombies.

"What did happen?" I asked.

"I told you. Somebody came in here and shot Dray Mattone, Dr. Banacek himself. In the head. Twice. Which was probably once too much."

"Twice too much, if you asked Dray," I said absently.

"I don't think he got the opportunity to have an opinion. He was shot in the back of the head and was dead before he hit the floor." Bostwick wasn't so much telling me as he was sizing up the room and the evidence being gathered to process it himself. Colored strings were being used to approximate shot trajectories. One uniformed cop — not Anderson by any means — was standing in traced footprints as directed by a plainclothes detective — not Bostwick — and holding his arms in front of him as if shooting a pistol.

"Can I get Barney out of here?" I asked the sergeant. I'm not sure if I was asking for my client or for me, because I sure as heck wanted out of the trailer as fast as possible.

"In a minute," Bostwick said. Then he leaned over, being careful to make sure none of the other cops could hear what he was saying, and very quietly asked, "Can you get the bird to talk?"

Was that code? "Huh?" I said. It was the best I could do on short notice.

"Can you get him to say something?" Bostwick repeated, still sotto voce but a little more urgently. "He saw what happened. Maybe he can help."

I had thought Bostwick to be a fairly intelligent, if off-the-rack, detective, but this was a little nuts even in my business. "You do realize he doesn't converse," I said. "He repeats phrases he hears."

"But he heard what was being said before the murder," Bostwick said, still practically hissing but now with an expression that indicated I just wasn't bright enough to get what he was telling me. "If you can get him to repeat it, we might have a really strong indicator."

Now, don't get me wrong: I wanted to help in the investigation if I could. But it was clear that Bostwick had a grand total of no experience with parrots. Mine had been somewhat limited, but I knew better than that.

"You have to train him," I explained. "Repeat the phrase over and over. Use a clicker to indicate to the bird when he's said the right thing and when he hasn't. It can take hours. It can take days. He can't simply hear something once and immediately integrate it into his vocabulary. Think of it as teaching a one-year-old how to speak."

Bostwick looked at me, then at Barney, then back at me. "I guess it was a stupid idea," he said.

"Not really." I was trying to be cooperative and, let's face it, kind. It *had* been a stupid idea. Well, not stupid, exactly. "It was just a question of your not having much experience dealing with parrots. It's understandable."

"Sorry," he said, looking away. He was embarrassed.

And then Barney looked over at me and said, "Put down the gun!"

CHAPTER THREE

I went through another hour and a half of questioning from Bostwick, a second detective named Baker (who never actually said anything), and a forensics expert whose name I didn't get but who seemed to be a fan of *Dead City* and just wanted to know backstage gossip, of which I had none. I'd been on the set for exactly one day, and it had turned out to be a doozy.

The bottom line was that I could not induce Barney to say anything more than the lines he'd been taught for the show, the few phrases I knew Patty had given him, and his new personal favorite, which had already gotten us detention after school. He seemed especially enamored of yelling, "Put down the gun!" every minute or so. This had not helped my cause, which was getting home in time to meet my parents for dinner.

After finally convincing the gathered cadre

of police masterminds that I could not simply get Barney to name the killer and wrap up their investigation, I was told by Bostwick that he'd be in touch the next day and asked to "see if you can convince him to say more by then." Explaining — again — that Barney would only repeat things he'd been painstakingly taught to say and not simply a random phrase he'd heard once seemed futile. I told the sergeant I'd talk to him the next day, picked up Barney's cage, tried again not to notice the signs of violence in the trailer, and left.

My first thought when I got into my car, Barney's cage safely strapped into the back seat, was to call Patty, and this time she actually answered the phone. The Bluetooth device hanging from my sun visor made her sound like someone whose upper respiratory system was waging war on her vocal cords. Which it was.

"How'd the day go?" she croaked.

I didn't want to add to her discomfort, but she'd no doubt be seeing news reports online and on television any minute now. Dray's murder had brought out the reporters in packs. News vans were everywhere when I left the sound stage, and intrepid journalists (we'll call them that rather than use the more colorful language I'm trying to avoid) had surrounded Barney and me as we left, shouting questions about our "relationship" to Dray, which had consisted of one conversation (me) and the repetition of a catchphrase on cue (Barney).

It was, in fact, surprising that Patty hadn't heard about Dray's murder yet, but her flu might have been keeping her away from the normal news sources. I knew she was speaking on a landline, not a cell phone, because the reception was much clearer, and besides, I had dialed her home number.

So when I told her what had happened, the stunned silence that followed was not a surprise. I wasn't sure if Patty had known Dray any better than I had — Barney had been working on *Dead City* for only a little over a week and had spent just one day on the set before I'd been drafted into service — but the murder of even a casual acquaintance is enough to stop a person in her tracks.

"Who killed him?" she asked finally. "Who do the cops suspect?"

"I have no idea," I told her honestly. "They tend to keep me out of their more secure conversations."

"What do you think?"

"Again, no clue. I didn't get to know anybody there, so I have no idea what their interactions are like. Dray seemed like a nice enough guy for a big-deal actor. I don't know why somebody would want to shoot him."

"What about Barney?" Patty asked. "Does he seem shook up?"

I looked in my rearview mirror and caught a glimpse of the parrot jumping up onto his perch, a piece of soft wood in his beak, shredding it as he would on any normal occasion. "It doesn't seem to have bothered him much," I reported. "But I had to stay late after interrogation because he's picked up a new phrase that he dropped at exactly the wrong time."

Patty's rasp sounded a little more interested. "What phrase?" she asked.

"Put down the gun!" Barney volunteered. He was being especially helpful today.

There was a moment of silence. I felt it was in honor of Dray Mattone.

"Where'd he get that one?" Patty said.

"Frankly, I thought you'd taught it to him. It's not in the script for *Dead City;* I checked."

"Nope, not me," Patty answered. "Maybe someone on the set?"

I was not convinced. "Maybe, but you know how long it takes to teach a bird new vocabulary. He wasn't alone long enough."

There was a pause. "Barney was alone?" Patty asked. "Where were you?"

Oops.

"He had to rest for a while, Patty. I went out and made a few phone calls and came back. Barney's fine, believe me." All of which was true.

"When did Dray get killed?" she said.

Time to own up, Kay. "When I was out. But believe me, he's not the least bit —"

"Oh, thank goodness," Patty said. "If you'd been there watching him, something might have happened to you."

That hadn't occurred to me. "You're the best, Patty. Other owners would not be that concerned with the agent's welfare."

"Well, you must be shocked after Dray got shot. Now that guy could get me out of bed. Or into it!"

Okay, that was weird. Best not to go too far into it with Patty, who was sick and after all making strange comments about a guy she hadn't known at all either. It's funny how we feel like we are familiar with the people who show up on our TV screens.

"Did you see anybody who was acting like they were mad at him?" Patty asked.

"Mad? I barely saw anybody except Heather talk to him. It was like the crew was afraid to get into his sight line. When he *wasn't* acting." If you're a crew member or anyone except another actor in the same scene, you don't want to stand right in an actor's view when he's working; it distracts some and mightily enrages others. When I was onstage, I so completely didn't care that I wonder if I was ever really an actress at all. I was a performer, sure, but an actress? Probably not.

"Well, there sure was someone there who didn't like the guy," Patty wheezed. Then she started coughing again. I told her I didn't want to tax her voice, and Barney made a comment about moving the key light to the left.

There was a fairly long pause during which Patty's coughing filled my sun visor and threatened to shatter my windshield. "I can hear you're feeling a ton better," I said when she finally managed to get control of her lungs back.

"Please," she croaked. "Maybe I'm not the best. I have to ask you something."

I knew what it was going to be and I felt the cage close around me. "What's up?" I asked in the sunniest tone I could manage.

"Can you take Barney home tonight? I'm not sure I could get out of bed enough times to take care of him. I promise it'll just be the one night, okay?"

I had already made the course adjustment and was heading for the Triborough Bridge (officially named the Robert F. Kennedy Bridge, but everybody in the tri-state area knows better). "I'll take him for tonight, Patty. You just get better, all right?"

"I'm already better. You should have heard me yesterday." She blew her nose. I made a mental note never to use the phone in Patty's house.

"I *did* hear you yesterday. It's when you asked me to take Barney to the set today."

"See? My mind is going."

"I'll take Barney, Patty. Feel better." We said our goodbyes and I immediately called Consuelo to tell her I was taking Barney back to my house and not visiting the office again today.

"I took care of the cat," she reported. "I think she's going to be a star."

Consuelo would like to be an agent instead of (or perhaps in addition to — the woman's energy knows no bounds) an office manager, and I'm all for it. So she was angling for me to let her handle a client. "I've told you a hundred times," I said. "You find a cat client you want to represent, go for it."

"I want to represent Celia," she said.

That was a problem because Celia the cat was already a client of mine and you don't just palm someone off to another agent because she wants to make a star. "You know I can't do that," I told Consuelo. "Find yourself a cat we don't already represent."

"Celia has a sister," she noted. "Roberta."

Roberta the cat? "Can you get Doris to change her name? Fluffy or something?" It was hard to picture head shots with a cat under which the name Roberta would be printed.

"So I can approach them?" Consuelo asked.

I wasn't crazy about the idea because we'd be splitting up two clients from the same owner, but I did want to help Consuelo start repping some talent and she appeared to have an eye for it. "What's Roberta like?" I asked.

"She's a beautiful black-and-white and she has tons of personality," my office manager said, already sounding more like a talent agent than I do. "I think she could —"

"Be a star, right?"

"Is it all right, Kay?"

I needed a moment. "I'll tell you what. You've already had contact with the owner and with the cat, whom I've never seen. So let me call Doris and ask her what she thinks about the idea. If she doesn't seem put off that we're splitting up the two cats, Roberta will be all yours."

"Oh, thank you!" If it was anybody except Consuelo I would have been worried about the tone, because it almost sounded like she hadn't heard the qualifiers in that sentence. But Consuelo is among the most practical, down-to-earth people I've ever met, which is why I was already dreading the idea of her not organizing my day as much as she was building a cat empire.

"Don't do *anything* until I talk to Doris and you hear from me," I said.

"Put down the gun!" Barney shouted.

"What was that? A gun?" Consuelo had no idea where I was or what I was doing.

"It's just Barney. You heard about Dray Mattone, right?"

Consuelo switched from exultant almost-an-agent to level-headed office manager in a nanosecond. "Yeah. We've already gotten four phone calls from TV reporters. I didn't tell them anything, but I figured you'd want them to go away."

"Yeah. They say there's no such thing as bad publicity, but I really don't want Barney to be the bird who saw Dray Mattone get killed."

"They know it's you, though," Consuelo

warned. "If they can find your office, they can find your house. Are your parents there yet?"

In the wake of Dray's shooting I'd completely forgotten that my parents, fresh off a gig on a Greek cruise ship, were flying into Newark International Airport today and were coming back to stay with me until their next booking in an Atlantic City casino three weeks from now. My father doesn't like layovers, but my mother wants what she calls "quality time" with her daughter, who is rather inescapably me.

"I forgot, but their flight was getting in at three. If the traffic isn't horrific, I might beat them back to the house."

"I had Peapod leave some groceries for you by the door, nothing perishable and nothing your dogs will be trying to scratch their way out for." Consuelo was the most efficient woman on the planet.

"Marry me," I said.

"Sorry, you're not my type. Dray Mattone was closer to my type."

I'd barely had time to think about poor Dray. I hadn't known him well. In fact I hadn't known him at all, but the one time we spoke he'd seemed like a nice guy. Why would somebody want to kill him? (Now that I think of it, why would someone want to kill *anybody*?)

"Yeah, he was very nice-looking," I said.

"If it makes you feel better," Consuelo said, "he was married, but they didn't have any kids."

It didn't make me feel better.

When I pulled up to my house in Scarborough, New Jersey, a full hour after having left the studios in Astoria, I felt like I'd spent the day being pummeled by Rocky Balboa in his prime. There was no car in the driveway, but that didn't mean much. I'd find out who was inhabiting my home once I started hauling Barney and his cage out of my back seat.

Sure enough, as soon as it was evident that I was carrying something bulkier than my purse and my iPad (which was actually in my purse), the door to the house flew open and I was descended upon by a horde of screaming Visigoths.

Or so it seemed.

My father, first out the door and already reaching for the now-covered cage (you cover the cage when transporting the bird for ease and safety), looked tanner and a little heavier than the last time I'd seen him two months earlier. The combination of night work, the Greek islands, sun, and cruise ship food certainly had affected him.

He was smiling broadly and looked happier than I'd seen him in some time.

My mother would have been next to the car, but she was beaten out the door by a wide margin. Eydie, my greyhound mix and queen of the house (according to her), bounded out as if I were a mechanical rabbit that had been put on a rail for her to chase. She was followed by Steve the dachshund and Bruno the ridiculously large and hairy mastiff, who had become great friends and were the strangest-looking double act you ever wanted to see. Steve is long and low to the ground. Bruno, whom I'd adopted after his previous owner had been slated for some governmental make-work, was roughly the size of a Volkswagen, friendly and rumbly where Steve was timid and stealthy.

All the dogs got to Barney and me before Dad, which made a transfer of the cage — something I didn't really need to do anyway — more difficult, so I just held on to it and handed my father my purse, which he didn't want. It was a gesture; he could help me if he liked, but I was still the one holding the parrot. As gestures go, it wasn't really a major one.

"Who's your friend?" he asked as the dogs barked and ran around me while I made my way to the front door, carrying Barney.

"A new client," I said. "He's had a rough day."

"Was he the one working on that TV set when the actor was shot?" My mother pretends to be a 1950s housewife and is in fact a savvy businesswoman, a gifted performer, and an Internet hound. She knows the news before it happens. Well, it seems that way.

We made it into the house as I admitted that yes, Barney and I (Mom hadn't actually understood that I was on the set) had been around on the day Dray Mattone was shot. Mom retro-actively worried about me and Dad looked concerned. I put Barney down on the coffee table in the living room, shaking my right hand just a bit to get the blood circulating again. That cage was not light.

Barney squawked and fussed. The dogs barked as Eydie circled the coffee table with a wary eye on this strange object. Steve actually hid under the coffee table and Bruno, being Bruno, went into the kitchen and plopped down on his dog bed because he didn't want to be a bother.

I gave Mom and Dad the *Reader's Digest* version of my day because I wanted to hear about their gig on the cruise ship, but Dad quickly dismissed any discussion about them because he said the situation with Barney was more important.

"So the bird was there when the actor got shot?" he asked. "That explains the phone calls."

I didn't like the sound of that. My cell phone had been buzzing, but when I don't recognize the number, I ignore the call. Let a prospective client talk to Consuelo at the office. They wouldn't have my personal number anyway.

"What phone calls?" I asked.

"Seven calls so far," Mom told me. "CNN, Fox News, the major networks, and News 12 New Jersey. They all want to know if you can tell them about Dray Mattone's murder."

"I can't because I wasn't there," I said.

"Yeah, but the bird was there," Dad noted. "They'll think he can talk."

"He *can* talk," I noted. "He just can't have a conversation. They'll think he can say who killed Dray, and he can't."

My mother looked out the front window. "I'm surprised they're not here already."

"Didn't you tell them I wasn't here and the bird couldn't help?" I said. I looked out the window too, because hey, maybe Mom wasn't seeing the *whole* front yard.

"We told them you weren't here," she answered. "We didn't know anything about the bird. We've been on a ship for two months." The way she said that last sentence led me to believe she hadn't absolutely loved the experience.

(And by the way, there were no paparazzi in my front yard looking for a yellow Amazon parrot.)

"What was the matter with the ship?" I asked.

"Nothing," Dad jumped in. "They treated us very well. We were out in the sun, we had great food, and the guests were very nice."

I looked at Mom. "But?"

Uncharacteristically she looked away. It's not like Mom to avoid a subject, but she hates disagreeing with my father, especially when it's about their careers. "I just get tired," she said. And she did not elaborate, but I saw Dad's face darken just a little bit. He looked away too.

This wasn't good.

There was no point in my pursuing it right now. They'd deny there was any problem and change the subject and I would find out exactly nothing. But I would revisit this topic, and soon.

It didn't matter anyway because my phone

rang and the caller was identified as NYPD. That's never comforting.

Turned out the caller was Bostwick, who was still on the Astoria lot questioning crew members. "Has the parrot said anything else?" he asked.

"Yeah, he mentioned something about bewaring the ides of March. Seriously, Sergeant, you need to get past this idea that Barney is going to tell you anything useful. He's a bird. He just repeats back phrases that are drummed into his head over and over again. He's not a brilliant conversationalist." While I spoke, I removed the cover from Barney's cage while calculating exactly what the risk of letting him out to roam around for a while might be. I decided against it for the time being. I was putting off a lot of things just at this moment.

"A lot of people want you dead, Dray," Barney said.

"What was that?" Bostwick asked.

Mom and Dad looked at each other in surprise. Whatever friction there had been in the room a minute ago was gone now.

"That was just Barney," I said breezily to the detective. "He said, 'People want bread, okay.' It was an exercise that he learned when he was just beginning training." It didn't make sense that Barney was coming up with these lines he could have heard only once. I needed time to think.

My father walked over to me and said, "Always tell the truth to the police, Kay." My father should have worked in civics films for third-graders. He could have written the dialogue himself.

"Who's that?" Bostwick demanded.

"That's my father," I answered. No sense elaborating if I didn't have to.

"What did he say about telling me the truth?"

Okay, so I had to. "He was saying I hadn't given you the correct phrase Barney just said. He actually said, 'A lot of people want you dead, Dray.' "

"And you didn't think that was something I should know?" Bostwick asked.

"Look, Sergeant. You have to understand. Barney just isn't capable of using a phrase he's heard only once. I don't know how he's coming up with these things and I don't want you jumping to conclusions based on what a bird says. There has to be an explanation other than Barney's hearing these words at the time of the shooting."

I sat down on the coffee table next to the cage. Barney really looked like he wanted to get out and spread his wings, but I was worried that one of the dogs (okay, Eydie) might misinterpret such a move as either threatening or delicious and take inappropriate action. I reached into my purse for the bag of parrot toys Patty had given me to find something that might occupy his attention.

So you can imagine my surprise when I felt something heavy and metal touch my fingers. Barney likes a nice chew, but he doesn't want to break his beak. Besides, this object was much too large. Much.

It was a gun.

I immediately withdrew my fingers. Like, my hand sped away from the crime scene at ninety miles an hour. My mother looked predictably alarmed and my father actually said, "Wha—"

"Sergeant Bostwick," I said, "can a forensic investigator tell the difference between a fingerprint that's a few hours old and a very fresh one?"

There was a pause on the other end of the conversation. "I'm not sure, but I'm guessing they can't make a distinction that small," he said. Then his voice took on a higher level of urgency. *"Why?"*

"Because I think there's a really good chance I just found the murder weapon in my purse."

My mother sat down.

CHAPTER FOUR

Detective Sergeant Joe Bostwick arrived at my home two hours later. What with rush-hour traffic, it was a minor miracle he made it there before midnight.

In the time we were ostensibly waiting for his arrival, I told my parents not to touch anything in my purse or Patty's bag — as if they needed the instruction — and took the dogs for a walk, an act that seems somewhat comical when you see it. These three dogs are a study in contrasts, and that does not end with their ability to yank on a leash. Steve just plods along, sniffing every blade of grass for information. He'd make a great forensic scientist. Bruno, big goofy pal that he is, trots at an excited pace, sure that everyone he meets will be his best friend forever. Eydie, the greyhound mix, is not given to running as you might think. She's suspicious and imperious, holding her head high and expecting nothing less than the admiration and obedience of all who cross her path.

We did our usual tour of Scarborough, heading out to West Roosevelt Avenue (the main drag) and nodding at people. I put my earbuds in but didn't turn on my phone's music app; it was more to stop idle chatter than to listen to something. I needed to think.

I'd been involved in a police investigation regarding a client — Bruno, actually — before, and it had not been tons of fun for me. In that case, of course, the client's owner had been murdered, which made it somewhat more personal, and I'd been accused of a great many things I had not done. So the whole dealing-with-cops prospect was an activity I preferred to avoid when I could.

Except now I couldn't. Barney had been present when Dray had been shot and killed. That didn't mean much to the investigation, I believed, since he was going to have roughly as much understanding about and knowledge of the incident as the overstuffed armchair Dray had kept in his trailer in which to read future scripts and think deep thoughts. In fact, given what had been splashed all over that chair, it would probably yield more information to Bostwick than Barney could.

But I had been unable so far to convince the sergeant of that fact. This was partially because people want to believe that parrots are actually conversing with them and partially because Barney insisted on shouting out some new gun-related adage every time I was insisting he could offer no help. Barney was a smart bird, but he was also becoming something of a pest.

I wasn't thinking about my route very much because I had not avoided the turn off West Roosevelt that would have kept me clear of Cool Beans, the local coffeehouse, where Sam Gibson was leaning on the doorframe. It's not that I had wanted to stay away from Sam, exactly, but I needed to think through my current situation and Sam wasn't going to help me do that.

I've known Sam since I moved to Scarborough and he had even asked me out once, but I'd declined. Lately I'd been rethinking that decision, but oddly, once I showed a flicker of interest, Sam had assiduously avoided asking me out again. It was the kind of thing that made a girl wonder. At least it made me wonder. And this wasn't the time to wonder about such things.

"What are you thinking about?" Sam

asked as I nodded to him, pretending to be listening to a great audiobook. Really, how could one interrupt me when I was enriching my mind so obviously? "Something's wrong, isn't it?"

I actually took one of the earbuds out to pretend I could hear him now. Which I could, because I had always been able to hear him. So maybe *pretend* wasn't the correct word. But you know what I mean, don't you?

"What makes you think that?" I said.

"The look on your face," Sam answered. He knelt down to pet Steve, since he could easily get to both Bruno and Eydie from a standing position. Sam thinks that Steve is the overlooked baby brother in the family, although Eydie would protect him savagely and Bruno would defer to him in all cases because Bruno defers to everybody about everything. Bruno is a pushover. "Also the sound of your voice, the fact that you're walking around with earbuds in while you're not listening to anything, and the news report about a murder I saw ten minutes ago that had a non-interview with you carrying a birdcage." One of the news crews that had gotten to me while I left the set with Barney.

"Oh, those things," I said.

"Yeah. You want to talk about it?"

"No."

Sam absorbed that and nodded. "Okay. Want an iced coffee?" He gestured inside his store.

That was not an opening. Sam will make me an iced coffee anytime. It's his job.

I smiled and it was genuine. "Not today, okay? I've got to think this thing through. I just happened to be there, not even when it happened, but my client was, and the cops are convinced he knows something."

"Your client's a bird?" Sam asked.

"Barney," I answered. "He's a yellow Amazon parrot."

"Does that mean you can get him free with two-day shipping?" Sam thinks he's funnier than he actually is.

"See, I'm not even concentrating enough to double over with laughter at that one," I told him. "I'm going to walk the dogs back to the house and meet with the police, and I imagine that'll be it. They'll find out who killed Dray, and I'll get back to representing Barney and other nonhumans like him."

"Sounds like you've thought it through pretty well," Sam noted.

Actually, that was true. "You're right. You made me see it more clearly." I watched as Sam stood up from his Steve-petting and made sure the other two dogs got some attention as well.

"I have that effect on women," Sam said. "I make them think."

"I imagine it's served you well."

"It's a blessing and a curse."

The four of us said our goodbyes to Sam and walked back to the house.

"You found the gun in your purse?"

Bostwick was drinking a lemonade (from the carton) my mother had gotten for him and sitting on my sofa opposite Mom and Dad, who wouldn't miss such a dramatic scene for the world. They'd say they were there to protect me. I have an active license to practice law in the states of New Jersey and New York, and they still think I need my parents to watch over me when a policeman comes to the house to ask questions.

"Sort of. I had a bag with all of Barney's equipment in it, and when I took everything out of the car, I put the bag in my purse to make it all easier to carry. I had the cage with me, after all, and that's not light. So the bag with the bird stuff was in my purse, and the gun was in the bag, which was in my purse. So if you want to say the gun was in my purse . . ."

Bostwick looked at me a little wearily.

"The gun *was* in your purse," he said.

"If that's the way you want to look at it."

Bruno, always the friendliest of the dogs, walked over and pushed his head under Bostwick's hand. Since Bostwick was sitting down and Bruno is the size of a Quonset hut, Bruno had to duck down to achieve his goal, but he got a few pats on the head and that was enough. It was evident, though, that the sergeant was a little nervous around dogs, especially Eydie, who just lay on the floor and watched him without blinking. Eydie is great at mind games.

"That's how it is," Bostwick said. "Now what you're telling me is that it was in your purse and you didn't know it. How could you not feel the weight when you picked it up? That is not a feather in there." The pistol, which Mom and Dad had definitely not touched, was now safely ensconced in an evidence bag and had been taken by a uniformed officer to Bostwick's car so it could be fingerprinted and whatever else it is they do back at the lab with the quirky medical examiner, who no doubt had a parrot in the morgue, because didn't I see that somewhere on TV?

"I was carrying a birdcage with an actual bird in it, and it wasn't my bag of bird toys, so how heavy or light it should normally be isn't something I'd just know off the top of my head," I explained.

Mom, of all people, looked thoughtful and pointed a finger to the ceiling. "Of course you had been carrying the bag all day, sweetie. So if all of a sudden there was a gun in it, you'd think it would be noticeable." My *mother*, ladies and gentlemen.

Bostwick held out his hands. "Yeah," he said, "what about that?"

"I can't explain everything. All I can tell you is I had no idea there was a gun in the bag." I petted Bruno and then Eydie aggressively to show Bostwick I wasn't afraid when even he might be. "Otherwise, why would I have told you that on the phone? If I'd shot Dray — and everybody you talk to on the set will tell you I was nowhere near the place when that happened — and then stashed the gun in Barney's kit, would I have been stupid enough to tell the detective investigating the murder?" It seemed like a pretty valid point to me.

"You could be covering for someone." Refreshingly, it was Bostwick and not my mother making the case.

"The question remains: Why tell you? Why not throw the gun into the Hudson River on the way home or have one of the dogs bury it in the backyard?" I couldn't have gotten the dogs to bury a gun in the back-yard if I'd promised to take them to Kibble-land for a year. If there was a Kibbleland. What do dogs know?

"I don't have the answers yet." Bostwick stood up as Barney fluttered his feathers in the cage. Letting him out would be a neces-sary risk I'd take later; he was getting bored and cranky and wouldn't be able to act tomorrow.

Wait. Was there going to be filming tomor-row? I hadn't heard from any of the produc-ers, but surely one of their stars being dead would be a crimp in the — pardon the expression — shooting schedule, wouldn't it?

"What does that mean?" I asked Bostwick.

"It means I'm not ruling anything out, but you have a point," he said. "It doesn't make sense that you'd tell me you had the gun if you didn't want me to connect you to it."

"She could just be clever," my father piped up. My parents are so anxious to be of help that they sometimes don't care who they're helping. It comes from decades of trying to please audiences.

I decided not to write them out of my will just yet, since that probably wasn't the best way to get back at them. Instead, I looked at Bostwick. "How about this, Sergeant? I left Barney's bag in Dray's trailer when I put him there because there was no sense in my having it if something was needed. So for that forty minutes, anybody — especially the person who shot Dray Mattone — could have put the weapon in Barney's supply kit. Yes, you'll find my fingerprints on the gun because I touched it when we were on the phone. But I'll bet that's the only set of my prints you'll find. Anybody else's on that gun could be your murderer." So maybe I have a flash of the melodramatic in my genes. I admit it. I just don't embrace it.

"I seriously doubt we'll find prints that aren't yours on the gun," Bostwick said, heading for the door, which was a remarkably short walk. Eydie stood up and followed him, perhaps as a warning and perhaps just to see what he smelled like close up. Bostwick was aware of her but tried very hard not to look down. "I don't think the killer is that stupid."

"Swell." I reached for my phone and texted Madolyn Fenwick, the producer of *Dead City* I'd been communicating with directly. She'd know about the coming schedule and what effect Dray's death would have on production.

Bostwick watched me tap on my touch

screen furiously for a moment. "Who are you texting?" he asked.

"It's business. It's not about Dray." It was sort of about Dray, but not in the way that the detective would have wanted.

"Pass me the birdseed!" Barney shouted from his cage. He loved that one because people tended to laugh when he said it. This time Mom and Dad chuckled, but Bostwick and I were way too intense for such a frivolity.

My phone buzzed. *Meeting tomorrow. Group text later.* Madolyn was efficient if not verbose. Some people text like they're writing long letters; Madolyn texts like she's paying by the word.

Bostwick watched my face for signs of interest but found none and did not ask any questions. He said his farewells to my parents, nodded at me, and left.

The dogs followed him and watched through the storm door as Bostwick got into his unmarked Chevrolet Impala and drove away. Bruno and Steve watched with wagging tails, but Eydie was far too hip for such a vulgar display. She sat down and scratched herself in any number of areas.

I breathed out, possibly for the first time in an hour. I closed the door, which disappointed the two male dogs, and turned toward my parents. "Remind me not to appoint you guys to my defense team, okay?" I said.

"What?" my father asked, apparently in earnest.

"You and Mom kept coming up with ways that I could still have killed Dray whenever I was explaining how I couldn't," I told him.

"We were just trying to help," Mom said.

I considered asking exactly who they were trying to help, but there was no point. They'd just gotten in from a long trip and a long gig, and they were, after all, my parents. It was starting to get dark, so I ordered a pizza and we were around the table (dogs circling like sharks for dropped pepperoni) in less than an hour.

When I had decided to "break up the act," as my father still puts it, and go to college, I had worried that Mom and Dad would suffer professionally. This was not because I thought I was such a gifted entertainer, believe me. On a good day I was adequate. But the idea that a three-person act was going back to a double act after all the years I'd been involved was risky.

They had not missed a beat. They'd sniffed a bit about my disloyalty (that was mostly Dad; I think Mom was secretly proud I wanted to be a vet, even if it hadn't turned out that way), but Dad had gone back to his yellow legal pad and started pounding out a new act. Frankly I don't think it was all that difficult, as I'd been an addition to the scenes rather than the focus. He took me out and there was still plenty for the two of them to do. They got laughs and sang songs. They've been booked fairly solidly ever since.

But the vibe I was getting from Mom, mostly, after this last cruise was not something I'd seen before. My mother has shown signs of a certain weariness with the traveling life, but anytime I'd seen them perform (all on land; I don't go on the cruises), she'd come alive when she hit the stage and seemed exhilarated after the show was over, just like always. Not this time.

"The ship was fine," she insisted. "And the audiences were fine too. I'm just tired, that's all."

"I don't think so," I said. "You've come back to my house after every gig for the last five years and I've never seen you look so relieved to be here."

"It got a little bit rough," Dad admitted, not looking up from his pizza. He actually dropped a piece of pepperoni purposely on the floor for Steve, who is Dad's favorite because he's the smallest. Eydie swooped in and stole it, but Dad was ready with another because he knew she would. Steve happily lapped the second piece up and I decided against admonishing my father for spoiling my dogs. "The facilities on the ship weren't always Class A."

"The facilities for performers are *never* Class A," I noted. "They keep you in steerage like the poor slobs on the *Titanic.* I always worry you guys are going to hit an iceberg."

"We were in the Aegean Sea," Mom reminded me. "They don't have icebergs."

"You know what I mean."

"Anyway," Dad said, "our accommodations were a little small and there were some slight problems."

"The toilet didn't work," Mom blurted out.

"That's worse than slight," I said. "Why didn't I hear about this on the news? You always hear about it when a cruise ship has that kind of problem."

"It wasn't the whole ship," Mom said, giving me a significant glance. "It was just *us.*"

Beat, two, three . . . "So why didn't you ask for a new stateroom or get someone in to fix it?" I asked. There had to be more to the story.

Sure enough, there was. "Your father

didn't want to ask for another room." Mom sniffed.

"They were booked solid," Dad said. "There was no other room."

"And the . . . facilities?" I asked, because I didn't want to hear my parents argue the point.

"Your father thought he could fix it himself," Mom told me, something like a moan in her voice.

Dad ate in silence even as Steve looked up hopefully for more. Bruno, who could have knocked over the table and had the whole pizza if he'd wanted to, sat patiently to the side. He was just happy to be included. "So what happened?" I asked, even though I knew the inevitable answer.

"The stateroom flooded," Mom said.

You could see that punch line coming from a mile away. Dad is a lovely man, but with a wrench in his hand he is an actual menace to society as we know it. "Why didn't you just ask the ship people?" I asked him.

"They're busy. They don't need to be bothered. It was a simple repair." Dad wasn't making eye contact with Mom. That wasn't good. This wasn't a raconteur story being told to an appreciative audience, like usual. This was the tip of the . . . well, you know.

"It wasn't simple when I was up to my ankles," Mom said.

Dad opened his mouth to answer, but I was saved by the buzz because a text message was coming in from Madolyn. *Special crew meeting tomorrow, 10 a.m. Don't bring Barney.*

That meant there wouldn't be any film shot the next day, which was not terribly surprising. The company was reeling, and decisions about how to replace Dray, if at all, were being made.

I texted back *See you then* and started to think about how to get Barney back to Patty's place. I could drive there before the company meeting and drop him off, then head to the studio if Patty wasn't up to the meeting. I was just the agent, after all, and not the parrot's handler.

I'd be out of this whole mess by this time tomorrow. I just had to keep reminding myself of that.

I was about to turn back to the soap opera unfolding at my kitchen table when my phone rang and Sam's number showed up in the ID. He rarely calls, so I was concerned and answered immediately.

"Is something wrong?" I asked. *Hello* just

seemed so mundane.

"Not with me," Sam said. "But you might want to look out your front window. Don't open the door."

Okay, so suddenly I'm in a monster movie and being told the call is coming from inside the house. "Why?" I asked, but I was already heading to the front window, which has adjustable blinds on it. At the moment they were adjusted down, but that was clearly about to change.

Before Sam could answer, and as my parents looked on doing what they do best — looking concerned — I pried a couple of the slats apart and looked out. There were four news vans outside my house. One was actually parked *on* my lawn.

"Oh," I said. "That's why."

CHAPTER FIVE

I would like it pointed out that I do not know anyone on the Scarborough, New Jersey, Police Department. I have dealt with some NYPD officers in the past, but this was actually my first time calling the local cops with a complaint.

The results were mixed. "The vans have every right to park wherever they want on a public street," the dispatcher told me.

"One of them is parked on my lawn," I said.

"Now *that* we can do something about. I'll get a cruiser out there right away and we'll see if maybe we can get them to move back or something, but there's no law against parking a news van in front of your house." My tax dollars at work.

Against my better instincts I thanked the dispatcher and disconnected the call. But before I could make it back to the kitchen, the doorbell rang.

"Don't answer it," Mom suggested. "Maybe they'll go away."

That seemed unlikely. "You want me to answer?" my father said. "I could say I'm a family spokesperson." Never get between my father and a spotlight; it's dangerous.

"I'll do it," I said. "If we let you out there, you'll do three encores."

Dad looked slightly wounded, but Mom grinned. It was one of the rare times I've seen them do anything but put up a united front. Now I was getting worried. "Let's move Barney out of the way," I said, and Mom took his cage into their bedroom, which was closest. It was showtime.

I walked to the door, took a breath, and opened it. That was a mistake.

At least five microphones and three digital voice recorders (those were the radio and print reporters) were within an inch of my mouth before I had stepped all the way out onto my front step. Lights flashed on. Questions were being shouted from people I couldn't see because of the klieg lights they were shining in my face. And all the time I was wishing I'd touched up my makeup before going outside. This was going live on CNN.

"What were Dray's last words?"

"Were you and he having an affair?"

74

"Did the parrot see anything?"

"Can you stand up taller?" That was one of the microphone holders who had been pushed to the back of the scrum.

Years of stage experience were not going wasted this time. "I have a brief statement," I said. "Is this going live to any of your affiliates?"

"Yes!" a couple of the reporters yelled out.

It was a pity. Because I didn't want to get into trouble with the FCC, my planned two-word statement was not going to be usable. They still get cranky about certain types of language, four decades after George Carlin. This is what we call progress.

"All right, here it is: We believe my client was present at the time that Dray Mattone was tragically shot, but we don't know that for certain. The bird is incapable of conversation; he can just repeat phrases he has been painstakingly taught over a period of days or weeks. So he has no useful information to give to the police and I have no information to give to you. That's all I'm going to say, aside from please get your van off my lawn. Thank you." I stepped backward through my front door as more questions were shouted at me and closed it in their faces, which wasn't nearly as satisfying as you'd think it would be.

"Nice," Mom said.

Dad, walking over to give me a hug, said, "You couldn't mention the act?" I raised my hand, but he caught it and kissed it. "I'm kidding, sweetie."

"So was I." Mostly.

But the doorbell kept ringing and the phone started to buzz with numbers I'd never seen before. The dogs barked each time the doorbell rang; they don't care about my phone but invasion of their personal space is definitely not cool with them. I wondered how I'd take them out for a walk after dinner.

Luckily that was the moment the Scarborough police decided to show up and get the van off the front lawn. The other reporters and broadcasters seemed to take that as a hint, but they didn't drive away. They just stopped ringing my doorbell, mostly because they'd probably figured out I wasn't going to open the door anymore tonight.

"What are you going to do now?" Mom asked.

"I'm going to have a normal evening and take Barney back to his real home early tomorrow."

I turned my cell phone to vibrate because I couldn't actually be unavailable if Consuelo had to get in touch or one of my clients' owners was frantic to find me (okay, so I'm afraid to be unconnected; you got me), so instead of hearing it ring off its virtual hook every few seconds I heard a buzz and glanced down at it. This in the modern world is what we call *managing.*

"I'm going to let Barney out of the cage for a few minutes," I told Mom and Dad. "He needs the change of scenery and the exercise. I'd appreciate it if you'd help me keep him from being eaten by dogs, because that would be a fairly serious breach of my contract with Patty."

Mom, who loves dogs and cats but has never warmed to any other animals, blanched a little, clenched her jaw, and nodded. My father, who never met an experience he'd prefer not to have, lit up. He rubbed his hands together. "Let's do this thing," he said.

With more than a little of my mother in me, I felt more than a flicker of trepidation but went into Mom and Dad's room to get Barney's cage, which did not have its cover on it. I decided his point of release should be the living room, so I returned Barney and his immediate environs to the coffee table and took a deep breath.

"Okay," I said, watching the dogs, who found this all incredibly fascinating. Eydie especially was showing more interest than I was used to seeing from her, which did not make me any more relaxed. "Here we go."

Barney barely reacted when I opened the cage door. That kind of thing happened dozens of times a day in his line of work, so he saw nothing unusual in the act. When I reached in to help him out, he seemed a little startled but not upset. He didn't try to peck at my hand or anything, which was a good sign, I thought. I didn't have the gloves that falconers use, but at the moment they seemed like a fine idea.

"Come on, Barney," I said. It was the tone that mattered, not the words. I could have said, "E equals MC squared," but that would have just confused my parents and possibly Steve.

Barney hopped onto my index finger, as he does with Patty when she's training him, and I eased him out of the cage, being careful to hold him up higher than even Bruno could jump if he felt like it. Bruno, big hairy floor mop that he is, was watching from his dog bed and seemed thrilled but not terribly threatening. He was about ten feet away.

I realized once Barney was out and sitting on my finger that I had no idea how to get him to fly. Then I wondered if I *wanted* him to fly, considering the rather extensive cleanup that could entail if he decided to make mischief or anything else.

But I knew it was better for the parrot if he had a chance to spread his wings a bit, and since going outside (for me and the dogs, not Barney) was off the table for the moment, this was the best moment for him to do so. I reached over with my free hand and tried to gently nudge him off my index finger. He wasn't exactly resistant so much as he didn't seem to understand what I was suggesting. I thought of calling Patty for instructions but thought of the rattle in her cough the last time we spoke and decided she could use the sleep.

I was a professional. I could get a parrot off my finger.

"Why don't you try tossing him?" Dad said, gesturing with his hand. Eydie thought that was a great idea and watched Dad's hand move back and forth with utter and profound interest.

"He's not a salad," I answered. "Besides, I don't want him to get hurt."

"I don't think your father means to throw the bird hard," Mom said. She could be annoyed with Dad and defend him at the same time. It's an art.

I got what he meant, but it's easier said

than done. I gave Barney another nudge with my free hand, but he just looked at it as he would at an invading Hun and ruffled his feathers, squawking a little.

"Easy there, big guy," I said. Bruno, who is used to hearing that nickname from me, stood up and walked over, expecting someone to pet him. Mom obliged; that was her contribution.

Finally I decided this couldn't be handled gently, at least not *this* gently, and did as Dad had suggested, just in a directional manner. I was guiding Barney into the air rather than trying to propel him, since that seemed the best way to keep my index finger unscratched.

And it was just when Barney got the idea and took off that I noticed something hanging off his left foot. Before I could get a close look at what that object or substance might be, he had taken wing and was circling my living room.

That caused a decent amount of hysteria among the dogs. Eydie barked, stood up on her hind legs, and shook her head in either wonderment or utter disgust. It's hard to tell with Eydie; she could also have been expressing some desire to make an appetizer of Barney.

Steve jumped up so his front paws rested

on the edge of the coffee table. He wasn't going to be able to do much, but he could see better from there.

Bruno, though, was terrified. Something was flying in our house! He didn't know whether to attack this bizarre creature or go hide in his bed and wait for it all to be over, so he stood absolutely still in the middle of the room, head tilted up to watch, and howled.

"What's that on his claw?" Dad yelled over the barking.

Barney did another couple of laps around the living room before exploring the kitchen, which *really* freaked the dogs out. Now this flying object was invading the space where the *food* was! It was barely imaginable.

"I don't know," I answered Dad as Barney flew from spot to spot in my kitchen, wisely never coming down to a level Bruno, the tallest dog, could reach. He was not, how-ever, gauging Eydie's ability to jump, but I was, so I held her collar and let her watch but not move. "I saw it just as I let him go."

Barney flew back into the living room — we had made sure bedroom doors were closed before I set him loose — and took up a position on the crown molding in the far corner of the room. He looked down and considered all he could survey, no

doubt wondering who all those odd creatures below him might be.

"Dinnertime for Barney!" he shouted. It
was a comfort phrase.

"I think it's hair," Mom said, pointing at
Barney. Clearly she meant the material
stuck to his talon.

There was no provision for bringing
Barney down right now, and that would
have defeated the purpose of letting him
out of the cage to begin with. So I let him
sit on the molding above us all but made
sure there was newspaper laid out on the
floor beneath where he sat, at least for the
time being.

"He's taking up residence," I told my
parents. "Do you think it makes sense to let
the dogs out in the back for a while?"

"Do you think there are any reporters
back there?" Mom asked. "It could be dangerous."

"For the dogs or the reporters?" I asked.

"I'm not sure you could convince them to
leave right now," Dad said, looking at the
dogs. "They're so excited I don't think
they'll be open to leaving."

He was right about that, but I was insis-
tent. I wanted the dogs to get out, and with
the platoon of paparazzi on the front lawn,
it was at best a dubious proposition that

we'd get out for a normal walk. They needed to do what they needed to do and it wasn't like we'd never used the backyard for that before. But Barney's escapades in the living room were just so incredible that getting the three dogs out of the area was a challenge.

Eventually it was achieved, with Eydie predictably being the most difficult to nudge. Luckily I'd already been holding on to her collar, so the addition of a leash was not difficult. The two boys were less obstinate, even if Steve did keep looking over his left shoulder at the bird and Bruno, still doing his tough-guy bark, seemed incredulous that we were not calling upon him to defend the house. Against a parrot.

Once they were outside, they naturally wanted to come back in and started to bark and cry. This was simple human manipulation, but it achieved two results: It made me feel bad and it attracted the attention of the hovering reporters, who ran around to the back of the house, no doubt assuming Dray Mattone's killer was revealing himself in my backyard, causing the dogs to bark.

I couldn't leave them (the dogs) outside alone with that group, so Dad and I stayed out for a while until it was clear all three had taken care of what was necessary and the reporters, shouting questions through the stockade fence, had exhausted what little there was of humanity within them. They started asking me if I'd shot Dray before or after we'd consummated our deeply felt lust, and I brought the dogs back inside.

The five of us found Mom in the living room, standing on tiptoe on one of the kitchen chairs, holding out a finger and trying to entice Barney to hop onto it. The finger in question was smeared with peanut butter and Barney looked like he was considering it.

"Mom," I said urgently, "get down off the chair."

"But it's working," she protested.

"I know; that's the problem. If he starts to peck the peanut butter off your finger, we're going to end up in the emergency room and the vultures outside will have a whole new story to tell."

Mom looked down sharply. "He has teeth?"

"No, he has a beak and it's strong enough to break branches," I answered.

Mom came down off the chair.

"Did you see what's on his foot?" I asked Mom.

"I still think it's hair. Dark brown and curly."

Luckily Patty had given me some instruction on the best way to get Barney back into his cage when he's been out because she knew I'd have to exercise him a little even while we were working at the sound stage. I reached into the cage and pulled out his favorite toy, a very sturdy strip of wood that already had a good number of beak imprints on it. This time I stood on the chair but did not offer any part of my own anatomy as an enticement. I extended the stick and cooed at Barney over the occasional bark from Eydie, the only dog left who found this the least bit peculiar.

"Come on, Barney," I crooned. "See the nice stick."

Barney saw the nice stick. Whether or not he was going to relinquish his position overseeing the rest of us was still a question.

"Wanna play with the stick?" I asked the parrot. Because in my business you have conversations with animals. There's a good deal of comfort in that because you never get an answer, so there's really no pressure to be witty or charming.

Barney flapped his wings a little and said, "Can't kill a zombie!"

Okay, so with Barney you *did* get an answer, but it wasn't actually relevant to the conversation, so the whole witty or charming thing still applied. "Come on, Barney," I repeated. "Get the stick!"

"Dinnertime for Barney!" Parrots never say anything that sounds subdued. They always seem to be shouting. They're not, but we're just stupid humans and react as if they were.

"Okay. Okay, Barney." I extended the stick a little bit farther, aware of the fact that I was standing on a chair and reaching for a bird who was sitting on my crown molding. I'd never noticed just how high the ceilings were in this house. This was not the way I'd wanted to find out.

He responded to my soothing tone the way I had hoped: He reached out for the stick with his beak and I let him have it while extending my right index finger.

Barney hopped on.

Breathing the inevitable sigh of relief, I made sure he was secure on my finger, didn't make any sudden movements with my hands, and accepted Dad's offer of help to get down off the chair. Eydie sauntered over to take a look, but I turned my back on her; I trusted Steve a lot more with a tasty-looking parrot on my finger.

I love my dogs, but I've become really attached to my right hand.

"Is the hair still on his foot?" Mom asked.

It was a good question. All the drama getting Barney from the ceiling molding back to his cage — and make no mistake, that's where he was going — had overshadowed the idea that he had something attached to him, possibly something that might have some relevance to Dray Mattone's murder. I looked carefully at his left foot.

"Yeah, it's still there. Give me a second." Mom and Dad fell back, like good troopers will do when ordered, and I got Barney to the door of his cage.

He held the stick in his beak, so he wasn't talking, but he seemed perfectly happy to be back in his familiar environment, the one that was there whether he was home at Patty's house, working at the studio, or having a sleepover here with his agent and her family. Barney's life was grounded in his cage and he was comfortable there.

Then he dropped the stick and yelled, "Put down the gun!"

"That one's getting old, Barney," I told him as he hopped off my finger and onto the floor of his cage, where he dropped the stick for further gnawing. I reached over and gently held his claw; then I reached in with my other hand (which wasn't easy in his travel cage with the smaller door) and extracted the stuff moving with his talon wherever it went.

It *was* hair, and as Mom had said, it was brunette and curly. I pulled out both hands and closed the gate on Barney's cage to avoid his deciding to take another tour of the house and to quiet him down for the night. I put the cover over his cage. He needed sleep, the dogs needed a break, and I needed a vacation in San Juan for about a week.

The only one who wasn't going to get what they needed? Guess who.

I took the hair over to the kitchen table where the light was better. The dogs and my parents trailed after me. Mom and Dad wanted to see what I'd recovered, and the dogs just follow people around in case something edible gets dropped. It's an eco-system.

As we got to the kitchen, me gripping the hair tightly so it wouldn't just blow into the air and end up part of the lovely patina of dust and neglect I have on every surface of my home, I asked Dad to turn on the overhead light and he did. I sat down carefully at the table and my parents followed suit. Even the dogs seemed to think this was an important moment and did not make a sound other than the clicking of their nails on the ceramic tiled floor — best for pet owners because it absorbs nothing.

It was so quiet in the room I expected Dr. Banacek to conduct an autopsy. But then we were actually sort of looking into Dr. Banacek's death, so it seemed oddly appropriate. I took a napkin from the holder on the table and spread it out, then put the hair on top of it.

The clump of hair was about half an inch wide and almost as long. It wasn't much, but it clearly was not something Barney would have naturally picked up in his day of hanging around in his cage and occasionally spitting out a quip about zombies. There was an audible exhale from all the humans in the room and then we all leaned over to look at what was on the napkin.

It was hair. That was about it.

"What do you think?" I asked my parents.

"It's curly hair," Dad said. "Did anybody at the studio have curly hair?"

I looked at him. "It was a television production," I reminded him. "The only thing you could say about all the hair was that it was gorgeous. Except of course for the teamsters."

I turned my attention to my mother, who

had been in charge of hair, makeup, and costume for as long as I'd known her (and to be honest, before that as well). "Do you think it's natural?" I asked her.

Mom takes her work seriously. "Do you have a magnifying glass?" she asked.

"No, but there's an app for that." I got out my phone and turned on the magnification application I'd downloaded once when trying to read the fine print on the contract for employment a chimp I knew was about to sign. I handed Mom the phone and showed her how to use the app.

She examined the hair for a decent interval, maybe seven or eight beats on stage (that's a long time if you're an audience member and worse if you're an actor). "If I had to guess, I'd say it's dyed, but there's something more interesting than that about it."

"What's that?" I asked. I was born to play the straight man.

"It's artificial hair, not real," Mom said.

CHAPTER SIX

"I can't tell if this is carpet fiber or a really bad wig." Janine Petinsky, the chief hairdresser for *Dead City,* looked over her half-glasses and into my eyes. "But it's nothing we'd use around here."

I had brought the sample from Barney's claw to Janine because I figured she would know even more than my mother about the composition of fake hair, and I was right. Mom had little to add other than it wasn't natural, but Janine, with one glance through her magnified lenses, had already determined its quality.

Bad.

The production meeting at which the measures taken following Dray Mattone's death would be discussed was going to start in a few minutes. I'd sought out Janine first even as I'd been dodging other company personnel, a few of whom actually remembered me from the day before. Without any information other than wanting an opinion, I'd asked her what this sample might be and she had immediately defended her department against even considering something so shoddy.

"Best guess, where would it have come from?" I asked. The group was starting to assemble on the sound stage adjacent to the makeup trailer where we were talking, so I didn't have a lot of time for subtlety.

I know what you're going to say: I had been determined to drop Barney off at Patty's house and get her to go to this meeting so I could continue my career and my life. You're right, that was the plan. But Patty had still been coughing and sniffling to beat the band — assuming one was for some reason angry with the band — and had pleaded with me to attend the meeting. She had agreed to keep Barney with her (at least for the time being) because he was certainly not going to be required for filming today. Besides, I was out of bird food.

"If I had to say, I'd guess it was a costume store, like for Halloween or something," Janine said. She looked me over. "Where'd you get it?"

"One of my dogs coughed it up," I said. "Don't worry, I washed it." She immediately handed me back the tuft of hair just as I heard commotion from the adjoining sound stage. The meeting was about to start.

I thanked Janine, who immediately used disinfectant on her hands, and went to the stage. Pretty much everyone I had seen the day before was there, and so were some additions to the crew.

The man at the center of the room, clearly commanding everyone's attention, was wearing a suit he did not pick up at Sears and was doing his very best to look absolutely devastated, but I know bad acting when I see it.

"Everybody settle down, please," he said in a quiet but authoritative voice. Sure enough, the company came to an almost complete silence; there was barely the sound of anyone's chair scraping on the floor. I felt conspicuous trying to find a place to be inconspicuous. It's funny how life works out that way.

"Who's that?" I whispered to the young woman immediately to my right, a production assistant (read: intern) I'd met briefly the day before.

She looked annoyed. This guy had told her to settle down and I was demanding she make a sound! Did I not realize how much she'd dreamed about this job when she was majoring in film at New York University?

"He's Les Mannix," she hissed. "The show-runner." Then she moved away from me, doing her best to be totally silent as she did so.

"I'd like to start by deferring to Nesha Pakresh," he said. "For just a moment of spiritual reflection on this solemn occasion." Dray's funeral wouldn't be for almost a week and would be held in Los Angeles, but the rituals were beginning now.

Nesha, whom I had not met the day before, stood up in front of the assemblage. She bowed her head and everyone in the room (except perhaps me) did the same. Then she chanted for a few minutes in a language I did not recognize, occasionally showing off a very lovely singing voice I'm sure she wanted the producers to hear. When she finished, the company didn't know whether to applaud, so they didn't. Nesha bowed once and walked backward without looking so Mannix could once again take center stage.

"I'm sure everyone has heard the dreadful news about yesterday," Mannix began. Of course everyone had heard the news; they'd been here and he had not. The only issue was whether *he* had heard the news, and he was certainly answering that question.

"We're all stunned. We're crippled and we're dazed."

That struck a chord before I realized he was quoting Elton John's (actually Bernie Taupin's) elegy for John Lennon, "Empty Garden." But Mannix wasn't anywhere near finished.

"What happened yesterday is something we would not wish on someone we despised, let alone someone as beloved as our own Dray. But I've learned something about love that I never knew before. You speak of love when it's too late." That was from *Stage Door.* I didn't know this guy, but he could quote with the best of them.

"The fact is, somebody killed Dray, and that has an impact on all of us here." Mannix rubbed his upper arms as if he was cold and stood to better be seen being troubled. He still wasn't convincing, but he was making all the right moves. "And that's sad and it's wrong and it's unfair. It's a bloody tragedy, but there's nothing we can do about it. Nothing!" He pointed in the air to emphasize his intensity and distract from his quoting a Peter O'Toole movie called *The Stunt Man.*

People hung their heads. Some were openly weeping. I don't think too many of them were sincere, and nobody was buying

Mannix's act, but they were show people and I know show people. If there's an opportunity to be dramatic, they are certainly going to leap on it and stomp it to death.

"And that means we have to consider reality even as we deal with the horror and sadness we're still all feeling, and will feel for a long time." You had to wonder if Mannix had consulted with Aaron Sorkin about the speech he was making now. Although I'm not sure Sorkin would work at television rates anymore, and he doesn't quote that much.

"I'm sorry, but we do have to think about what we're going to do next. I know the adage is that the show must go on, and we agree with that, but it's not always possible." There was an audible gasp from the crowd, which Mannix clearly heard, because he looked up from his facedown "brooding" pose with a slightly surprised expression. "Now, hang on. No decisions have been made yet." The crowd relaxed, but not much.

"Believe me, nobody wants to shut this show down. But this is a business. We're still reeling from the shock of yesterday, and so is our fan base. We have no idea yet whether they'll follow us without Dray, who as you know was a very popular feature of

Dead City."

A hand went up somewhere to my right and I heard a woman's voice ask, "Are you going to recast the part of Dr. Banacek?" That was met with some grumbles and the hand went down, probably in fear of physical attack.

Mannix's mouth twisted a little, probably involuntarily, since he wanted to look wounded, not angry. "No, that is not a consideration," he answered, and a few in the crowd actually applauded. "This is a very delicate situation. Dray Mattone was a special talent who connected to viewers in a unique and wonderful way. It would be an insult to him for us to recast the role."

"What about the crew?" a man to my left shouted. "Are we still working?"

"Not today," Mannix said, holding up his hands, palms out. "Let me tell you what we are doing.

"We'll be suspending filming on the first unit immediately, but the second unit will continue for this episode only. We had almost all of Dray's scenes shot before . . . this happened." Mannix closed his eyes a moment to get back into character. Good: mourning. Right! The eyes opened again.

"So for scenes that don't require Dr. Banacek we will continue filming, but not until tomorrow, out of respect," he went on. "After everything is in the can we will be suspending filming temporarily while the creative team makes a decision about how to proceed."

"The creative team," muttered Heather Alizondo, who had appeared just to my left, arms folded. "Like the rest of us are just manual laborers and don't have a useful idea among us." I don't even think she was talking to anyone in particular. She certainly couldn't be heard more than a few feet away.

"How long will it take to decide?" asked someone I couldn't see at all. I'm not that tall and I was standing in the back. So sue me.

"We hope not very long," Mannix said, not really answering. "We'll be meeting with some studio people and some network people to get their input, and we'll figure something out."

A burly looking grip a couple of rows (such as they were) in front of me stuck up a paw. "Do we get paid while you people *decide*?" he asked.

Mannix raised an eyebrow to indicate he'd gotten the note of defiance in the man's question. "Yes, you will," he said. "Every-body on the crew will continue to be paid at least for a week, and we expect that our path will be clear before then. Okay?" The defiance was on the other foot now.

"Okay," the grip said. He knew the union rules. Everybody got paid as long as the show was considered in production. If it went on the dreaded "hiatus," meaning it was probably canceled, everybody would be making phone calls and polishing up résumés. Not that they weren't doing that already, but after a cancellation, the activity would be considerably more overt.

"But for the moment," Mannix said, composing himself again, "let's concentrate on our lost friend Dray. Reach out to Denise if you can." Denise Barnaby was Dray's second (third?) wife, whom I had not seen on the set. "She's having a rough time, as you might imagine. If any of you need counseling, we'll have a therapist here on the set for the next couple of days or for however long it's necessary. No expense is being spared." That was nice; Dray Mattone was dead and Mannix wanted us all to know it was costing him money.

"And one last thing," he said, holding up his hand like a traffic cop again. "The police will be here today and probably tomorrow and, frankly, for as long as they want. We're telling everybody to cooperate with them to the fullest extent that you can. The priority here is to find the bastard that killed Dray and bring him to justice. Are we clear?"

There were some nods and a few mumbled words of agreement, but for the most part everyone was studying the floor, or as much of it as they could see with an entire company of television people crammed onto one sound stage. Those things look huge until you bring in the whole crew, from the executive producers to the guy who locks up the doors at the end of the day.

"Good," Mannix said, as if there had been unrestrained shouts of assent. "Now we'll have a short memorial service today at noon, right here on the stage. Everyone is invited." He made *invited* sound like it was spelled *required to show up for fear of termination.* Which, to be fair, it probably was.

I didn't have to worry about future employment by the production company because I wasn't working for them; I was working for Barney, and by extension Patty. So I made up my mind on the spot to skip the memorial service and move onto more productive things, like heading to my office and seeing if there was a talented otter or something that could get work without running into a murder just by accident.

But heading for the exit was something of a gauntlet. Even after Mannix left the floor and the meeting was clearly over, people were milling about, no doubt gossiping about Dray's shooting and wondering how long they would remain employed in television.

Janine stopped me first. "I've been thinking," she said. "That fake hair you've got? Could be from a mannequin, you know, a department store dummy? I've never seen anybody try to get by with something that bad, but I have seen it in party stores and whatnot. You might try there. What do you want more of it for?"

I didn't want more of it — in fact, I was hoping to get rid of what little I had, but I thanked Janine and pressed on toward the door, which seemed farther away than it had been the day before. Before I could make much more headway through the crowd without a machete, Heather took hold of my arm.

"I don't want to bother you, but do you think Barney might be able to come back tomorrow?" she asked. "With Dray gone, I might want to cut to more close-ups on the bird."

Nice that the company was so grief stricken at the loss of their star. "I can tell Patty to get him here tomorrow," I said. "But he has only one facial expression. If you have old footage it'll look like the new footage."

"Not after I get done lighting it." Everybody wanted to make sure they were doing great work now; they had to line up another job.

We agreed on a time and I noted it on my phone to tell Patty when I got there, assuming I could make it through this jungle and out the door. Sure enough, Les Mannix himself stood in front of me and beckoned with his index finger for me to approach. I looked around, but no, he seemed to be pointing toward me, which made very little sense. I was just the parrot's agent.

"What did you think of the eulogy?" he asked. And that stumped me more because I had no idea it had been a eulogy so much as a status meeting for the crew.

"Very touching," I said. It's my responsibility to keep my client employed, so insulting the boss was not part of my game plan.

"I'll say more at the memorial service. You're coming, right?" He glared with the kind of intensity that I'm sure had crushed more than one personal assistant into a fine powder.

"I'm just the bird's agent," I blurted.

"Yeah," he said, looking past me to see if anybody cooler was there. And by my own reckoning, there pretty much had to be. "You were the one who suggested the parrot should stay in Dray's trailer, right?"

Oh, no. I wasn't about to get saddled with that one. "As a matter of fact, no," I said. "Heather asked if Barney could stay a while longer. When I said he needed to rest for a while, it was her idea that we take his cage to Dray's trailer." I was in second grade and Juanita Lewis had been copying off *me,* not the other way around!

Mannix's gaze did not return to me; he was playing the room. What was his sudden interest in figuring out why Barney had been resting at the scene of the crime? "The faster this murder gets solved and somebody gets arrested, the faster I can figure if we still have a show on our hands," he said without prompting. "So anything you can do to help, I'm hoping you'll do it."

"I would have anyway," I said. "I have no reason to hold anything back." I felt into my pocket for the tuft of what now appeared to be very bad fake hair and considered giving it to him, but Mannix simply nodded and moved on, shouting to someone named Billy as he did. I removed my hand; there was no point.

Just as well, because I made it to the door and the welcome feeling of cooler air when

Detective Sergeant Bostwick, who was walking in, stopped me before I could make my escape.

"Has the bird told you anything else?" he asked.

"Yeah, he said to bet on Seabiscuit in the fifth at Aqueduct." There just wasn't much point in explaining the whole parrot speech thing again.

"Nobody likes a wiseass," Bostwick said.

"Then explain Bill Maher's career." I was just in that kind of mood. I didn't like being among a group of people who would have told you they were a family when they were all figuring ways to save themselves, possibly at the expense of others. It wasn't that I didn't understand or would have reacted differently in their position. In fact, that might have been what was making me uncomfortable. I needed to get home and talk to normal people like my parents, who had spent their lives pretending to be other people for the amusement of hotel and cruise ship patrons.

"Who?" He waved a hand to tell me not to answer, which was wise. "I just want to know if you have anything else to tell me that might help."

I could think of the larger whole, after all. "Yes, I do," I told him, reaching into my pocket. "I found this on Barney's foot last night." I searched a little harder.

"What?" Bostwick asked, suddenly interested.

"Um . . ." That was weird. "I'd swear it was here a minute ago . . ."

His eyes got suspicious. Of me. "What was there a minute ago?"

"This little piece of something you should see." My jacket pocket wasn't that deep or that wide. I should have found the evidence by now.

But it wasn't there.

"Somebody stole my hair," I said.

CHAPTER SEVEN

By the time Bostwick had agreed to believe I'd once had a small piece of physical evidence — one that I could not begin to explain in terms of significance — but now it was gone, the memorial service for Dray Mattone was about to begin. And I saw no graceful way to extract myself from the sound stage, so I was stuck.

I'd actually gotten Janine to come over and verify the fake hair had existed and had been in my possession. Bostwick had not exactly been skeptical, but he had seemed a little afraid to approach me, like I might next tell him Dray's killer had escaped to Saturn, but I had a ship in the parking lot if he wanted to pursue.

He'd gotten a full description of whatever it was that tuft was made out of from Janine, but without the sample itself to test (and possibly even with it) did not seem to think it was much of a lead. "The bird could have picked that up anywhere," Bostwick said to me. "Maybe he found it in your house."

"There wasn't anything like that in my house." I was oddly miffed at the suggestion, like Bostwick was somehow insulting my admittedly shoddy housekeeping by suggesting fake hair could be found in my residence. "Besides, the only time he was out of his cage there was after he'd gotten that thing stuck to his foot."

"I guess it's worth checking if there was any similar evidence found in the trailer," the detective admitted. "I'll call the precinct when I'm done here."

"What's your agenda on the sound stage today?" I asked him after Janine, hearing that the memorial was about to start, headed toward the makeshift theater that had been constructed on the stage where Barney (and Dray) had been shooting the day before. It seemed there'd be a full house; whatever Les Mannix wanted, Les Mannix got.

"Following up," Bostwick answered. "It's a big company, there were a lot of people questioned after this happened yesterday. We have a few more questions that need answering." Like, for example, who had killed Dray Mattone. Stuff like that.

"Anything for me?" I asked.

"No."

That was definitive enough. I was swept up in the tide of people heading toward the memorial service, which I imagined Bostwick would want to watch anyway. I read in a detective novel once that the funeral (or as close as you were going to get) was a good place to look for suspects.

If that was the sergeant's plan, he had his work cut out for him. There were at least seventy people crammed into the room. Temporary bleachers had been constructed since the meeting this morning, not long ago at all. I hoped the stagehands had been paid well. Wouldn't want them to leave out a bolt or something due to their disappointment.

I sat all the way to the side, closest to the exit, about six rows up. This was a bigger group than simply the day-to-day workers on a TV series. Clearly every writer, producer, actor, and executive had been added to the usual list of technicians, stylists, and set decorators, and the army of production assistants who were paid either in college credit or at minimum wage for the endless hours they put in.

The magic of show business. Who wouldn't want in?

The lights dimmed, which I hadn't realized was possible, just as Bostwick slipped in behind me by two rows. I figured he would follow the book, even if it was a book by Raymond Chandler.

It would have been logical to expect Les Mannix to run the memorial service, but he was seated front-row center, with a very tasteful key light positioned to make him visible without being the center of attention. Film companies are stocked with very talented people, and TV companies have the same, only faster.

Instead of Mannix, a woman I had not seen before stood up from the same row where he was seated and walked to the center of the stage, where an actual spotlight was being directed by a tech guy in the top row. Apparently there had not been enough time to create a lighting system that could be run from the booth.

She was tall and willowy, which was not the least bit unusual for a TV crew, and I took her to be an actress. I was not a huge fan of *Dead City,* unless a huge fan was someone who had never watched so much as one episode of the show. I had read the script pages Barney needed to learn and that was about it. So I did not recognize the woman and I got the feeling I should have.

"Good afternoon, everybody," she said in a voice just as sheer and flowing as her top, which had no doubt been made for swirling. It was not black, which you might have expected, but was blue. I guessed that was the closest she could come on such short notice. "For those of you who don't know, I'm Mallory Jenkins."

There was a small chuckle from the gathered group. Who could possibly not know Mallory Jenkins?

She acknowledged the response with a nod. "Les asked me to lead the ceremony today, and I haven't had time to prepare, you know. This all happened so . . . suddenly." Now, Mallory happens to be a good actress, and I knew that because I couldn't tell whether the tear she was wiping away was one she'd produced for effect or a genuine one. I was not that far away and I can spot a phony from much farther distances.

"I'm not going to make a speech," she went on. "You know me — I can't really improvise too well." Again, a knowing titter from the group. "But I didn't ask the writers to give me words to say. Today is about saying what's in your heart." I'll bet the writer she had asked to put together a speech had thought hard about that passage. It played beautifully.

"All I can say is that I know we all loved Dray very much. He was such an open spirit. He would listen to your troubles and he would care, you know? Not like in a way that he wanted you to see him caring. Like, for real." She was going off-script now, unless her ghostwriter had intentionally made her sound like a nineties Valley Girl.

"So let's all think good thoughts about our dear friend and wish his safe passage to wherever he might be going now." Mallory was back with the program now. She sounded more confident and more sincere, which was weird because these clearly were someone else's words she was reading. Actors. They're better at being someone else than they are at being themselves.

She bowed her head, skillfully leading the others to do the same. Then she looked up and said, "We've got a few people who have asked to be given time to speak now. But if you want to say something too, please just come on down here and take the mic. We'll let you know when, okay?

"Our first scheduled speaker is one of Dray's best friends on the show and someone I'm sure you're understand —"

She never got the chance to mention who this close friend and constant companion might be because a young woman on the other side of the bleachers, far to my right, stood up and pointed dramatically (what else?) toward the stage area. "Murderer!" she shouted. "Murderer!"

This was probably the worst time and place to audition for a part ever, but this young brunette, slim and petite, was over-playing her role to an unconscionable degree, I thought. Who yells, "Murderer"?

The voice was vaguely familiar, but I couldn't place it. But the most disturbing part was her hair.

It was dark brown and curly and looked really fake.

Mallory, down at the center of attention in what now might be taken as a boxing arena, looked up, confused. Her head went to one side, then the other, then back at the pointing woman, who continued to shout, "Murderer!" at the top of her lungs. "Me?" Mallory asked, seemingly baffled.

"No, not you!" the accuser shrieked from her spot in the bleachers. *"Him!"*

She was pointing directly at Les Mannix, who stood up and pointed at himself in some confusion.

"Yes, you!" the woman shouted.

I saw Bostwick, whom I had turned around to face, tense up his arms. His hands were in his pockets, with his jacket open and the lower end of his shoulder holster visible on his left side. He didn't reach for it, but he wanted to be sure it was handy. It was.

Mannix was the showrunner, meaning he was an executive producer with the final say on the program from beginning to network (which always has the *final* final word). So he had two priorities in this situation: showing he was still in charge and effective, and not being implicated in the shooting of the star of his series.

As one might expect of a television producer, he chose to demonstrate his authority.

"I'm responsible for everything that happens on my show, so I guess you're right that I take some blame for the tragedy that befell our own Dray," he said. No microphone, no amplification. The man was a professional. The *befell* was unfortunate, but it communicated the gravity and formality Mannix was trying to maintain under the circumstances.

"No!" The brunette wasn't buying his passive-aggressive bit. "You killed him! You went to Dray's trailer and shot him!"

There was something of an uproar in the room. People stood in all sections of the bleachers and began screaming, either at Mannix or at the woman making the accusation. I was still sitting — I figured there was no way I was going to see what was happening anyway, and it had already been a long day — so my view was somewhat obstructed. If I'd paid for this seat I would have been profoundly disappointed.

I did see that Bostwick had heard enough. He started working his way right to the end of the row, where he could more easily reach the woman who was accusing Mannix of pulling the trigger on Dray. People were not exactly standing in his way, but those who hadn't spoken directly to the sergeant the day before wouldn't have known he was a detective and therefore might not understand why he needed to question her immediately. They didn't simply fade back and let the cop through.

So it took a little longer than it normally would for him to reach the woman he had wanted to question. And that was a problem, apparently, because after about a minute I heard him shout, "Did anyone see where she went?"

That couldn't be good.

Chaos, or at least the TV equivalent, ensued for some minutes. I kept my seat because I didn't see how I could be of much help. There was, I'll confess, a moment where I considered trying to walk down the bleachers and out the sound stage door, but I felt that might look somewhat suspicious, and besides, there was a wall of people everywhere I looked. If there'd been a back on my seat, I'd have stretched and tried to shut my eyes for a bit, but these were uncomfortable metal bleachers.

So I did what any self-respecting agent would do under the circumstances: I got out my smartphone and checked my email.

While I did I heard various shouts from the crowd: "Did you see her?" "Who was that?" "Where's Les?" "Did he shoot Dray?" "Who's your agent?"

My ears perked up at that last one, but none of my clients or potential clients is able to actually conduct a conversation, so I just kept checking messages. There was a text from Patty reading *Can you take Barney again tonight?* This was not exactly the thing I had been dearly hoping I'd see. I considered my options, realized I didn't have any, and sent back *If you need me to,* which was about as passive-aggressive a response as I could conceive. I knew Patty would not back off on the request and I knew also that it was not my responsibility to take care of her parrot while she was ill even if he (the parrot) was a client.

Thanks so much, she sent back.

Swell. I sent a text to Mom telling her we'd have company for the evening again and once again considered trying to escape so I could at least stop by my office after picking up Barney at his home again. But now the crowd was starting to climb down the stairs to the stage area and the bleachers were therefore emptying out. Before too long it was just Bostwick and me situated at opposite ends of the sound stage.

I looked over at him. "Come here often?" I asked.

"Lately, yeah." He stood up and started to walk toward me. "How come you're hanging around?" There was an edge to the question. He wasn't bantering; he was asking with a purpose.

"I was texting and didn't notice everybody was leaving until just this minute." Now *I* stood up, to prove I was planning on doing the same. "I'm on my way to my office."

"I'll walk you," Bostwick said. We met in the center and began walking down toward the floor, which took only a few seconds. The bleachers were wide but not high.

"I'm just going to my car," I said in case he thought I was a permanent member of the company and had an office on the lot.

116

"My office is in East Harlem."

We started toward the sound stage door as stagehands began dismantling the bleachers and some production assistants, clipboards at the ready, shuffled around the sound stage, no doubt having been told to find an authentic leprechaun for the leading actress or a 1940s Moviola for the editor despite his having no intention of using one. Bostwick was looking down, perhaps wondering if the solution to Dray Mattone's murder was resting on the concrete before us waiting to be picked up.

"Why is your office in East Harlem?" he asked. "The show shoots here in Queens."

For a detective, he had a lousy memory. "I told you yesterday, I don't work for the production company. I'm the parrot's agent."

He nodded to indicate his comprehension. "Of course."

"Why aren't you chasing after the woman who yelled that Les Mannix killed Dray?" I asked.

"There are uniforms for that. They chase. I detect. It's all in the union contract." Bostwick thought he was being charming. I got the impression he believed that helped him get people to confess their guilt or something.

"Did anybody know who she was?" Outside it was sunny and warm. In the bleachers during the memorial service it had felt close and constricting. The weather outside was a pleasure, except I had a cop on my right acting strange. "She had the same kind of hair as the piece I found on Barney's leg. You could test it if I could find it and you could find her."

Bostwick shook his head. "Nobody had ever spoken to her, but a couple said they'd seen her before. Even the guy sitting next to her in the bleachers, the head gaffer, whatever that is, said he didn't see where she went after all the yelling started."

"A gaffer is an electrician," I told him. "As you might expect, they need more than a few around here. Don't you think it's odd that *nobody* recognized this woman, but there she was pointing at Les Mannix and accusing him of murder as if she knew him really well?"

The detective shrugged. "Maybe she's his vengeful ex-wife," he said. "She doesn't have to be a member of the TV crew to be annoyed with the guy."

"No, but she has to be a member of the TV crew to get admission to the sound stage, and for that matter, the lot," I said. We reached my car and I got my keys out

118

to open it. "Was she wearing a lanyard?" I held out my own to prove I had one, I guess. "I couldn't see from where I was sitting."

"I couldn't either," Bostwick said as I opened my car door. "The real question is, did Mannix have access to Dray Mattone's trailer?"

I slid into the driver's seat. Bostwick, for a detective assigned to a case on a TV studio lot, didn't seem to know anything about the television business, which I guess wasn't terribly surprising. "He's the showrunner, the producer who's in charge of everything," I told him. "He has access to anything he wants."

"You going straight to your office?" he asked me without acknowledging the information I'd given him.

"First to pick up Barney, then to my office, then home," I said. "Do you want to be my chaperone?" I closed the door and started the car so I could open the window.

"Does the parrot's agent always take him home with her every night?" Bostwick said.

I could feel my left eye twitch a little; there was something in the way I was being questioned that . . . well, what's a comfortable way to be questioned?

"No, but in this case the parrot's owner isn't feeling well and needs the time to sleep, so I'm doing her a favor." His gaze was unnerving me, and not in the way a guy's gaze can unnerve you just under normal circumstances. "What's the interest in my business all of a sudden? Am I a suspect?"

"Mind if I follow you to the parrot's house?"

What can you say to a request like that from a member of the NYPD? "You suspect Barney?"

"Until I know who did it, I suspect everybody. Do you mind if I come along?"

I didn't see a way around it, so I agreed. I waited until Bostwick brought his dull-looking car around and followed me off the lot. Every time I looked into my rearview mirror or the side mirror, there was the dull-looking cop in his dull-looking car, right on my tail.

I felt a lot like a suspect.

CHAPTER EIGHT

Patty Basilico was not up to having guests, but here I was in her bedroom, with Barney's bigger "home" cage on a stand in one corner, and I had brought a New York City police detective with me. Not only was I nervous about getting whatever Patty had, but I also felt rude for having burdened her, in this condition, with an unwanted intruder who had questions about Dray's murder that he wanted to ask her parrot.

Honest to goodness, Bostwick was busy questioning Barney within three minutes of having essentially barged his way in (okay, I knew where the spare key was kept, but it was the effect that mattered), and he was both wasting his time and trying my patience. Patty, being a very sweet-natured person, was pretending this was a completely normal occurrence, like she had detectives in to interrogate her bird twice a week.

"Barney," the detective said into the cage, "who had the gun?"

"It doesn't work like that," Patty rasped for the fourth time. "He doesn't answer questions."

I sat down in the easy chair next to the bed, moving Patty's jacket out of the way as I sat. This had become tiresome.

"Then what *does* he do?" Bostwick asked. "I've heard him talk, and I've heard him say things I don't think he'd spent hours learning."

Patty coughed a little, so I jumped in to save her throat. "You have to be mistaken on one of those points, Sergeant," I said. "Barney simply isn't capable of saying something if nobody has taught it to him and taken a long time doing it."

Bostwick shot me a look that stopped me in my tracks, if you can make tracks sitting in an easy chair. "I wasn't asking you," he said brusquely. "I was asking Ms. Basilico."

I could have argued that he was being rude, but Patty has an instinct for defusing tense situations. "The sergeant is right, Kay," she said. "He's already heard everything you can tell him. I've known Barney a lot longer."

"That's right," Bostwick said. I noted that he did not jump on the opportunity to apologize to me. "So tell me, how does the parrot's being in the room when Dray Mattone was shot help me find the person who killed him?"

"It doesn't," she answered. "Barney has a repertoire of phrases that I've taught him. No one else has ever had him long enough to teach him a new phrase." She coughed again and a gray strand of hair fell forward. Patty rushed to push it back, making sure she continued to look all blond. "Even Kay couldn't have given him new words to say in the time she had him; it just takes longer than that."

"Ms. Powell had the bird overnight yesterday," Bostwick noted. "Does the process take more time than that?"

"Under some circumstances it wouldn't, but in this case I'd say it's pretty much impossible," Patty told him. She was propped up in the bed at an angle that made her look as attractive as a patient can, and she was using it on the detective. I wondered whether she had a crush on Bostwick, although his charms were certainly eluding me. "Kay doesn't have enough experience with Barney to teach him quickly and hasn't ever tried it before. Not to mention that the bird can't work for long periods of time. He'll get tired and cranky and then you're just working against yourself."

Bostwick turned his attention back to the cage and its occupant. "Barney," he said, "the gun. Who had the gun?"

Patty and I exchanged a look. Some men just aren't ever going to admit that they can't solve the problem without help. "He's not going to tell you, Sergeant," I said.

"He's talked about the gun a couple of times," Bostwick said. "I want to see if maybe I can get him to say something else."

"Can't kill a zombie!" Barney informed him. Bostwick did not look amused.

"It's the newest thing he learned," Patty said. "He's proud of himself and wants you to know he can still do it."

The detective turned to face her. "Can you get him to say something about the gun?" he asked.

"The only way to do that would be to say it myself and have him repeat it to me," Patty told him. "I don't see how that's going to help you much." She coughed lightly, but it didn't escalate. I was hoping that meant she was getting better and maybe I wouldn't have to take Barney home with me tonight.

"But you're not the only person who can get the bird to say his lines," Bostwick pointed out, finally giving up on the cage and walking closer to where I was sitting but paying attention to Patty, which she appeared to like. "You were sick yesterday and had someone else prompt him when he needed to say the line for TV, right?"

I didn't know how I felt about being referred to as "someone else," but kept quiet, which is an underrated skill for agents. Believe me, I use it more often than not and it has served me well.

"That's right," Patty said. She played the pleased teacher well, knowing it would make Bostwick easier to deal with if she appealed to his ego. "You understand, Sergeant. Once the teaching has made an imprint on Barney's memory, meaning he knows the phrase, someone with a knowledge of the bird, someone like Kay, can get him to repeat it once I let her know what's most likely to work. In this case, because we knew the lines from the scene in advance from reading the script, we could teach him to say his line when he heard the prompt from the other actor. How did Barney do with that, Kay?"

They turned their attention to me, which startled me a bit. "Well, you know I told you yesterday that Barney had been a pro from start to finish. He never flubbed a line or missed a cue. But I don't think that's what the sergeant is concerned with, is it, Sergeant?"

Bostwick had been given the chance to act like a cop in charge and he wasn't about to let that one go by. "No, you're right. I'm more concerned with the parrot being in the trailer when Dray Mattone was shot, and the fact that after it happened, he started using the phrase 'Put down the gun.' Can you explain that?" He had directed the question at Patty.

"Actually, yes I can," she said. "It's a phrase I've been working with Barney on for a few days. It's in next week's script, so I was introducing it into his vocabulary."

That was odd. When I'd told Patty what Barney had said after the shooting, she had seemed surprised. What was she doing now, covering for the parrot?

I felt it would be wrong to call her on it, so I said nothing. Bostwick nodded since the explanation seemed reasonable. He looked back into the cage and exhaled a bit wistfully.

"I guess you're not going to tell me much, are you?" he asked Barney.

"Kill Les Mannix!" Barney shouted.

There was a very long moment of stunned silence. I looked at Patty, who was staring at the cage, astonished by what she'd heard.

Bostwick, who had been leaning in toward the cage to better discuss the matter with the resident parrot, stood up straight with his back still to Patty and me. He took another moment.

Then he turned and regarded Patty, who was wheezing a bit in her bed and still gaping at her talking bird.

"Is *that* in next week's script, too?" Bostwick asked.

CHAPTER NINE

"The bird said he wanted to kill the executive producer of the TV show he's working on?" Sam Gibson sat on a lawn chair in my backyard watching the dogs do laps around the perimeter for no discernible reason. Dogs like to run.

Sam had entered through the back gate to avoid the two news vans still staking out the front of my house. The rest of the horde, having grown tired of sitting at my curb watching the house not do anything, had taken off for the greener pastures of Manhattan or at least Passaic, where there had been a nice juicy fire that day just to give the TV reporters something to do.

I was going to give the dogs their regular walk tonight, and if the news vans wanted to follow me, they were . . . okay, *welcome* might be overstating it, but if that was how they wanted to waste their time, it was theirs to waste. I would be walking my dogs.

But Mom and Dad had gone out to a movie (with Dad saying he wanted to get some tips from Will Ferrell about timing, because my father's only been in the business since John F. Kennedy was president and Dad was a toddler) and the dogs had gotten restless watching me eat reheated pizza. Sam had closed his store early and dropped by ostensibly to see how I was holding up under the strain. The way I saw it, it wasn't my strain.

"Well, he didn't so much say *he* wanted to kill Les Mannix as he said someone should kill Les Mannix," I said, swirling the red wine in my glass because I'd seen people do that in movies and it looked classy. "It was either a command or an opinion. It was hard to tell."

"But there's no way he could have learned that in such a short time, and you had him all last night." Sam looked over at me. He wasn't drinking wine but had a cup of his own iced coffee from which he'd been sipping steadily. It never seemed to deplete the amount of liquid in the cup. Perhaps Sam had a secret supply stashed somewhere. "Where could he have picked *that* up?"

"I have no idea. I thought Patty was going to cough up a lung when she heard it. She barely spoke for five minutes, she was so stunned."

"Is that how she got you to take the parrot overnight again?" Sam asked. Barney was lounging in his travel cage in my bedroom tonight. I wasn't about to let him fly around the house again, so we'd let him do his winging at Patty's place before I'd packed him up to leave. Tomorrow Patty was getting her parrot back even if she was so sick he had to stay in her hospital room.

"No, we'd agreed to that before Bostwick even suggested coming along when I went to pick Barney up." I stretched out on the chaise longue while Steve, always the first to tire in the more strenuous games the dogs played, lay down at my feet and drank from the water dish I'd left there. Steve knew he had to get to the water first, and he was no dummy. "But that was weird. All of a sudden the detective wants to take a ride with me to talk to a bird he knows can't tell him anything."

"And then the bird tells him something." Sam rested his coffee cup on his stomach, holding it with both hands. "It doesn't make sense that he'd start spouting all this new stuff right out of the blue, and it's always about the murder."

A microphone started to insinuate itself between two posts in the stockade fence.

"That's right," I told Sam. "Clearly Barney has begun to hallucinate and anything he says is completely without any merit. I'm only worried someone will take something he spouts seriously." Off Sam's confused look, I nodded in the direction of the mic and he looked, nodded, and smiled.

"I didn't know birds could become delusional," he answered. "What do you think caused it?"

I made sure my voice was audible to the microphone, which was now clearly visible through the fence. "I think it's too much exposure to TV reporters," I said. "It's obvious Barney has taken up with a group of people who will believe anything they hear and have no powers of intellect so they just parrot back whatever is said to them."

"Very funny," came a voice from the other side of the fence. The microphone was withdrawn. "And we're radio reporters." Well, that taught me a lesson.

Sam grinned and took another minuscule sip of coffee. "I still don't get how Barney could get new phrases if you're not teaching them to him and Patty's not teaching them to him. Was he alone on the set with anyone who would have had the time?"

"I can't think of anyone. I was there for

only one day, but I was with him the whole time."

"What about Patty?" Sam asked.

"She's been sick in bed for two days," I reminded him. "She couldn't teach Barney anything except how to cough."

"Well, it must have been someone from the show," Sam said, leaning back as much as he could in the lawn chair. Bruno, who misses Steve when he stops playing, came over and nudged Sam's hand with his head. He got the stroke he was looking for; Bruno is a crowd-pleaser. Maybe I should start putting him up for roles again, but that's a full-time job and one I don't especially want. "That's the only thing that makes any sense," Sam went on.

"You know what's nice?" I said.

"That it's really not our problem who killed Dray Mattone?"

"Exactly. I'm sure Bostwick will be around another time or two because he has this odd idea that Barney holds the key to the murder, but after tomorrow that'll be Patty's responsibility. And from the looks she and Bostwick were passing to each other, I don't think that'll be too much of a burden for her."

"Really!" From the glass doors to my kitchen I heard my mother's voice. I turned, and there she and Dad stood. I had no idea how long they'd been watching us, but it couldn't have been much because the dogs ran up to my parents as soon as they were aware of new sources of treats and pets.

"What are you doing here?" I asked them. I stood up as Mom and Dad, dodging various canines, walked down the stairs from the deck to the yard. "Did the movie sell out?"

"There was no movie," Dad said. My parents passed a look between themselves that wasn't at all encouraging. "I guess we sort of lied to you, Kay. Sorry."

"But I see the two of you are having a nice evening," Mom said, gesturing to Sam, who came over and shook hands with my father. Men do that. I'm not sure why; the whole showing-you-don't-have-a-weapon thing has been outdated for at least a couple of years.

"Yeah, but I want to hear why you told me you were going to the movies when you weren't going to the movies." I wasn't about to let them off the hook. I am not at all a fan of suspense, but luckily Alfred Hitchcock isn't around to be insulted anymore.

Again, they exchanged a glance that was of the nervous variety. "I think that can wait until later," Mom said. She was professional enough not to telegraph her thoughts with a sideways look at Sam to indicate it was a family matter.

But he got the message. "I have to get back," he said. "It's getting late, and I have to open bright and early." That was true, except that it was only eight in the evening. Sam was being gracious and clumsy at the same time. It's not easy, but he can pull it off.

There were the usual protests that it wasn't necessary, but Sam was outside my compound gates within five minutes. He hadn't made much of a move out of the just-friends mode we were in now, even when my parents weren't around, so I assumed that ship had sailed and it was just as well. It would have been so awkward after we'd broken up and I still came in to get coffee in the morning. I like Sam, but I love his dark roast.

"Okay, spill it," I said once he was gone. "What's the deal here?"

"Don't you have to walk the dogs?" Dad asked. "It's about that time."

"The dogs have been out here in the backyard with me for an hour and you're stalling," I said. "You're getting me worried. Now tell me what's going on. Right. Now." Before there was time, I added, "And don't pass one of those guilty looks between the two of you. That's what's making me most nervous. Talk."

I looked at my father, who is always the spokesman for the team. He nodded, looking solemn. This was going to be a big one, I could tell.

"We're breaking up the act," he said.

"I need cake," I told him.

We went back inside and the dogs of course followed, no doubt worried about the end of the entertainment dynasty that was the Powell family. I had more concrete concerns, like whether my parents were actually going to move in with me permanently. I'd been considering looking for a larger house, but was on the fence about it financially given the mortgage I still had on this one. Did they have *any* money saved up? I'd never asked my parents about their retirement plans, and now it seemed they were retiring.

I headed directly for the refrigerator and took out a store-bought chocolate cake with white frosting that I hadn't actually managed to completely eat yet. There was about half of it left. There were three of us. It would be tight, but I thought we could manage.

Nobody said a word as I went into the bedroom (mine) and checked on Barney, who was still a parrot. It seemed you couldn't count on anything these days, but that had remained a constant.

I stood there a moment and took a nice cleansing breath that I'd learned in a yoga class ten years earlier (and that was all I remembered). Then I went back into the kitchen to talk to my parents and (mostly) eat cake.

Mom had already put out plates and cups and started coffee brewing. I knew it was chocolate cake with white frosting, so I got a glass to fill with milk. I was a rebel.

"Okay," I said as I sat down, "what's all this about retiring?"

Dad had taken off his jacket and stopped halfway between the table and the silverware drawer. "Retiring?" he asked. "Who said anything about retiring?"

"You did," I reminded him. Were there memory issues I wasn't aware of going on here? "You said you weren't going to do the act anymore."

He shook his head. "No, I said we were breaking up the act."

I felt my eyes narrow to slits. "So you're going to do two solo spots now?" Had they decided they could make more money charging as two acts?

My mother put her hand over mine, which

was unfortunate because my hand was holding a forkful of cake and that meant I had to stop eating. "No, Kay," she said. "What it means is that your dad is going to go out on his own, and I'm going to stop doing the act."

"Why?" I asked, and she withdrew her hand. More cake for me.

"I'm tired," Mom said. "I don't feel like going back out on the road anymore. The audiences are getting smaller, and frankly I'm not that interested. It was different when it was the three of us, and even in the last few years when Dad and I were working steadily, but the cruise ships have just started to wear me out. I don't want to be onstage anymore."

Now you have to understand the way my family operates. When I'd told my parents I was going to give up performing to pursue veterinary school (which thankfully hadn't worked out at all), you would have thought I'd told them I was repudiating happiness, oxygen, and the human race. Well, I was choosing animals over humans, but it wasn't that definitive.

So hearing my mother say she didn't want to be on a stage again was devastating. I actually stopped eating cake for a moment and stared at her. "Are you sure?" I asked.

"Very sure."

I looked from parent to parent and the seriousness of their expressions was enough to give Ingmar Bergman a sense of dread. "Are you two splitting up?" I asked, but I'm not sure my voice was actually audible. To my ears I sounded like a client I'd once had who was up for a live-action version of *Cinderella.* He was going to play one of the field mice. Convincingly.

But my parents must have deciphered my squeak because they both burst out laughing at the same moment. "No!" my mother shouted, and I heard a squawk from the bedroom; she must have awakened Barney. "Where did you get that from?"

"I just can't imagine one of you onstage without the other," I said.

They exchanged another of those glances, but this one was more personal and less ominous. Dad walked over and gave me a hug. "It was hard for us to imagine too," he said. "We spent the whole night walking around in the park trying to work it out. But what it comes down to is that your mom really isn't happy on the ships and I'm not happy without an audience. So this is the only way we can figure to satisfy both of us."

"We'll be apart a lot of the time, and

neither one of us is pleased about that," Mom said. "There are a lot of details we haven't decided on yet. But we thought we should let you know before Dad booked himself onto a cruise and suddenly he was gone and I was here."

The frosting was a little too sweet, I decided. This cake was good, but for earlier in the day. I put the rest back into the fridge. "Well, I certainly would have had some questions." I still had a few, like whether Mom was planning on staying in my house full-time now. But perhaps this wasn't the exact time. "Do you have your first solo booking, Dad?"

I'd thought it was a safe thing to ask, but apparently I had inadvertently stepped on a live wire. My father winced a little. "We just decided," he said. "I haven't had a chance to get the word out yet."

Rarely have I been as relieved to have my phone ring. The ID suggested the caller was Heather Alizondo, which I thought was unusual, but I answered. Heather immediately apologized for calling at night, which was also unusual. Most directors, even in television (which is a writer-producer's medium), couldn't care less whether they're disturbing you at an inopportune time.

This was not one, and I told Heather that.

"Good," she said. "I did ask you if Barney could be on the set tomorrow?"

Was she just calling to remind me? "Yes you did, and yes he can," I answered. "What time do you need him?" I was still puzzled, since this would usually be the task given to an assistant director or, more likely, the producer's assistant.

"Well, that's the thing," Heather answered. "We're going to need him a little earlier. Can you do seven in the morning?"

That *was* early, and would require me leaving home somewhere around the crack of dawn. I swallowed. "Sure," I said. "Are you trying to get all of Barney's work in early so you can shoot around Dray the rest of the day?"

I heard Heather hesitate. "No, this isn't a production company request. I'm asking because Sergeant Bostwick requested we all be in Dray's trailer at seven. He wants to reenact the crime."

Maybe just a little more cake.

CHAPTER TEN

"Okay, so the vic was standing here, according to the forensics." Detective Sergeant Joe Bostwick stood in Dray Mattone's trailer, which had been sealed from the time the police had left two days ago until now and smelled like it. Working from a diagram he held in his hand, Bostwick was sizing up the space. Between him, another detective named Baker, who seemed never to speak, and the camera crew — Bostwick had asked that Heather film the reenactment for reasons I didn't understand — it was a tight fit *before* I'd been instructed to place Barney's cage "exactly where it was that day." That was something of a test for me because I didn't remember precisely how everything had looked. I had been a trifle distracted by the blood on the carpet, which had now dried to a very unattractive brown.

Barney's habitat had been positioned on the table about six feet from the trailer door.

It's important to know that just because actors operate out of trailers, these are not your typical RVs. Stars like Dray would be given a double-wide version that wasn't ever going to be moving while he was inside it, so it was outfitted with considerably more luxury than a person might expect in a home on wheels.

Everything was compact or stowable, to be sure. But the seats were leather, the countertops were granite, and the carpet, at least before the brown stains, had been tasteful and luxurious. If you didn't know better, you'd believe you were in a classy if tight hotel suite, not a mobile home. Television stars lived well. If it hadn't been for the bloodstains on the carpet, the piece of wood on the table that had ricocheted from the gunshot, and the yellow police tape, I would have gladly moved in here and left the house for Mom and Dad. The chemical toilet was probably a negotiating point.

Now Dray Mattone wasn't living at all and that was why we were gathered here. Bostwick was sizing up the scene like a director. I almost expected to see him frame the area with his hands to better duplicate what it would appear like on the screen.

"He's got his back to the door," the detective went on. Baker, standing to his right and positioned toward the door, looked at it as if the killer was about to walk in and announce himself. Alas, that didn't happen, so we went on with Bostwick's little stage play. "He's doing something near the table, but I don't know what." He looked at a sheet attached to a clipboard in his hand. "Was there anything found on the table?" he asked no one in particular.

Nobody answered him. Baker simply didn't react at all, perhaps assuming the question must have been meant for someone else, because Bostwick never seemed to want anything of his colleague. I didn't answer because I had no idea what might or might not have been left on the table, and the film crew, each doing a job, wouldn't have answered if someone had asked whether the trailer was on fire. They were engrossed.

It didn't matter anyway because Bostwick pointed at the clipboard and nodded. "Right," he said, answering his own question. "There was a butter knife and a plate, like he was about to eat something." Amazing, Holmes! The powers of deduction were staggering!

Then Bostwick turned toward the trailer door and asked, "So where is Dray Mattone?"

It was now clear that the sergeant had lost his mind. I was doing my best to be invisible in the far corner from the door, and still I believe my gasp was audible from anywhere in the room. If Bostwick thought Dray was going to walk through the door, why did he think he'd set up this reenactment in the first place?

And then, son of a gun, Dray Mattone walked into the trailer.

All right, that was how it seemed on first glance. The man who entered was Dray's size and had his build. His hair was colored and fashioned just as Dray's had been when I'd met him on the set two days before. He walked with the same tightly controlled gait. His face was serious but showed the ability to be softer and more frivolous.

But it wasn't Dray.

"This is Dray's camera double," Heather told Bostwick.

The man stuck out his hand toward the detective. "Gary Norwood," he said. "I stand in — stood in — for Mr. Mattone when they were lighting the set."

Heather led Gary in by the shoulders like a proud mom. "He's too modest by half," she said. "Gary did almost all of Dray's stunt work as well."

"Not that much," Gary said, eyes down.

"Dray did his own stunts whenever he could."

"You don't have to keep that fiction alive anymore," Heather told him. It was odd the way she was promoting Gary to the gathering, most of whom had certainly known him a while. "Dray didn't like to do stunts and you are very good at them."

Gary just grinned goofily and kept searching the floor for something.

"Okay," Bostwick said, impatiently waving Gary toward him. "All I need you to do is stand here where we think Mattone was standing when he was shot. You can do that?"

"I did it all the time," Gary answered, his voice a little more combative. Do not dare impugn his ability to stand still!

"Good. Right here." Bostwick pointed to the spot. "Face that way." He indicated the wall away from the trailer door. "Now let's see how that looks." The detective stood back and took in the scene. David Lean on his most detail-obsessed day couldn't have looked more intense.

He pronounced himself pleased and motioned to Heather, who was directing the documentation process. They spoke quietly for a few moments and then she walked back behind Dan, the guy with the Steadicam, which was the only professional camera that would have fit in this tight space with this many people and gotten a decent image.

Personally I thought a uniformed officer with an iPhone could easily have handled the filming here, but Bostwick appeared to be making his demo reel in case Heather wanted to recommend someone as a director on a cop show. Bostwick might not solve the case, but he was going to have the absolute best crime scene video ever shot.

"Ready when you are," he said to Heather.

She looked a little surprised and answered, "We're rolling. Do what you need."

Bostwick must have expected to hear "Action!" or something, because he kept looking at Dan the cameraman for a moment, shrugged, and went back toward Gary. "Okay," he said, "you're Dray Mattone."

"I'm Gary Norwood," the double replied.

Bostwick waved a hand dismissively. "I know. But for these purposes, you're Dray Mattone, okay?" Gary nodded, although I'm not sure he had understood. "So you are alone in your trailer except for the bird, right?"

"Can't kill a zombie!" Barney insisted, just to make sure everyone knew he was there.

"Yeah," Bostwick said absently. He turned

back toward Gary, pointing. "So you're pointed in that direction and you're doing . . . what?"

Gary stared at him. For a while. "I dunno. What?" he asked.

"I'm asking you."

Gary, obviously very confused, looked around. "What do you want me to be doing?"

"That's not the point," Bostwick told him.

Gary looked from face to face, no doubt searching for some assistance. Because I was not bright enough to avoid eye contact (as the others were), he settled on me. "Do you know what he means?" he asked.

How to say this in actor-speak? "He wants you to ad-lib," I said.

The poor kid looked absolutely terrified. "I'm a stand-in," he hissed at me. "I don't know improv."

"Fake it."

He looked at the table in front of him. "Should I use the stuff on the table?" he asked Bostwick.

"Do whatever you think Dray Mattone would have done" was his answer, and I expect it was not the one Gary had hoped to hear.

Gary examined the table, which still held a plate and a dull knife. "Okay," he said as unconvincingly as I've ever heard it said. He picked up the knife and stood there holding it as if waiting for a piece of toast to pop so he could butter it. Naturally, he looked down at his hands while holding what I'm sure he considered to be props.

"According to the angle of the bullet, his head was up when he was shot," Bostwick said. "Hold up your head."

Immediately Gary's neck snapped upward and he stared directly ahead. "Is this better?" he asked. I wanted to give the kid a cookie and tell him it would be okay in a little while.

"Well, now you're not doing anything," Bostwick noted.

Heather finally came to poor Gary's rescue. "I'm here to direct, Sergeant," she said. "I don't know anything about the forensics you're trying to do. Why don't you concentrate on that and let me get the whole thing on video for you? I promise we won't miss anything."

Bostwick, having been reminded he was a police detective and not Martin Scorsese, nodded brusquely. "Okay, kid," he said to Gary. "You just stand there and relax. Mattone didn't know anything was coming."

"Is something coming?" Gary squeaked.

"Not really, no." Heather jumped in

before Bostwick could frighten the young man any more thoroughly. "This is just a run-through, Gary. We're not doing anything for real."

That seemed to satisfy the stand-in, who just stood (because that was literally his job) and waited. Bostwick looked at Heather, who nodded. The detective then gestured toward the trailer door.

"Now in accordance with the angle of the shot, this man is the proper height for the shooter," Bostwick said to the camera, apparently believing he was now the host of a true crime TV show. "If we can see how the crime went down, we might be able to get a better idea of who might be the killer."

I naturally looked toward the door expecting another stunt performer or one of the production assistants, whose job it is to do everything nobody else wants to do. Instead, the door opened and Les Mannix entered.

"You wanted me in here?" he asked Bostwick.

"Just for a moment," the detective told him. "We're reenacting the crime and you are the right height to stand in for the shooter."

This was all seemingly news to Mannix, who looked both surprised and concerned. His voice deepened to convey responsibility and portent. "Should I be calling my attorney?" he asked.

"You're not being asked to do this because you're a suspect," Bostwick told him. "You're being asked to do this because we need someone exactly five foot eleven, and you're that height. I'm sure we could have found someone else to do it, but I'm betting you'll want to be in on this so I don't have to tell you about it later. Am I right about that?"

Mannix thought it through and you — or at least I — could see him weigh his options. If he insisted on seeing his attorney, he'd look like a suspect in Dray's murder. If he didn't, he might do something that would give Bostwick the upper hand. There is nothing television producers like less than letting someone else call the shots.

Eventually he fell back on his first line of defense — seeming to be reasonable while continuing to monitor the situation. "Of course," he told Bostwick. "I'm happy to help the investigation in any way I can."

"Good," the detective said. "Now our friend Gary here is pretending to be Dray Mattone. You're the person who shot Mattone."

"No, I'm not." Mannix was pretending to be witty, but it was clear he wanted that on

150

the video record. He'd been near enough cameras to know when one was running. Heather had the Steadicam operator back himself into the threshold of the open door so he could widen his angle.

Bostwick gave Mannix his intended chuckle but did not directly address what the producer had said. Bostwick would be the determiner of who had shot Dray, and Mannix's denial, on the digital record or not, meant nothing.

"So you're standing in for that person," he said, nodding once in Mannix's direction. "Now if you would just put your feet onto the marks that have been made on the floor, I'd appreciate the angle."

Mannix obliged, saying he knew how to "hit his marks" from a brief career as an actor before he'd moved behind the camera. "What do you want me to do?" he asked Bostwick.

The detective once again referred to the diagram on his clipboard. "The killer is right handed, and so are you, Mr. Mannix. So, here." He reached into his pocket and retrieved a pistol. "This is the model of gun that we found in Ms. Powell's purse yesterday and that we are assuming, pending confirmation from the ballistics department, is the murder weapon. It's not the same gun, but it came from your prop shop, so it's the same type and caliber."

Mannix studied the weapon as Bostwick handed it to him, and it was clear the producer had held a gun before. "We have a number of weapons on set," he noted. "It is a cop show. This is one of the guns we keep for our detectives to carry." He hefted it, held it as if aiming. "It's not loaded, right?"

Maybe Mannix thought he was being funny — his grin was of the bad-boy variety — but Bostwick was not laughing. "Of course it's not loaded," he said. "Well, it is loaded with blanks because we want the weight to be the same. We take every precaution."

He repositioned Mannix in the role of killer behind dear sweet Gary, who had not moved a muscle the whole time. "Now stand like you've just walked in. You pull the gun out of your pocket — yes, put it in your pocket first, Mr. Mannix, good — then aim it at Mattone here." Bostwick referred back to his ever-present clipboard. "No, the angle is lower. Like this." He adjusted Mannix's right arm so the gun was being held at hip level, but was pointed upward. "That's it. Now let's see it in one swift motion. Come in from the door." Bostwick looked up to see Heather and the Steadicam operator in the doorway. "Okay, just take a couple of steps back and then pull out the gun and fire it. Let me see what that would have looked like."

Barney was fussing a bit, so I walked over and gave him a peanut to keep him sociable. During that time Mannix got himself into "character," stepped back, and looked to Bostwick for some direction. Bostwick stood and stared at him.

"So?" he said.

Heather Alizondo rescued him. "Action," she called from the doorway.

Mannix knew what that meant. He took a breath, straightened his shirt, and took two steps toward the spot where Bostwick's team had marked the killer's stance. Not being a professional actor, he had to watch the floor for his mark, but he hit it, which was all that mattered.

The producer was taking his role seriously. He reached into his pocket for the gun, which he found fairly easily. It had been conspicuous in his suit jacket just out of sheer weight. His face took on an angry snarl and he pointed the gun straight out, then remembered the correction Bostwick had given him and held it at his right hip, angled up severely.

"Put down the gun!" Barney yelled. He

dropped the peanut as he spoke.

That might have been what startled Mannix, or it might just have been his general awkwardness in his role, but he looked toward Barney and not Gary as he pulled the trigger on the gun. The problem was that instead of the click we expected to hear, we got the loud report of a live round being discharged as Mannix's gun, handed to him by a detective of the New York Police Department and guaranteed to be unloaded, shot a bullet when it shouldn't have.

Gary hit the floor face first, and for a sickening moment I thought Mannix had shot him. It must have seemed that way to the producer too, because Mannix looked at the gun and flung it to the floor. "I didn't do that!" he shouted.

Bostwick looked absolutely astonished, but his immediate reaction was to reach into his pocket for a pen, which he used to pick up the still-smoking pistol from the trailer floor.

"A lot of people want you dead, Dray," Barney said.

CHAPTER ELEVEN

Luckily, Gary had simply fainted and fallen to the floor because he'd been facing away from Mannix and the last thing he'd expected was for the gun to go off. Bostwick did notice a hole in the roof of the trailer that he called yet another team of forensic experts to come and examine. He said they would be at the set in a half hour.

Mannix, relieved that he hadn't killed a stand-in (the unions frown on that), sat down on the leather sofa and got an assistant to bring him a scotch without asking Bostwick whether it would be all right. Gary came around after a minute or so, and the group of us sat him on one of the other leather seats in the trailer. He was pale and asked for water; Mannix's scotch got there first. There is a hierarchy in Hollywood and it is not pretty.

Heather, after her boss and Gary were squared away, offered to show Bostwick her video of the event so he could see from her angle exactly what had happened. They huddled in a corner watching the footage on Heather's camera monitor. (Fun fact: The instant video monitor for movie cameras was invented by . . . Jerry Lewis.)

I tended to Barney, who seemed none the worse for wear after the loud noise. Hearing a gun go off anywhere can be startling; when you're in a small enclosed space it can seriously mess with your hearing for a good couple of minutes. So I couldn't hear what Bostwick and Heather were saying as they screened the footage.

Mannix, however, was within earshot, and he was constantly stating his innocence in the shooting of Gary, which had in fact not happened, mostly because Mannix was a lousy shot. Gary, on his part, sipped the water that came after a few minutes and looked at the bullet hole in the roof of the trailer.

"This job isn't worth it," he said. I was probably the only person who heard him and I did not argue the point.

Bostwick walked away from Heather's monitor with his hand to his chin. "It's not what happened here in the trailer that's the problem," he said to no one in particular. "It's the time between when I left the station and when I walked into this trailer that someone either switched guns or loaded the one I had on me. That's what I wish I had on video."

He didn't have it on video.

"Look, I have an agitated client here," I said. Barney had just made a perfectly normal squawking noise that I was using as an excuse. "Is there any reason I shouldn't take him home?"

Before Bostwick could answer, Heather stepped in front of him. "Barney's still got scenes to shoot today," she reminded me. "I'm going to need about two hours of his time."

"When can you start?" I asked.

She looked at Bostwick, who shrugged. "Don't leave the studio," he told her. "Aside from that, I don't need you right in this trailer."

Heather turned back toward me. "Give me an hour," she said.

I nodded. "Okay, but I'm going to take him onto the sound stage if that's okay. I think he's spent enough time in here, probably for his life." I reached for the cover to put over his cage.

"The stage is being lit," Heather said. "It's better if you're there, actually, so they can work around Barney being in the cage on set."

"How are you going to work around Dray not being there?" I asked.

"We got all Dray's stuff shot already. I just need some reaction shots of Barney."

Reaction shots? Did she expect the parrot to look different on command? But if there's one thing I've learned in my showbiz life, it's never to argue with an artist or, worse, someone who thinks she's an artist.

"Okay," I said, "I'll get him there." I put the cover over Barney's cage, something you do whenever transporting a parrot. On the way to the door, which admittedly wasn't a long walk, I passed Bostwick and said, "See you, Joe." Actually I hoped I wouldn't see him again because that would mean I'd be staying on set after today, but why bring it up when he clearly had a lot on his mind?

"Yes you will," he answered, which seemed ominous.

Instead of heading directly to the sound stage, though, I took Barney to my car and settled him into the back seat. I wasn't planning on driving anywhere, but I did want just a little chunk of time when there wasn't anyone else bustling around. Film sets are insanely difficult places to think.

And I had a good deal to think about:

Barney was working on a TV series that might or might not be ending thanks to the death of its star. That death had been brought about with Barney in the room, and while he didn't seem especially traumatized by the whole thing, he had strangely picked up a number of new phrases when that simply shouldn't have been possible.

Dray's murder had also meant the kind of suspicions and tensions that follow any company of entertainment professionals had been multiplied by a noticeable degree. People were looking at one another in ways they had not before, wondering who might have been the one to walk into the trailer and pull out a gun. The rest were assuming this gig was coming to an end and scrounging around for the next one.

But what I found myself circling back to, no matter what track my train of thought had started out on, was the idea that my parents were breaking up their act. That was such a staple in my life I found it hard to imagine it would not be continuing. The act was something I'd known literally all my life, and now instead of being a stable unit, Mom and Dad were becoming two separate individuals, one of whom would probably be living in my house all the time.

I wasn't sure I knew how to handle that.

We hadn't really had time to discuss it the night before. The call for Bostwick's botched reality show version of Dray's shooting had been for a very early hour, and that meant I had to get to sleep early last night. Once I'd taken the call, despite my wanting to iron out all the plans for Mom's retirement and Dad's transformation to a solo performer, I had asked for a day to process the information and gotten myself into bed. I hadn't actually slept all that much, but it was the intention that mattered.

All this rumination wasn't getting me anywhere, and I was in fact sleepy from the night before. So I decided to act like a mature adult business owner and call my office. Consuelo, as ever, answered on the second ring. Not the first, not the third. Always the second.

"I was wondering when you were going to call in." One of the disadvantages of caller ID is that for people like Consuelo it has eliminated the need for something so prosaic as *hello.*

"Things have been a little busy," I told her. I filled her in on the morning's laugh-filled agenda so far and asked her what was new at the office, which I remembered as a place I used to frequent but now couldn't clearly picture.

"The woman from Giant Productions called and is interested in Bagels," she reported. "The dog, not the food."

"Yeah, I sort of figured that. Do they want to see him?"

"They do. You want to take a ride over there and schedule something, or do you want me to do it?" Consuelo never asks as if she was unwilling or unhappy about taking care of the errand; she just wants to know which one of us will be handling it.

"I'll go. But call Miriam and tell her to make sure Bagels's schedule is free, okay?"

"No problem. Um . . ."

Oh, damn. "I'm sorry, Consuelo. I forgot to call Doris about the other cat, but I'll do it right now, I promise."

"Oh, it's okay," Consuelo said. She didn't want to seem like she was putting pressure on her boss, which was wise.

"No, I will. I'll call you right back."

I had Doris Kappel's number in my contacts, but I took a minute before calling just to figure the right tactic. On the one hand, I wanted Consuelo to have a fair shot at being an agent. On the other, I didn't want my client's owner to feel I was foisting her off on my "assistant" so I wouldn't have to handle both her cats. It was a tricky situation.

I'll admit it; I chickened out. I called Consuelo back.

"Listen," I said, "I'm not comfortable trying to separate the two clients between us."

"I understand," she said. Not even a tinge of resentment in her voice.

"But here's what we're going to do. The very next cat owner who gets in touch with us gets you, not me. The sign on the door says Powell and Associates. You're Associates. Okay?"

Consuelo's voice lightened, even if she wasn't elated. "Okay," she said. "Thanks, Kay."

"I mean it. The very next cat. Keep me informed." We hung up.

There was no problem with splitting things that way. The key was to get Consuelo established as an agent, and the best way to do that was to start her off with a fresh client, not someone we'd worked with before. I told myself that it was a better idea and that I wasn't actually a sniveling coward.

To be fair, it actually was a better idea. That last part . . .

I drove over to the Giant Productions and held another five-minute meeting with Harriet, Barney knocking around in his cage on the floor next to my chair, during which

Bagels the sheepdog was confirmed for an audition the next day. Bagels, whose main talent was looking goofy while being pretty smart (but not brilliant — he was no Bruno), was up for the part of Roger, a big shaggy dog who was going to befriend a bear in a family movie, thus teaching small children that bears can be friendly creatures tamed by dogs. Rated PG because, for all I know, the bear uses a mild curse word.

When we got to the *Dead City* sound stage again, only the back half of the morgue set had been put up; without Dray, there would be no need for the front part. This was to be a number of shots of Barney in his cage, presumably reacting to various stimuli, both good and bad. I guessed.

Heather was not yet present, but the crew was working on the lighting and I did notice a boom mike being prepared for use, which was interesting. Barney could be recorded at any time and didn't have to be in sync with any special audible cue. Why Heather would have called for a mike to pick up whatever he felt like saying was puzzling, but directors are nuts, and in my experience it's best to just give them what they want.

Mandy, the actress who had been playing the freshly deceased but actually still walking around zombie, was standing by but out of costume. The slab on which she'd been lying the day she shot the scene with Dray was set up, and that was as far as the set went today. Perhaps Heather wanted to get some longer looks at the scene as a whole, but without Dray in it, the shot would look weird. Maybe she wanted to get some reactions from Barney and still have Mandy's voice on the track. There wouldn't be any way to edit Dray seamlessly into the overall scene without some pretty expensive computer-generated imagery (CGI), which television doesn't usually like to do because remember how I said it was pretty expensive?

I put Barney on a prop table not near the craft services area. The smells from the food probably would have driven him crazy, and the baked goods there weren't going to serve me all that well either.

There wasn't much to do until Heather decided the set was ready for shooting, which probably wouldn't be all that long from the looks of things. Another couple of lights in place and we'd be all set to film a bird being himself. Playing herself, I guess. Mandy wandered over from the other side of the stage as I took the cover off Barney's cage and let him look around for a while.

"Hey," she said as if we'd ever spoken before. She looked into the cage. "Hi, birdie." She was about to extend a finger when I held up a hand.

"Give him a minute to acclimate," I said. "He might decide your finger is a peanut, and you don't want that."

Mandy laughed daintily. "No, I don't." She stuck out a hand. "I'm Mandy Baron. I don't think we met the other day. You're an agent?"

I took her hand. "Kay Powell. No, things were pretty hectic that day. Yes, I'm Barney's agent."

"I'm sort of . . . between agents right now. Are you looking for clients?" Mandy was very good at looking cute when she wasn't being a zombie. She could use it on men or women too.

I shook my head. "All my clients are animals," I said. "The kind with fur or feathers."

Mandy laughed. "I've met the other kind. Too bad. Know anybody who's looking? I work pretty steady."

"I'll ask around," I said, although I don't really deal with agents for humans very much. "Pretty tense around here, huh?" Change the subject so the actress doesn't make another pitch.

"I know. What happened to Dray." She shook her head at the senselessness of it all. "I mean, I thought he'd gotten himself back together, you know?"

I won't say I didn't consider the option of pretending I knew what she meant, but I felt it wouldn't actually give me any information at all, and what would be the point of that? "What do you mean?" I asked.

Mandy turned her attention away from Barney, whom she'd been watching intently, to me. "I guess I shouldn't have said anything."

Yes you should, I thought. "I don't think it's speaking out of school now. Is it anything you didn't tell Sergeant Bostwick when he questioned you?" If it was, I was heading to the front of the class. If not, there was no harm in telling a nobody like the parrot's agent.

"He didn't question me," Mandy said. "The other detective did, and I think he asked maybe one question, like, 'Who killed Dray?' The guy doesn't talk much."

True enough. "What did you mean, Dray had gotten himself back together?" Best to keep the conversation on topic.

"Drugs," Mandy said. She tried to be casual in the way she moved back to peer into Barney's cage, but as an actress, she was in the business of conveying emotions and being noticed. Right now she was exhibiting nervousness. "Dray had supposedly cleaned up. You remember."

Of course I did *not* remember, so I looked at her blankly for a moment. It's one of my best things. I'd ask my mother what she could find online about Dray using drugs later. Mom is a whiz on the Internet.

"When Dray went into rehab? It was on all the shows." Mandy searched my face for signs of recognition, so I gave her one despite my not having any. Recognition. "See? He went in for alcohol, they said, but I'm pretty sure it was cocaine. Anyway, he came out and they said he was doing well, but I guess he relapsed."

Before she could ask me to recall anything else I hadn't paid any attention to, I asked, "What makes you say that? Do you think the shooting had something to do with drugs?"

"There were people on the set the last week or two," Mandy said. She was making such a show of playing with Barney that it almost convinced me until I realized Barney was asleep on his perch. "Not all the time. Someone would be close to Dray as soon as a take was finished. Walk over to a corner and just huddle up like they were trying to decide how to break through the defensive line, you know?"

I was pretty sure that was a football thing. I nodded. Later I'd wade through what she was saying and try to figure out exactly what the subject matter might have been.

"It wasn't the same person all the time," Mandy went on. Once given to talking she needed little encouragement to keep going. Actors love nothing better than attention. It makes a little more sense when the actor, like my client base, is not a human. "But it wasn't like there was a new one every day."

"Did you ever see them doing drugs?" I asked. It had been so long since I'd heard my own voice I decided to try it out and see if it still worked. And sure enough, it was in perfect operational order.

Mandy actually glanced at me for a moment with a face that didn't quite make it to disdain but stopped somewhere around pity. "Of course not," she said. "Nobody's going to get high right on the set; there are too many unknowns and eyes on you here. But there were plenty of trips to the trailer, and it wasn't simply because that's where the comfy bed with the drink holders in the frame is kept."

I tried not to speculate on how Mandy knew about the drink holders in Dray Mattone's bed. I had sunk so deep into the none-of-my-business zone here that plunging further seemed to invite the danger of drowning.

"Are any of the people who were meeting with Dray here now?" I asked, looking around the sound stage and watching technicians stand around because apparently the work was pretty much done. There are always stragglers on a film set. Friends of the producer's children. Starstruck financiers. Aspiring actresses looking for . . . ways to further their careers. People who believed in their hearts that this was a glamorous, exciting business and not complete drudgery. Television series shoot incredibly long hours every day for weeks on end. Yes, the money (especially for the producers and actors) is really good. But anyone who thinks it's nothing but fun and thrills is in line for a tremendous disappointment.

"No," Mandy answered without even turning around to look. "None of them has been around since the day he died. In fact, I didn't even see one that day. I thought it was weird that he was actually doing his job without the security blanket he'd seemed to have with him every day before that. Then it made sense."

Sense? That would be a refreshing change

of pace. "What made sense?"

Mandy finally gave in to Barney's need for rest and faced me, resting her hand on her hip and fixing me with a significant gaze. I surmised she hadn't made it to the leading roles in TV shows yet because she tended to play everything a little too big.

"The fact that Dray got killed in his trailer. I figure he set up a meet there for after the scene was done, and something went wrong. That's when he got shot."

That was a lot of guessing. "Sure," I said, "but it could have been anything. A jealous husband. A crazy fan who thought Dray should be in love with her. An accountant who knew too much about Dray's tax return. Could have been anybody."

"Except I saw a woman go into the trailer and then a minute later I heard the shot," Mandy answered.

Okay, maybe she wasn't overplaying that part so much.

CHAPTER TWELVE

Mandy insisted she'd told everything about the day Dray Mattone had been shot to Detective Baker during questioning, that he'd written it all down and walked away without saying anything. I began to wonder if Bostwick and Baker were the police equivalent of Penn and Teller, and Baker was simply the silent partner in the act, but maybe the one who knew more than he was saying. Because he wasn't saying anything. See what I did there?

I was going to go look for Bostwick to ask, but it was barely a minute later that Heather Alizondo informed me that Barney should be made ready for his close-ups. Naturally the bird was asleep but I managed to rouse him pretty easily and being the trouper that he is, Barney managed to act exactly like himself in the cage under lights for about an hour and a half before Heather deemed herself satisfied with the amount of footage they had and dismissed Barney for the rest of the day, saying they might not need him again this week.

That led me to wonder what the status of *Dead City* might be at this point, but Heather, a director for hire, had not been privy to the high-level meetings about the show's future. I looked for Les Mannix on the way out of the studio but didn't see him. I figured I'd hear from the production company as soon as there was some news. The parrot who played Babs probably wasn't first on the call list to disseminate the news. The bird's agent was only a step or two beneath him on that list.

There were no cops on the set at the moment (which was refreshing), but I didn't make it all the way to my car free and clear. I wasn't exactly thinking about what was next on my agenda, which was taking Barney back to Patty's house and making sure he stayed there this time. Dray's murder, despite my ignorance of most of the facts, was occupying my mind.

I knew he'd been a famous television actor and therefore grossly overpaid, but even with the police around for the past three days and the usual sniping and gossiping of a theatrical company, I hadn't heard one word that had addressed the central question when someone walks up to a man and shoots him in the head on purpose.

Why?

Dray Mattone had been killed and people were trying very hard to find out who had done that. The repercussions of the act would no doubt be felt all the way back to Los Angeles, California. There was a widow who would be expecting to see Dray's estate. But what everybody on the set was doing, as they should, was working to complete the episode that they had been filming when the killing occurred. They couldn't afford to lose the whole week's work.

From what I'd seen of Bostwick and Baker, the Bobbsey Twins of the NYPD, they were working angles, figuring out forensics, and occasionally setting up re-enactments that went disturbingly wrong very quickly. The process was all about how and who. Nobody was focusing on why, and that seemed odd.

When a person is wealthy and famous, is it simply assumed that everybody wants him dead?

From what Mandy had told me not long ago, there had been a drug problem in Dray's past and possibly in his present. Was that a reason someone might shoot him? I couldn't imagine that he'd gotten too far behind in his payments. A star actor on a hit series that means a lot to the network can make as much as a million dollars for each episode. Between seasons there would be films that paid equally extravagantly. Dray couldn't possibly have spent so much or used so much that he couldn't afford the habit. Had there been something else?

The two big motives for violence, I'd been told, were money and sex (or jealousy about sex). Had Dray been cheating on his wife? Might she have found out? Was I just guessing that based on the idea that it was a woman who walked into the trailer? Was Mandy trustworthy? Could jealousy be a motive to perhaps stop into his trailer one day and empty a prop revolver into his head? Would Dray's wife, Denise Barnaby, have done it herself? It seemed from what the entire company was saying that she was in L.A. Maybe she'd hired someone to do the deed.

I didn't know enough about Dray as a man to guess what things he might have done that could have incited this kind of violence, but maybe it wasn't his fault at all. There is a lot of envy in show business. There's a lot of money in show business. That's not ever a good combination.

This musing was getting me absolutely nowhere, but it was short-lived. I stopped and put down Barney's cage so I could get out my car keys and get him settled in the back seat. But behind me I heard a voice say, "Excuse me?"

I turned. Next to the car, directly in line with Barney's cage, was Harve Lembeck, the assistant director who had asked, what seemed like four years ago, whether Barney wanted a cracker. "Hi, Harve," I said. Snappy repartee seemed not only unnecessary but impossible.

"What did the bird say about Dray?" he said. Apparently niceties like a greeting or an acknowledgment of the other person were not in Harve's conversational arsenal.

"What?" So he caught me off guard. It's not the kind of question I got on a regular basis. Until recently.

"The bird. They say he knows who killed Dray." Harve shifted his weight from one foot to the other like he was torn between running off at top speed and starting to dance the samba. "Is that true?"

Instinctively I reached over and moved Barney's cage away from the crazy man. "I'm not sure what Barney knows," I told Harve, "but there's no possible way he could tell anybody because he just repeats what someone has taught him to say." It was getting really old having to explain this over and over, and I was fairly sure this would not be the last time.

"Okay." Harve seemed to settle on his left foot and stood there looking at me a moment. Then he pivoted and began to walk away. That wasn't really helping.

"Hey!" I yelled after him and Harve turned to face me. "What was that all about?"

He took two steps back, assumedly so we wouldn't have to shout such confidential communications to each other in a parking lot. "I didn't want the bird saying anything that would get me in trouble," he said. "I need this job." He pointed his head in the direction of the sound stage in case I'd forgotten where he worked.

"What would get you in trouble with the company?" I asked.

Harve looked at his shoes, a move that I'm sure had gotten him out of situations when he was five, but wasn't flying today. "Nothing," he said.

"Oh, please. You practically just confessed to Dray's murder." I realized as the words left my mouth that this was probably an unwise thing to say to the man's face.

But he looked absolutely shocked by the

very suggestion. "What?" he squeaked.

"Well, I'm not saying you shot him, but you're sure making a case you did."

"I didn't shoot nobody." Well, that did it; I was convinced.

"You didn't shoot *anybody,*" I corrected without thinking.

"Exactly."

It wasn't my job to figure out who shot Dray Mattone, and even this exchange wasn't convincing me it was Harve anyway. But somehow it seemed the faster this murder was solved, the sooner Barney would be back in Patty's hands and working again, which meant I would be getting 15 percent of his salary. So I figured anything I could find out and pass along to Sergeant Bostwick would be helpful not only to the NYPD but to me personally. It's how an agent gets through the day.

"Look, Harve, you know something about what happened when Dray was shot. I'm guessing from the way you looked a minute ago that you probably didn't tell the police. But you're in the clear as soon as they find out what happened. So here's what we'll do: You tell me what you know and I'll tell the cops without mentioning your name at all." His face had blanched just in the split second I'd mentioned the police. "That way the murder gets solved, you don't have to worry about losing your job, and you don't get in any further trouble. How's that?"

It was a complex set of principles for a guy like Harve, who was still trying to puzzle out why I might have thought he had been asking Barney if he'd wanted a cracker. So it took a few seconds for him to process everything I'd said.

"I don't like it," he answered. "How do I know you won't tell the cops where you heard this when they ask you?"

"I'm a lawyer, Harve." That was actually true; I have a license to practice law in New York State. "Anything you tell me is subject to attorney-client privilege, which means I don't have to tell them anything. Give me a dollar."

Harve looked suspicious, but he reached into his jacket for a wallet and produced a fairly greasy picture of George Washington with the proper artwork attached. "Now I'm your lawyer for this matter," I told him. "I'll go to jail myself before I'll tell the cops where I heard whatever it is you're going to say. So spill it."

There was the usual interval during which Harve translated my words from English into whatever form of communication went on in his brain. "Okay, here's the thing," he said. "I wasn't there when Dray got shot, okay? I'd never been inside his trailer in my life. I just usually stood outside the door and knocked, trying to get him to come out in time to shoot the scene."

"Was Dray difficult that way? Did he get temperamental and stay in his trailer when it was time to film?" You hear of testy actors throwing tantrums, but sexist society that this is, they usually seem to be women. The men are deemed "tortured artists."

Harve shook his head. "Nah, he was a good enough guy and a pro. But he liked it for someone to come knock on the door and remind him, if he fell asleep or something, and I was the one who got the job. You know, I don't like to tell tales out of school, but sometimes he wasn't alone in there."

"He had women in the trailer?" I asked.

Harve did a head tilt. "Not a lot. Once in a while. They'd go in there in costume and come out wearing street clothes, and I don't think they were just using the place to change, if you know what I mean. There are still some costumes in there."

"So what happened that day?" I could hear Barney flapping in his cage. It was probably getting hot under the cover, so it was time to cut to the chase.

"It was getting close to the time to shoot,

so I went out to knock on the door like usual. But I stopped when I got to the door because I heard voices inside."

That probably wasn't terribly unusual, I thought, and Harve must have been anticipating that point because he didn't let me talk. "I heard voices in there before, of course, but this time they're yelling at each other and I don't want to get involved, you know? But I know Dray's gonna want to know it's time to come out and act, so I wait for the moment when there's a break in the yelling. Except there *is* no break in the yelling. Then there's a shot."

Barney squawked but did not speak.

"You heard the shot?" I said. "Did you see who came out of the trailer after that?"

"No! I didn't want nobody to know I was there. I didn't knock or anything; I just ran. Right back into the building so nobody would see me, especially the guy with the gun. I don't want no trouble." Harve, whose face overall resembled a callus, looked like he might cry.

"So why were you concerned about what Barney might have seen?" I asked him. "If you were outside the whole time and you didn't see the person who shot Dray, there's no way you could get into any trouble with the police or the killer."

"I lied before," he said. "When I said I never went into Dray's trailer in my life. I did go in that one time. Before the cops came. Because I was afraid they'd find something inside that was mine." Harve looked away and squinted despite the sun's being behind him.

"What?" I asked.

"The gun. The one that shot him. I'd given it to Dray because he said he wanted to get comfortable with it, you know, for his character. He's a medical examiner, so usually he's in the lab. But he knew there was a scene coming up in a couple of weeks where he'd have to handle a gun and he didn't want to look stupid with it."

"What does Dr. Banacek need with a gun?" I asked. "How do they get to that point?"

Harve looked at me. "A lot of the people in the show are zombies," he said. "Even after they're dead, you have to shoot them sometimes."

Under the cage cover I heard Barney mention that it is not possible to kill a zombie.

"So you gave Dray a gun?" I asked Harve.

He nodded. "From the prop stock. Maybe a week before this happened. It wasn't registered to him and he didn't have a license. I figured if the cops found out I'd

181

given him an illegal gun I could be back in jail."

"*Back* in jail? When were you in jail?"

"Got out about two years ago. Minor drug offense."

"But wait," I said, "you didn't have the gun. The gun ended up in Barney's equipment bag and the police found it with me."

"Yeah," Harve answered, still looking away as if searching for the missing piece of his soul in the distance. Everybody on a set is so *dramatic.* "I heard someone coming as soon as I got inside. I figured even if they saw me walking out, it was best if I didn't have the gun on me. So I stashed it in the bag next to the bird-cage and figured I'd come get it later. Except there were cops there forever, and by the time I got back, the bag was gone."

Yeah, guess why. "I'd already carried it away," I told him. I opened the door to my car, got in, and started the engine so the air conditioner could start working. I wanted Barney out of the heat. "So how come whoever shot Dray with that gun left it lying around in the trailer for you to drop into Barney's bag?"

Harve broke his leading-man-brooding pose and looked at me. Then he shrugged. "No idea," he said. "I actually got out of

182

the trailer before anybody got there. I don't even think they saw me coming out of the trailer."

"I'm guessing not or the cops would definitely have mentioned it," I said, making a mental note to tell everything in this conversation to Bostwick if I saw him again. And I was pretty sure I'd see him again. You don't get rid of a cop that easily.

I assured Harve that his secret(s) would remain untold, a pledge I had no intention of honoring if there was any need whatsoever to break it. Harve thanked me profusely while I once again informed that Barney would make no incriminating statements about him at all and (without any help offered from the kind gentleman) heaved the cage into the back seat of my car. Then I drove off with Barney before Harve could tell me anything else that would make me uncomfortable.

I drove straight to Patty's house, mustering a level of determination I usually reserved for difficult negotiations with producers. I was not keeping this bird another night and I didn't care what Patty said about it. She was Barney's human owner, she was the person who was going to receive 85 percent of his earnings, and cold or no cold, she was going to be seeing to her parrot that night and every night from now on.

Parrots can live to be eighty years old. Barney was six. I wasn't making that kind of commitment to any male, particularly one who had to be kept in a cage. No offense, Barney.

Steeling myself for the whole trip to Sunnyside, which would take only eleven minutes if not for the Long Island Expressway, I avoided calling Patty to let her know Barney and I were on our way. I didn't want to give her time to put together a really strong pathetic plea.

And that's why it came as something of a surprise — okay, an enormous shock — when I arrived at Patty's house to see two police cruisers parked in front, lights flashing. There were also two unmarked cars, one of which I recognized as Bostwick's, parked in the driveway. A crowd of neighbors was standing outside on each stoop, no doubt hoping to be the first to tell the others the real story about what was going on. There's nothing New Yorkers like better than knowing something first.

My first horrible thought was that whoever had shot Dray Mattone had done the same to Patty. But the logic, as I double-parked half a block from the house and left Barney in the car, windows open, eluded me: You have a grudge against a big celebrity actor and shoot him. So then you shoot the owner of the parrot who works on his show? There was a bridge to be built there, for sure.

It got both less stressful and more perplexing just as I got close enough to be held back by one of the uniformed officers. They hadn't yet gotten yellow police scene tape up to keep back the crowd, but it seemed unnecessary, since I was the only one actually trying to approach the house.

As strenuously as I argued that I was, after all, the parrot's agent and should be allowed into the crime scene (and yes, it sounded stupid even to me), the officer was not moved. "If there's a reason to get in touch with you, I'm sure the detectives will call," he said.

As it happened, that was when the front door opened and out walked Patty, dressed in sweats and with her hair uncombed. She was alive, though, and that was certainly something.

The thing was, she was also wearing handcuffs behind her back.

Holding her left arm, the one closest to where I was standing, was Bostwick, and Baker, who astonishingly was not doing the talking as they walked, had the right. They were maneuvering Patty down the stairs to make sure she didn't fall, and Bostwick seemed to be keeping up a running commentary in her ear as they moved.

I didn't know what to do. There wasn't a logical explanation for Patty's being arrested and there wasn't time to think about it right now. They were just about to make it to the sidewalk level when she looked over and saw me. Her face became animated — until now she'd looked like she was in a daze — and she called over to me.

"Kay!" she yelled. Bostwick's face indicated amazement that she wasn't paying undivided attention to what he was saying and he looked over toward me to see what might have diverted her. "They're arresting me! If I don't get out in time, take Barney for the night, okay?"

I might have opened my mouth once or twice. That just didn't make sense. "Uh . . . sure," I said. Patty leaned to my side, indicating she hadn't heard what I'd said. "Okay!" I shouted. "What are you being arrested for?"

"Shooting Dray Mattone!"

They hustled her into the car.

CHAPTER THIRTEEN

"They arrested Patty for Dray Mattone's murder?" Consuelo looked as puzzled as I'd ever seen her, and I've walked into the office with a boa constrictor on occasion. Okay, once. But she was usually unflappable, is what I'm saying. "How does that make sense? She was sick in bed when he got shot."

"Oddly, the police are not in the habit of explaining their arrest protocols with me," I told her, placing Barney's cage on the floor next to my desk. Maisie, the macaw who lives in the Powell and Associates office full-time, looked down from her suspended cage at the interloper and honked. Maisie does not work and play well with others. "I don't know what kind of evidence they have against Patty."

I know what you're thinking: My client's owner and a friend had been taken into custody and said it was for the murder of a man I'd met the other day who just happened to be a famous television actor. My parents were breaking up the act they'd had together for close to forty years. I had custody of a client whose species is not in my area of expertise (he's not a dog and I'm pretty good with cats, but beyond that I'm basically flying by the seat of my pants) for what now appeared to be an indefinite period of time. The set of *Dead City* was in complete chaos: Nobody even knew if there was going to be another episode shot or if the current one would ever be aired. I had responsibilities and obligations and I had some information for the police that they might or might not already know.

So you want to know why I went to my office and not anywhere else. A fair question.

The fact was, I really couldn't help Patty in her current situation. I wasn't her lawyer, and I'm not a criminal attorney at all, so looking into her arrest on her behalf was not an option. The information I'd gotten from Mandy (which she'd said she'd told Detective Baker) and Harve (which he definitely hadn't) wasn't going to help or hurt Patty as far as I knew, and with a suspect in custody, Bostwick surely wasn't going to take my phone call, let alone see me in person. And the news vans had already started converging around Patty's house before I'd managed to slip away.

There wasn't anything I could do about my parents' decision. Besides, I would definitely see them tonight whenever I managed to get home. The work to be done there was really more in my own head than in the actual world. They'd made their choice and I just had to figure out how to cope with it.

I had other clients who had been neglected the past three days, and that was not acceptable. Consuelo had not laid eyes on me for that same period of time, and although she is a remarkable office manager, she can't do everything all by herself. And frankly being at the office was a source of comfort for me. Right now comfort was not the worst thing I could experience.

"But what about Barney?" Consuelo wanted to know. "He's stuck without his mom, and we don't know how long that's going to be." Consuelo refers to the clients' owners as if they are the clients' parents, which is not only a little twee for my taste but also zoologically impossible.

"I guess I'll have to take him on," I told her. "It's not the best solution, but it's the only one I can think of right now."

Consuelo shook her head. "You don't know anything about birds," she said. "I know about birds. I'll take Barney."

I considered the crush of publicity that would unquestionably result from the arrest, and the horde of news vans that would once again appear outside my house now that the crazy parrot's owner had been taken in for the murder. "I can't let you deal with that," I told Consuelo. "It's more than you signed up for."

"It's exactly what I signed up for," she answered. "I knew what was going on with this agency when I interviewed for the job. And besides, nobody is going to be looking for Barney at my apartment." It was a good point. If we could get the parrot out of the office unnoticed — which so far had not been a real problem, as when given a choice, reporters appeared to want to ambush you at your home rather than your place of business — there would be no reason anyone would make the connection and stake out Consuelo's place. Not to mention her son, Diego, who prefers to be called Dee, would probably be able to convince anyone who came by that this was not in fact the bird they were looking for. Dee has Jedi mind powers, I'm pretty sure. He's that smart.

I resolved to find a cat client for Consuelo ASAP.

I texted Mom and Dad to expect a bunch of reporters despite the fact that Barney would not be joining us for dinner. Mom got back to me moments later saying they were going out for dinner and I'd have the place to myself.

Great. Me alone with my thoughts after the way this day had gone.

Consuelo insisted on introducing Barney to Maisie, and as usual with one of her ideas, it went incredibly well. The two birds shared Maisie's much larger cage for a while and seemed absolutely tickled with each other. Barney even gave up chewing on his piece of wood for ten minutes, a new record in my presence.

I thanked Consuelo, got the rundown on four more clients I'd be dealing with tomorrow, and texted Madolyn Fenwick to confirm that Barney would not be needed the next day. She answered that there would be no need for the bird tomorrow or the next day and thanked me for "being so understanding." She did not comment on the arrest of Patty, and I wondered if the company had been alerted.

That freed up a lot of time for me. I thanked Consuelo sixty or seventy more times, wrote a couple of emails that I'd been putting off because I'd been Barney-sitting, and walked down the three flights of stairs from my office to the street feeling oddly free, considering a man I'd met had been murdered and a client's owner was currently under arrest for the crime. Right now I could just be myself for a few hours until my parents got home; that seemed the near equivalent of a two-week vacation in Monaco.

Note the word *near.*

I had already unlocked the car and was settling into the driver's seat when my cell phone rang. I swear I considered not even looking and letting the call go to my voice mail but thought it might be a client's owner in need of service. I'm a one-person business except that Consuelo does half the work; if they can't get me when they need me, they will surely move on to someone else.

So I looked down. Dammit. The caller ID indicated I was being called by the New York Police Department, an organization rarely interested in bringing you a glass of wine or awarding you millions of dollars just for being a nice person. Still, you can't just ignore a call from the NYPD, and given the current circumstances, it was extremely unlikely the call was a mistake.

Sure enough, I heard Bostwick's voice on the other end of the line. "We have arrested Patricia Basilico in connection with the murder of Dray Mattone," he said, no doubt being sure to word his information properly. "She has requested the services of an attorney during questioning and said you are her attorney of record."

That made even less sense than anything else that had happened in the past seventy-two hours, and I told Bostwick exactly that. "I'm not a criminal attorney, Joe," I said, remembering he insisted on being informal. "Patty must be mistaken or so shook up that she doesn't know what she's doing."

"I'm not in any position to determine if the suspect is capable or incapable of determining right from wrong," Bostwick told me. I wondered if a captain or somebody of higher authority was watching over his shoulder. He sounded like he was reading off an officially distributed NYPD guideline. "She requested you, you are in fact a practicing attorney licensed in the state of New York, and she is entitled to your services if you're willing to provide them."

I started feeling the environment close in around me as if I had turned on the engine and siphoned the exhaust into the cabin.

But trust me, I hadn't done either of those things. "Let me talk to Patty," I said.

"She has already used her phone calls, but I'll allow it," Bostwick said. Which I thought was damn nice of him, given that he pretty much had to do that no matter what. The police are not entitled to stop a suspect from communicating with her attorney, and that was, at least for this one minute, what I appeared to be.

There was the usual jostling of the phone receiver — it appeared the NYPD was still operating on landlines — until I heard Patty's tentative "Kay?"

"Patty, I'm not a criminal attorney," I said. "They have to let you get in touch with one. I can look up a couple while we're talking if you want . . ." I started to search on my phone while the speaker feature assured me I was still on the line with Patty. I never trust the smartphone to do anything it's supposed to do.

"I want you, Kay. You understand about me and Barney and you know that I was nowhere near Dray's trailer when —"

I cut her off. "Don't say anything about Dray," I said. "They can use anything against you, even stuff they overhear when you're on the phone to me. I'll recommend a criminal attorney; I'll even call one or two for you, Patty. But you have to know that I'm not the person you want to be defending you on a murder charge."

"They haven't charged me yet," Patty said. Her voice was a little foggy as if she were on medication or just dazed from the events of the day. "But I trust you. I want you to be here. Please? Kay, I don't know where else to turn." And then she started to cry and that was just dirty pool.

"Patty. Listen to me. I'll do a bad job. I don't know what I'm talking about. I'm an agent for parrots and dogs and cats, not someone who can stand up in court and prove you didn't shoot somebody. Just let me find you someone who can do the right stuff. Are you going to have trouble paying? Is that the problem?"

She just continued to sob. "Please, Kay. Please. I've got no one else. *Please.*"

I was on my way back to Queens in two minutes.

CHAPTER FOURTEEN

It took me six minutes to locate my New York State Bar Association membership card in my wallet and my license in a separate credential folder I keep buried so far down in my purse it was under a lipstick I hadn't worn since my last actual date, which had been eleven months earlier. Lesson learned: I need to clean out my purse more often.

The lesson about dating more often I chose to ignore.

I needed the ID to get into the holding cell and the interrogation room where my "client," Patty Basilico, was sitting still in her sweats, hands not cuffed to the desk, the hideous fluorescent lighting making her seem like a murderer even to me. Anybody would look like a killer under those things.

"What evidence do they have against you?" I asked her after I had sat down, once again mentioned how I was the worst person on the planet to defend her in a criminal matter, and been rebuffed simply by her horrified expression.

"I don't know," she moaned. Patty is usually very even-tempered, but this was an ordeal on top of an ordeal and her voice was starting to show it. "As soon as I said I wanted a lawyer they stopped questioning me and started getting on the phone to you."

"This is crazy," I told her. "You weren't physically capable of killing Dray. Did you have any reason to want him dead?"

"No! I barely knew the guy." Patty shook her head too vehemently. I could see now that my impression of her from the phone must have been correct: She seemed like she was on some medication and was reacting a little more slowly than I was accustomed to seeing. "I worked with him for a few days to teach him how to deal with Barney like they were old friends. He'd been working with the previous Babs, so he knew something about parrots, but each one has a personality and Dray wanted to know what Barney's quirks were so they could show a rapport on camera." Actors, ladies and gentlemen, are nuts.

"Where did you work with him?" I was hoping it wasn't Dray's trailer because then it would be less likely Patty was familiar with the surroundings and that would at least be a point to bring up.

"Dray's trailer." There's a reason I'm not a criminal defense attorney. There are in fact thousands of reasons I'm not a criminal defense attorney.

"And what did you think of him?" I asked.

Patty shrugged. "He was a nice enough guy. You know actors — it's all about them. But you should expect that in this business. If you don't have a gigantic ego you won't make it past community theater, and maybe not even that far."

"Anything unusual you noticed? Something that might have indicated he was in some sort of trouble or someone was mad at him?" Patty's pretty smart and perceptive; she might have seen something that I could tell Bostwick to get him off the idea she had shot Dray.

She thought for a long moment. And then shrugged again. "Nothing special. People in and out of the trailer all the time needing something from him. Makeup, hair, agents, accountants."

Accountants. "Did they seem to think he had some financial trouble?" I asked Patty.

"Nothing I heard about, but they were always huddling in another corner of the trailer away from where I was sitting, so I didn't really get much of the conversation." Patty was trying to be coherent through what must have been the haze of illness (fading) and medication (I had no idea). "I was mostly dealing with Barney anyway."

I figured it was best to stay with her area of expertise. "How did the training with Barney and Dray go?"

"Well, I thought. Barney seemed to like him and Dray was attentive to Barney. You saw how he was on the set, right?"

Dray had been professional about working with the bird, I'd thought, but hardly like they were pals. "I thought they got along well enough to work together," I said.

"That's just about right. After I think three days of training on and off when Dray wasn't filming, they knew each other and Dray could cue Barney pretty well, which is really all you want. I didn't want him to think he was responsible for Barney, especially since I thought I'd be on set every day, not you. Sorry about that."

I shook my head and held up a hand. "Don't worry about it. You needed help and that's my job. But here's the thing: I'm still not a criminal attorney and I want you to have one."

Patty looked firm in her conviction. Probably a bad word to use. "I want *you,*" she said. "I can't explain the whole thing about a parrot to a new attorney. Besides, you've already given me advice about not saying anything in front of the police and all. I think you're cut out for this."

But I wasn't going to let an idle (and probably false) compliment condemn Patty to a long jail sentence. "I'll tell you what I'll agree to do," I said. "I'll be second chair on your case, if they charge you with the murder. But I'm going to contact a real criminal defense attorney and you're going to work with him just as you would if it were me. That way I'll know that my inexperience isn't going to be the thing that sends you to prison. And I won't agree to any other arrangement because that's how strongly I feel about it. Is that okay with you?"

Patty drew in her lips like she wanted to object, but she saw the look in my eyes. "Okay, deal," she said. "So far they haven't charged me with anything as far as I know, so maybe it won't come to that. But I want you at that table if we get to court, yes?"

"Yes." I wasn't happy about this, but I was considerably less anxious knowing I probably wasn't going to have to do much of anything about defending Patty if she needed defending.

I told her I'd be in touch as soon as possible with the name of a lawyer and that she should get in touch with me if anything changed with her status. I left the interrogation room and went immediately to look for Joe Bostwick because I still couldn't believe Patty had been arrested at all and figured he could best explain.

The officer who had brought me into the room showed me to Bostwick's desk where the sergeant was sitting and talking on the phone. I couldn't hear exactly what he was saying, but he looked agitated and hung up quickly after he saw I was there. He did not offer me a chair despite there being two in front of his desk. I stood.

"Since when are you a defense lawyer?" he asked.

"I'm not," I told him. "And I just spent a decent amount of time telling Patty that. Are you charging her?"

His face, which usually bore a look of slight amusement at the spectacle that is we civilians, was closed. I couldn't tell if he was annoyed with me for pretending to play Perry Mason — which I was assuredly not doing — or if there were some outside pressure, maybe from others in the department, that he was feeling on the Dray Mattone case.

"I'm not going to tell you anything," Bostwick said. "Get it straight: I'm not the friendly cop who tells you all you need to know to solve the crime yourself. It's not your job to solve the crime; it's mine. If you're representing Basilico, you'll get your information from the D.A. in discovery. If you're not, I have absolutely no reason to give you anything at all. Are we clear?"

I folded my arms because that seemed the best gesture of either indifference or resistance, and at the moment I couldn't tell which I was feeling. "That was very impressive," I said. "Did you rehearse it or are you that good off the cuff?"

"I'm serious. You'll get nothing from me. I'm not even sure why you came back here at all. Are you the attorney of record on this case?"

As I've said, I had absolutely no intention of trying to defend Patty against a murder charge. And as far as I knew at that moment, there had been no charge filed. But the way Bostwick was talking to me was so condescending and dismissive that I didn't want to just turn tail and run.

Besides, I wasn't 100 percent sure why I'd come back to talk to him either.

"Right at this moment I am," I said. "So let's pretend you're a cop and I'm a lawyer and maybe you can stop treating me like the dumb blonde in a burlesque sketch. How's that?"

Just to be clear: I am not nearly old enough to have worked in burlesque, at least not the classic definition that included so many characters of that ilk. But I was well versed enough in my showbiz history that I could make the reference without even considering whether my audience — in this case, Bostwick — would understand what I was trying to communicate.

"Huh?" he said.

That's what I mean.

"What I'm saying is that I am the attorney of record until such time as I find another lawyer who Patty agrees should represent her in what I'm fairly sure will at the very least be a suit against the city for false arrest. So suppose you start offering me the same courtesy you would any other lawyer who walked in here representing a client, okay?"

A small hint of the familiar smirk crossed Bostwick's face and then vanished. "I'm already treating you that way," he said. "I'm not telling you anything I'm not required to tell you by law. And right now that's absolutely nothing." He pretended to be interested in a piece of paper on his desk, which I could see was a memo from the department having something to do with saving money by sending memos via email.

"Okay, since you're going to be a jerk about it, let's just make one thing clear: Right at this minute you have not charged my client with a crime, is that right?" I asked.

He did not look up. "Not yet."

"So why is she still sitting in an interrogation room?" I said.

"Because we're still interrogating her."

"Then I want to sit in."

Bostwick looked up. "Wouldn't you be better served looking for a real lawyer for that?" he asked.

"Let me in with my client while she's being questioned or don't question her," I told him. "And if you're not going to question her, you need to release her."

"That's not my decision," Bostwick mumbled. Even though I'd heard him, I pretended I hadn't so he would have to repeat it. That's the kind of mood I was in by now.

"Then whose decision is it?" I said, moving my hands to my hips like Wonder Woman. I played Wonder Girl in a sketch with my parents when I was eleven. The costume was humiliating.

"Captain," he said, and pointed to a door behind him and to the left with his thumb. "Feel free to state your grievance."

"Captain who?" I said. "Kirk? America? Crunch?"

"Henderson," Bostwick grumbled.

Without saying anything else to him I walked to the door, which was marked *M. Henderson, Captain of Detectives,* and knocked. There was no response.

"He's not there," Bostwick said.

Now I was mad. I stomped back over to Bostwick's desk and stared at him. "Why are you jerking me around, Sergeant?" I demanded.

"Call me Joe."

"No. Now what's your problem?"

He stood up and looked me in the eye. "I don't have a problem with you," he said.

"You have a funny way of showing it."

"Connect the dots. If I don't have a problem with you and I'm acting like I do, maybe there's a reason," Bostwick said. "In the meantime, nobody's going to be grilling your client without a lawyer present because that's against the law once she's requested an attorney. I'd advise you seriously to find a criminal lawyer to be here when they do because you don't want to be in over your head at that time. Okay?"

Much as I hated to admit it, he had a point. "How much time do I have?" I asked.

"Best guess they'll release her for tonight and request she show up for more questioning tomorrow. They could keep her for up to forty-eight hours, but I don't think that's the way this is going to go. If I knew for sure, I would tell you that because you're the attorney of record. Got it?"

Going home was not an option until I knew for sure what Patty was facing tonight. I nodded my thanks to Bostwick — he had just given me a useful tip — and told him what I'd heard from Mandy and Harve, which he seemed to have filed away from previous interviews, but thanked me anyway. Then I walked over to a corner of the room, sat on one of the uncomfortable molded plastic chairs, and tried to think of a criminal attorney I could call.

I had never actually operated in those circles before, so the only name I could conjure up was Jamie Wallace.

Jamie had been in my class at Rutgers Law in Newark, both of us studying at night while working in other businesses during the day. He'd been so intent on getting into criminal defense that it was almost comical. Jamie was born to argue and loved nothing better than doing moot courts, a practice the rest of the law students absolutely hated. He wore suits to his; the rest of us were considered adequately dressed if we showed up at all.

I hadn't really kept in touch with Jamie since we'd passed the bar, but I did have his phone number in my contacts because once someone is on your contact list they don't ever come off even if they're no longer alive. That is one of the rules of twenty-first-century communications etiquette.

After going through the inevitable secretary Jamie picked up almost immediately. "Kay!" It was nice to hear the voice of someone actually happy to find me on the other end of the phone line. Phone satellite. Whatever. We exchanged the obligatory pleasantries and caught each other up (he had a wife and a baby son; I was me) and then he asked, being astute, why I was calling.

I explained about Patty and could hear Jamie's excitement level rising with each word. For a fairly young attorney like him to be involved in the defense of an accused killer — and one who had (allegedly) shot a TV star! — would be a career-maker. Jamie's a nice guy, but he's also really interested in being a hotshot lawyer.

"Okay, here's what you do," he said as soon as I had brought him up to speed. "Stay there until I show up, just in case they charge Patty or want to question her again. She doesn't say one word to the cops without one of us present. Got that?"

I'd already had it, but I liked the feeling of someone else being in charge, particularly someone who might actually know what he was doing. It was a refreshing change of pace.

"Got it. Then what?"

"Then you sit back and let me handle it. I'll consult with you along the way, but I'm willing to bet you want no part of that courtroom, and I'm happy to be there. Am I right?"

He was right.

"Meanwhile," Jamie continued, "I'll get some people here working on discovery. Even if they don't charge her today, they had enough to bring her in and question her. From what you've told me, they shouldn't have anything. Patty wasn't able to be in the trailer when Mattone got shot, and you can vouch for that. She also didn't appear to have a motive. We'll find out if she has a permit to carry a gun."

"The gun was probably from the prop department at the studio," I told him.

"Yeah, but I'll bet the bullets weren't, and she might or might not know anything about firearms. It's not as easy to shoot somebody dead with one shot as you think, even that close up. It's worth knowing, anyway." I was starting to think I'd called the right number.

"You're on your way?" I asked. The sooner he got here, the better.

"I left already," Jamie said. "Don't let her talk to anybody." And he hung up.

Jamie was coming from Hackensack, easily a one-hour drive and longer if he took public transportation, which he wouldn't. My plan right now was to blend into the appalling green paint job and wait for Jamie while following Hippocrates's lead and doing no harm. So even when I saw the heretofore absent Captain Henderson unlock his office door and go inside, I did not storm in and demand justice for my client. For one thing, I had no idea whether she was getting justice now or not, so I might just end up looking silly, something I have tried to avoid even when walking a seriously groomed poodle (she looked like topiary) into an audition for a *Lassie* reboot (she didn't get the job and the show never got made).

Then Henderson, a tall man roughly

resembling a rock-climbing wall, walked out of his office and to Bostwick's desk. He leaned over (imagine a rock-climbing wall leaning over) and talked quietly to the sergeant, who looked impassive. Bostwick nodded once or twice and then pointed.

At me.

Henderson drew himself up and walked toward me. His voice was exactly what you'd expect from someone that imposing — deep, sonorous, and generally intimidating. The guy was born to boss other people around.

"Ms. Powell?" he said, knowing full well that Bostwick had told him who I was. I stood, which didn't help that much; my head came up somewhere south of Henderson's shoulders. I decided not to wait and began disliking him immediately. But I admitted to him who I was.

"I understand you're representing Patricia Basilico," Henderson said. Again he was telling me something both of us knew. I wondered where this was going, but stuck to my policy of agreeing that true stuff was indeed true. "We are releasing her in a little while, but we want your client to remain available. Can you vouch for her reliability? Can we be sure that she won't leave the state of New York?"

"I'm representing her only until her criminal attorney arrives, and he is on his way," I assured the captain. They were releasing Patty, but they wanted her to stick around? What did that mean? "It might be best to wait for him."

"It will probably take that long to get her processed and ready to leave," he answered. This guy was being disturbingly agreeable. "Just wait here and I'll alert you when we have all that done."

And that was the item I was supposed to overlook. "I don't think so," I said. "If you're planning on having any contact at all with my client, I'm going to insist on being present the whole time. I'm sure you understand that she has exercised her right to an attorney. This of course means she can have one present whenever the police are going to be there to possibly question her or overhear something she says. It's my job to protect her rights until her lead attorney gets here."

Maybe I should have gotten into this criminal defense business after all. I was starting to impress myself.

Henderson's mouth tightened visibly, but he said, "Of course," and gestured for me to follow him.

We walked through the halls back past the

interrogation room where I'd left Patty. When we kept walking down the corridor, I said to Henderson, "My client was moved and I was not informed. You know better than that."

"Your client asked to use the restroom. Should we have come and gotten you for that?"

I sort of thought they should have but didn't actually know so I kept my mouth shut. I'd ask Jamie later.

Finally we reached a door marked simply 6, and Henderson nodded to a uniformed guard standing there. The guard unlocked the door and opened it.

Inside, Patty Basilico was sitting on a bench. The room also held a sink and a toilet. It was a holding cell. I gave Henderson a dark look.

"I thought you weren't charging her," I said.

"Not yet."

"Then what's she doing in a cell?"

Henderson shrugged. "She needed a restroom. This was the closest one."

I pushed past him and had a sudden jolt wondering if the door would be locked behind me; that seemed like the worst thing that could happen. Literally. But it didn't. The door was left open. I walked to Patty and sat close to her on the bench.

"Did you say anything to them?" I said quietly.

She shook her head. "But they said stuff to me."

I held up a finger. "Wait until we're outside," I said. Patty nodded and went back to looking at the floor. Ten minutes in a holding cell and she was damaged. I couldn't let her go into a cell for any longer than that.

I looked at Henderson in the doorway and said, "Is there any reason she needs to be in here while she's being processed?"

He said there was not and ushered us into the hallway and then back to his office, where he started punching keys on his computer to begin the paperwork process of getting Patty out of the building. It's amazing what happens once you're in the system; it takes nothing short of a miracle to get you out.

Sure enough, the red tape kept us there until (thankfully) Jamie Wallace arrived and I could immediately fade into the background again. Jamie did not kick up a lot of dust with his entrance; he loved the courtroom but wasn't the flamboyant performer a lot of litigators are, so he had a reputation for being reasonable. Until he beat you in court without making you mad. It's a peculiar but valuable talent.

"My client has not been charged," he told Henderson. "You can fill out whatever paperwork you want after she's left, but she is definitely leaving. You have her contact information. When you need her back here, you know where to look, and it's my office." He handed the captain a business card, gestured for Patty to stand up, and we left the precinct without so much as a peep from any of the cops.

I wish I could do that. The attitude would make it so much easier to get work for cats.

Jamie made sure we kept up a very quick pace — so no time for talking, because Patty and I were essentially following him and trying to keep up — until we reached the parking lot. Patty of course didn't have a car, so I was going to drive her back to her house.

"What did you say to them?" he asked her. "Don't be embarrassed, just tell me the truth because that's the only way I can help you."

"I didn't tell them anything," she answered. "It's what they said that scares me."

I could tell Jamie didn't care for that statement or didn't believe her. "What did they tell you?" he asked.

"They said they knew I killed Dray because they had physical evidence that I was in his trailer."

"What physical evidence?" Jamie asked.

"I don't know; they wouldn't tell me."

Jamie shot me a look that essentially said I knew the client better than he did and I should step in. It was a very eloquent look.

"*Were* you in Dray's trailer?" I asked Patty. Best to get to the heart of the matter.

"Not the day he was shot, no. But I told you, I did some training for him and Barney there a few days last week. They can find my DNA or whatever all over the place, I guess."

I didn't know much about crime, but I knew DNA evidence wouldn't have come back that quickly. "What else did they find there?" I said.

"They found a letter I sent Dray," she mumbled.

That was new, and I shot Jamie an equally loaded glance. "What's in the letter, Patty?"

"I sort of . . . told him I was pregnant with his child."

Jamie closed his eyes and breathed in.

CHAPTER FIFTEEN

As it turned out, we all went back to Patty's house, but I drove alone and Jamie made sure Patty rode with him. He didn't want to miss anything.

But it was clear when we arrived that she hadn't said anything more about her rather stunning claim. Jamie looked at me and said, "We've been waiting until we were all together," before we walked into Patty's house and sat down.

I had explained where Barney was staying before, but Patty seemed distracted (imagine!) and asked me again. I said he was with Consuelo, whom Patty knows, and she appeared to be pleased with that, but kept looking at Jamie as if he were going to execute her if she gave the wrong answer. He was on her side. And he hadn't even asked any questions yet.

She offered us pound cake, but we both declined. Patty was coughing less and seemed to be largely recovered as she sat on the sofa, just as she had at the police station. Which was odd, since she'd told me this morning that she was not feeling a lot better yet. I mentioned that to her.

"I guess the adrenaline rush from being arrested sped me along," she said. "It's a new experience, and not one I'd like to repeat if possible." She looked at Jamie. "How do we do that?"

"We start by you answering everything I ask you completely and honestly, no matter how it sounds," Jamie answered. He had a yellow legal pad (which seemed appropriate) that he had taken out of his briefcase (see previous parenthetical comment) and held poised on his lap awaiting the notes to be taken.

"I'll try," she told him quietly.

"There is no try. Do or do not," Jamie answered in a relatively awful impression of Yoda. Patty looked a bit puzzled as if he had somehow insulted her. "Sorry. Bad joke. Let's start with this: Were you in Dray Mattone's trailer the day he died?"

"No," Patty said. "I was sick in bed." She turned toward me. "You remember, Kay. I asked you to come take Barney because I couldn't get out of bed that day."

Jamie did not look at me for my confirmation of Patty's statement. He wasn't interested in things he already knew; he was just getting her ready for the rest of the questions and gauging how honest Patty was going to be. I admired his technique.

"Okay," he said. "Now, you said before that the police had a letter you'd written to Dray informing him that you are pregnant with his child. Is that right?"

Patty nodded and bit her lip. "Yes. That's what the officer told me, that they'd found the letter in the trailer after Dray was shot."

Jamie shook his head. "That's not the part I was asking about. Sorry if I wasn't clear." He was being kind and observant of his client's state of mind. I'd called Jamie because I remembered him from law school. Now I was finding out just how good he was, and he was good. "I meant, is it true that you are pregnant with Dray Mattone's baby?"

Patty closed her eyes. "Yes," she said. She did not whisper it or say it so quietly we had to strain to hear her. Patty was owning her situation even as she sat there not looking at us. It must have been difficult to do that, but she wanted Jamie to know he would get true answers from his client.

"Okay. So you had a relationship with Mr. Mattone that wasn't just about training your parrot to work on his show." Jamie stated the obvious fact but left it hanging for a response.

"That's right. I've actually known Dray for a couple of years. We met at an awards dinner. I was there with Barney as part of an act they were doing with the emcee that night, and he was there as a nominee. We just hit it off, and . . ." Her voice trailed off.

"Did you know he was married?" I asked. I should have kept my mouth shut and let Jamie conduct the interview, but I also wanted to feel like there was a reason I was there.

He didn't seem to mind and nodded in Patty's direction.

She opened her eyes again. "Yes, I knew. Of course I knew. I mean, it was in the newspapers when they had the wedding and Dray told me about it. I wasn't trying to steal her husband, you know. I just . . . we just . . . fell in love. Denise was in L.A. and I was here in New York, where he was filming most of the time. I knew it wasn't right, but it didn't feel wrong. Does that make sense?"

Nobody answered her question. Instead Jamie leaned forward. "So you were having a relationship with Dray Mattone. And you found out you were pregnant with his child.

Why did you have to write him a letter? Why not just go to him and tell him?"

"We'd broken off the . . . we weren't seeing each other anymore and he stopped taking my phone calls."

That rang a bell in my head. "So what you told me about training Barney with Dray last week was a lie?"

"No. We broke it off last Tuesday, before I knew about the baby. We were working with Barney that day, and that's when Dray told me he was trying to work things out with his wife and that meant we weren't going to be a thing anymore. That's the term he used — a *thing*. Can you believe it?"

"When did you find out you were pregnant?" Jamie asked.

"Saturday. And I tried calling Dray, but like I said, he wouldn't take the call." Patty didn't seem angry so much as puzzled about her ex-lover's behavior. "He kept having his assistant Tracey send me emails telling me he was unavailable."

"So you wrote him a letter?" Jamie asked.

"I couldn't email. Tracey would get it; she checks all his incoming email. And I couldn't talk to him on the phone or go to the trailer anymore. So I thought, Well, a letter would do it because I could send it directly to his house. I had the address and

I knew Tracey didn't read the mail he got at home."

"But the letter showed up in his trailer," I said.

Patty shrugged. "He must have brought it there. I don't know."

"What was his reaction?" Jamie asked. His pen was poised over the pad; this was an important question.

Patty's face hardened a little. "He didn't react at all," she said. "I never heard from him again."

Something occurred to me. "Did Barney get the job at *Dead City* because of your relationship with Dray?" Jamie actually gave me a slightly sharp look. The question wasn't relevant to the case he was building, but it had leapt to my mind and I didn't curb the impulse because, well, I'm me.

"I guess," Patty answered. "I mean, he told me the old parrot had died and they needed a new one, so I suggested Barney. Next thing I knew, they were calling you to bring him in for an audition, Kay." Her eyes flashed. "But if Barney hadn't been able to do the job, it wouldn't have mattered that I was with Dray; he wouldn't have gotten the job."

Jamie's glance at me softened. Maybe there had been some value in what I'd asked after all, although I certainly couldn't think of what it might be.

But he wasn't going to let me get in another question for a while; this was Jamie's show and he wanted that to be made clear. "Okay, Patty," he said. I sat back to indicate I would not be a distraction. "You find yourself carrying Dray Mattone's baby after he breaks off the relationship. You try to contact him to let him know and he won't answer your letter or take your phone calls. Can you see how the police might think you had motive to want him dead?"

Patty looked a little surprised and took a moment to think it over. "Not really," she said. "I can see why they might think I was mad at Dray, but I really wasn't so much as mad at myself. I was so stupid to think I was going to be different to him. But what's the advantage to killing him? What do I get from that?"

I wanted to say *revenge,* but I restrained myself. Give me points for that.

"Some people would call it a crime of passion," Jamie said. "But I don't think this has the hallmarks of that term at all. Whoever went into Mattone's trailer was already carrying the gun. That indicates premeditation."

I shook my head because Jamie needed to

have the facts straight. "The gun was already in Dray's trailer because Dray was using it to get comfortable with it. He had a scene coming up where he carried a gun and wanted to look like he was used to it. So the gun was there. The real question is where the bullets came from, because the prop man who gave Dray the gun had loaded it with blanks. But the same thing happened with the gun Sergeant Bostwick used in reenacting the crime."

Jamie mulled this new information over, but I was looking at Patty to see if she reacted. She seemed to be listening intently but absorbing. The information seemed to be new to her, but she did not seem shocked or worried. One of the pillars of Jamie's defense had just fallen — albeit not a huge one — and she didn't seem to be connecting it with her own situation. It was like she was watching Jamie and me on TV.

"Okay," Jamie said, processing, "so the gun was there, but we don't know how the live bullets made it to the trailer, although it's definitely worth checking if all the guns in the prop shop are loaded with live ammo. That's something we'll have to research. I'm going to get an investigator on this case right away." Then he started talking to Patty about retainers and hourly fees and suddenly she *was* connecting it to herself.

"I . . . I'm not sure I can afford you," she said. Patty's house was not lavish, but it was sturdy. Her car was not new. Barney's new gig at *Dead City* was bringing in some money, but it had just started. I knew she still had her day job as a tax preparer for a storefront chain of accountants, and while that paid the bills, it didn't pay for a criminal defense attorney. The truth was that most people in Patty's position would probably have had to take out a second mortgage on the house or face the music with a public defender if she ended up being charged with Dray's murder.

"Don't worry about that right now," Jamie assured her. "I'm sure we can work something out." He wanted this case for the spotlight it would shine on him, not for the fee. The money would come after the case was over. If it got to court, he would be a nationwide celebrity. Patty could probably get a book deal if she wasn't convicted. The money would be there for sure. "In the meantime I'm going to get to work."

"What will you do first?" I asked. This was practically a tutorial in criminal law for me.

"First thing is to find out if Patty is actually going to face charges," he said. "But if the cops drag their feet and don't give me a definitive answer, we're going to have to go the other way."

"What's that?" Tell me more, teacher.

"Find out who we can pin the murder on in a jury's mind."

CHAPTER SIXTEEN

I left Patty's house not much later, actually hoping there would be heavy traffic going home because I desperately needed time to think.

Jamie and I conferred briefly on Patty's sidewalk after we left her house. He said finding the real killer wasn't the lawyer's job, but giving a jury a plausible alternative would be helpful if the case ever got to trial. This was an esoteric area that I'd never actually confronted in my representation of furry animals who just wanted to be appreciated as artists.

I didn't even turn on the radio during the drive home. There was way too much to process after this marathon day. But the fact was, I really didn't feel like thinking about any of this stuff.

There was no avoiding it: Patty had put herself in a very tough position because she was the only person thus far that the police could attach to a strong motive for killing Dray. This, coupled with the fact that she had been in his trailer before — even if there was no evidence she was there the day he was shot — could produce fingerprints and physical proof. That wasn't good.

Jamie wanted to find a viable alternative to present to jurors. I suddenly wanted to find out who had actually killed Dray Mattone because I needed to help my friend and her parrot. That sounded weird even to me.

If the police truly believed Patty had shot Dray, they would not be concentrating on finding another suspect, but on gathering evidence against the one they had. That meant Patty was essentially in this on her own except for Jamie and me.

Suddenly I very much wanted to talk to my father. He's great at making plans, and I felt like I needed one.

It took more than an hour and a half to get home and I'll confess that after about an hour I finally put on a CD. The strategizing and the struggle to think of all possible contingencies had finally filled up my brain and threatened to leak out my ears, which I felt would be unfortunate. Maybe a little distraction wasn't the worst thing.

Darkness had fallen with a loud thump

when I got home and remembered my parents wouldn't be there. The serenity I'd hoped for before I saw Patty carted away was no longer tops on my agenda; now I wanted to have people around, and for once there were none here.

Except there were, of course, news vans in front of the house. No doubt the word of Patty's arrest had spread in nanoseconds and the parrot angle was back in the Dray Mattone story. I very loudly proclaimed, making sure to fill my speech with profanity I knew they couldn't possibly air, that I would not be answering questions and that Barney was not here. I was especially colorful in my proclamation that there was no #$@&ing way I would tell the reporters where he was, and felt good about myself as I walked into my house.

But after getting the requisite ecstatic greetings from the dogs, I leashed them up and decided to take them on one of our longer walks just to get my blood moving around and kill some time until Mom and Dad got home from their dinner. Maybe we'd go see how Sam was doing and be friendly without flirting, which seemed to be the new normal.

It wasn't long into the walk, with Eydie trying to yank my arm out of its socket every now and again because she'd been cooped up too long, that we ran into Lorraine Toscadero, the prototype of a Jersey girl who works at L'Chaim!, a kosher bar and grill on West Roosevelt Avenue.

I'm told many women named Lorraine prefer to be called Rainey or something of that ilk. Since moving to Scarborough and meeting her, I've always called her Lo, which seems to befit the woman: "Lo! Here comes Lorraine!"

Perhaps I do have a streak of the vaudevillian in me after all.

"Hey, Lo," I said after the dogs finished greeting her with sniffs, hand-licks, and in Steve's case, a vehement attempt to climb Lo from the knee up (which failed).

"What's up with this Dray Mattone thing, Kay?" Lo doesn't waste time with the niceties; she jumps right in, which is perfectly fine with me. She'd earned it with some late-night glasses of wine, support during rough times, and the occasional free kosher drink after the doors have been closed. "You were on the news yesterday. You looked like you were being hunted by zombies."

"I was. The newspeople have their job, but it's no fun being part of the story. They swarm after you and ask some really stupid questions."

"Did you actually know Dray Mattone?" We started to walk again because Bruno had stopped doing what walks are for and was now moving on with his life. I was moving on with a plastic bag because I am a good citizen who owns dogs.

"Not really, no. I met him the day he died and we talked for about five minutes. He seemed like a nice enough guy, though." I felt there was no need to mention his unborn child and the fact that a woman who wasn't his wife was carrying it, particularly since she'd been on television being arrested earlier today.

"Who do you think killed him?" Lo asked.

Walking with dogs is not a great form of exercise because the dogs are not aware that you want to raise your heart rate. They *are* aware that the grass smells like another dog has been here recently, or that someone dropped a chicken leg in this spot two weeks ago, or that it might rain and make the grass smell interesting later. So you have to stop periodically and stand while the dog investigates. When you have three dogs on their leashes, multiply that stop-and-start action accordingly.

Lo instinctively took Bruno's leash and walked alongside us, decreasing the tension on my right arm, which was welcome.

"I honestly have no idea," I told her. "There are rumors he had relapsed after getting out of rehab, but I didn't see any evidence of that, so I don't know if it's true." Normally I would not have even mentioned such a thing, but I know Lo is trustworthy, and besides, Jamie wanted to deflect suspicion from Patty. How did I know Lo wouldn't be a potential juror (despite her living in another state)?

"I think it was his wife," she volunteered. "I've been watching the news shows. She doesn't seem that upset."

"She was three thousand miles away," I reminded Lo.

"Yeah, I don't care. It's always the wife. I'll bet he was hooking up with someone else and she paid somebody to whack him." Lo was staring straight ahead as she walked Bruno, always looking for the next interesting tidbit of life. I tend to walk the dogs looking down at the dogs. Bruno is big enough, though, that you can do both at the same time.

"Don't believe what you see on TV," I told her.

Lo gave me a "meaningful" glance. "What do you know?" Her voice was low like Natasha Fatale's, assuming I had dirty secrets I was about to share.

Instead I chuckled in what I supposed would be a convincing manner to a civilian. "I don't know anything," I answered. "I'm just the parrot's agent."

And of course that's when my phone rang. Jamie, so I had to take it.

"She isn't charged yet," he said in lieu of greeting. "Part of it is that their forensics people are saying the killer was five-eleven and Patty is nowhere near that. But I'm calling about this guy Les Mannix. How well do you know him?"

Lo could see the look on my face, but I had the phone in one hand and two leashes in the other and didn't have the wherewithal to consider my expression at the same time. "What do you mean?" I asked.

"I mean, I heard someone called him out at the memorial service and said he was the one who killed Mattone. Think that's true?" Jamie said.

"Honestly, I've had maybe forty-five seconds of conversation with the man in my life," I said. "I couldn't tell you whether he was likely to get a parking ticket." I didn't mention Barney yelling, "Kill Les Mannix!" That seemed a little too on the nose, and I was positive Barney hadn't shot Dray.

I could practically hear Jamie thinking through the phone while Lo looked at me with an expression that indicated we had a lot to talk about when the phone call was over. Which I should have seen coming. After a moment Jamie asked, "Do you think you could find a way to get back on the set to ask around tomorrow?"

My first impulse was to say I couldn't. I'd so been looking forward to not dealing with this and letting Jamie handle it. "Wouldn't your investigator be a better choice?" I asked.

"With cop stuff and official things, yeah," he answered. "On the set he's going to sound like an idiot because he doesn't know the business. I'll send him after you've laid the groundwork, but come on. We're splitting the fee on this one." That was news to me. "I'm not asking for much. Talk to two or three people. An hour at the most."

Well, if we were splitting the fee . . . "I have to take a dog to an audition at another production company on the lot tomorrow," I said, which was true. "I'll spend the hour, but no more than that. Fair?"

"Perfect!" Jamie is really good at getting what he wants, and there's no reason for me to tell you how I know that. "Just give me a call when you're done and tell me what you've found out."

"Wait. What am I asking? I can't just walk

233

up to people and start with, 'Did you shoot Dray Mattone?' "

Lo raised an eyebrow.

"No," Jamie admitted, "but you can see if anybody knew of a grudge, particularly one this guy Mannix might have had. I mean, he was, like, the executive producer on this show, right?"

"*One of* the executive producers, but he was the showrunner, which means most of the decisions were his. He was the guy who probably set the salaries and negotiated the contracts, so he would have had most of his dealings with Dray's agent, not the actor himself."

"Well, he's the boss, and everybody hates the boss," Jamie said. "There are plenty of possibilities there."

Lo and I passed Cool Beans, where Sam was not visible from the street. She noticed me looking for him, but I did not hesitate as the five of us kept walking.

"Anybody else?" I asked.

"If you could find the woman who called Mannix out, that would be good," Jamie said.

"Haven't the cops figured out who that was yet?"

Now Lo was *really* interested; her mouth was practically twitching in anticipation.

There wasn't anyplace on West Roosevelt where we could stop and sit with the dogs, and Lo would turn left in two blocks if she was walking home. She wasn't going to let that happen without finding out what was going on.

"Not that they're telling me," Jamie said. "Keep in mind that I have virtually no contacts in the NYPD, although I am licensed in New York. I'm going to see about hiring a freelance investigator who might have better ties than me and be able to talk to cops he knows. I'll let you know about that tomorrow. Meantime, talk to Mannix and to this Heather Alizondo, the director. She worked most closely with Mattone; she might know something. And you said there was a woman who thought Mattone had a drug connection on the set?"

"Yeah, but Mandy was a guest actress trying to get noticed," I told him. "She would have said she'd seen Godzilla in the commissary if she thought it would get her hired."

"So don't talk to her. Talk to other people around the set. See if they knew what his connection was. Maybe ask like you're trying to score something."

"Yeah. Maybe not." My luck I'd ask an undercover narcotics agent and spend the next ten years in the big house because Jamie wanted to know if Dray had a connection on the set.

"Okay, I'll let you wing it. You're an actress. Get out there and act." Jamie hung up just when we were reaching Lo's corner, which she could not have appreciated more.

"You need help walking the dogs back to your house?" she asked. Butter could have melted in her mouth but probably wouldn't have gone to the trouble.

"No, it's all right," I said, reaching for Bruno's leash.

She snatched it away. "Forget that, Kay. I'm walking back with you and you're telling me everything you know about Dray Mattone getting shot."

So I did. She's Lo. She's a force of nature.

By the time we got to my back fence in an effort to avoid the news reporters at the front of the house, I had regaled her with my version of the Dray Mattone saga. Lo had not interrupted once — she listens intensely, as she does everything else — which led to my probably telling her more than I would have if she'd stopped me frequently. It's a cute trick. Try it if you ever want to get someone to talk. Just listen.

She digested the sordid tale for a few moments while I let the dogs into the backyard and closed the gate behind them. They did a couple of laps after being let off the leash just to show me what they could do if they decided to ignore my human rules. It was pretty impressive, even for Steve, the smallest and slowest of the bunch.

"So who do you think did it?" Lo asked.

I hadn't really considered that before. Having been so intent on proving that Patty *didn't* kill Dray, the fact that someone else had was sort of a forgotten side issue. I thought about it.

"If I had to put money down on it, I'd guess it was Harve," I told her. "He admits to putting the gun in Dray's trailer. He claims he doesn't know how it got loaded with live bullets, but he'd be the one to find them if he needed to."

"Okay, so the first thing you want to do when you're asking around tomorrow is make sure you stay away from Harve," Lo said definitively.

That seemed counterproductive. "You sure? If he's the most likely suspect, shouldn't I be trying to find something that proves he did it?"

"You're forgetting," she said.

"Forgetting what?"

Lo looked at me with a dash of pity in her eyes. "If he did it and you're snooping around, he might not hesitate to do it again."

"Oh, yeah," I said. "That."

CHAPTER SEVENTEEN

Bagels the sheepdog did remarkably well in his audition for the Giant Productions film, which I knew he would. The audition had basically been to sit, stay, lie down, and stand on command, and Bagels can do that in his sleep. I'm not sure he hadn't done it in his sleep today; the hair over his eyes makes it hard to tell. Bagels isn't the brightest bulb on the Christmas tree, but he's far from stupid, and once he's shown what to do, he can do it without ever hesitating. He's not quite the pro that Bruno is, but as his current guardian, I have decided that Bruno is retired. He's been through enough.

Once Bagels finished going through his incredibly furry paces with assurances we'd hear about the role in "a couple of days," I called his human owner, Miriam, and gave her my report, which was that the dog had done well enough that I thought we had a very good chance for a hire. I asked Miriam if she minded whether Bagels got home an hour later than she might expect, and she said it would be fine.

Dammit. Now I had to go onto the set of *Dead City* without Barney and ask questions.

Mandy was no longer on set, since her part had been filmed and she was a one-week guest actress, although she'd be needed on location later in the week. There was no reason for her to hang around; she was either at her next job or on the hunt for one. So I moved on to finding Les Mannix, who I was told (by the stage manager Bonnie Prestoni, who was *always* around) was on the set today, although he would be in meetings with the producers and the regular cast for much of the afternoon.

It was ten-thirty in the morning, so I had some time if Les did. I found him in the craft services (that's food) area, of all places, having a chocolate-frosted doughnut. That indicated to me it was not a great day — people in the film business consider sugar to be synonymous with cyanide, and technically they're close to being right, but I don't care. In this case, Les eating a doughnut was much like seeing a normal person holding a bottle of sleeping pills too longingly.

He nodded at me and then saw Bagels and

looked concerned. "Did we hire a big dog?" he asked. "I don't remember one in the script."

I shook my head. "He's here auditioning for a movie elsewhere on the lot. I just wanted to see what was going on with the show, whether it's been decided if you're going to keep it on the air."

He grimaced a little; I took it the news was not going to be good. "I'm not ready to make an announcement yet," he said. "And I don't want to offend you, but I think some of the long-standing cast and crew members should hear what's going on first."

Bagels sat, right next to a platter of his own name. "I'm not offended," I told Mannix. "I do need to know whether Barney's schedule is opening up or if he has a steady gig. But I completely understand your need to tell the others first. I'm not trying to be a problem; I'm sure you have enough to deal with." The key to dealing with producers especially is to remind them what a colossal big deal they are.

"Yes, I do." Mannix agreed he was tremendously important and therefore terribly busy. He leaned over confidentially and spoke very quietly. "The network wants to cancel the show. They think it's too expensive and that nobody will watch without

Dray because he had the most followers on Twitter."

"Oh, that's a shame," I said, thinking of how Patty could have used the income from Barney's job to pay some of her legal fees. "I wish it wasn't going to happen that way. How soon?"

Mannix looked a little offended. "I said the *network* wants to shut it down," he reminded me. "I haven't given up on it yet. Even if they do, I could find a home for it on cable or maybe Netflix. They get really good numbers from us, you know."

I nodded. "You have a lot of platforms to choose from." It's best to stay positive in these conversations. If there had been a grizzly bear carrying a chainsaw advancing on Mannix, the best way to tell him to get going would have been saying that he was doing so well the president of the United States wanted to talk to him in the next room. He'd move much faster. "Does the way Dray died hurt your chances of catching on somewhere else?"

Interestingly it never occurred to Mannix that my question was at all inappropriate. He was a show business professional and his loyalty was to the show. It was too bad one of his stars had been shot, but the rest of the company relied on him. So what I'd asked had been a totally legitimate question in his view.

He put on a "thinking" face and moved his head back and forth like a beagle trying to decide which pose was more adorable, which I have seen happen. "Actually I'm not sure," he said. "On the one hand, it hurts to lose a star the audience loved that much. It wasn't the Dray Mattone Show, you understand, but his presence was a large part of the audience appeal, especially among women eighteen to thirty-four." There is nothing a TV producer cares about more than demographics.

"But on the other hand, by the time the show gets picked up by another platform and we have product ready to deliver and air, I'm sorry to say the coverage of Dray's death will have gone away." Mannix looked both wistful and irritated. "After the first episode or two, the novelty of it will have worn off. We'll probably get huge numbers that first week, but if we don't deliver a blockbuster show to keep them watching, it might be a problem."

"So a really strong first episode would be key." I didn't actually care about the first episode — other than to ensure that Barney had a steady source of income — but I wanted Mannix to feel that I was on his side. "Would it be too tacky to have the team investigating Dr. Banacek's murder?"

I know for certain, based on years in show business, that Mannix had considered that very question before. There's no way he hadn't, even if for just a moment. But he stared off into space as if it were the first time the subject had been breached. He might as well have been Columbus's crewman in the crow's nest searching desperately for land.

"We will have to explain the character's absence," he said. Mannix, like most television producers, had begun his career as a TV writer, so he had a strong sense of what would and would not work on the screen. "But I don't want to look like we're exploiting what happened to Dray." He broke his pose and looked at me. "I'm getting ahead of myself. First we have to get through negotiations and find the right outlet for the show, assuming the network definitely cancels us."

"There were some scripts in the pipeline before Dray was shot, right?" I said. "I heard there was one in which he would have to carry a gun."

Mannix turned his head to look at me as if I'd said there was a rumor Dray was really a unicorn. "Never! Dray had it written into his contract. No guns. And we respect our actors' feelings, especially when it's in their contracts."

This was perplexing, but I had to move on. "So would you have scripts you could rewrite to exclude Dray, or would you have to start from scratch with a new network?" I asked.

"Still depends on whether our current network cancels us," Mannix reminded me.

"That's not certain yet?" Bagels plopped down on the floor and put his head on his paws. A lot of dogs would have been attacking the meats and cheese available not far from his head. He was way too classy.

"Nah." Mannix curled his lip. "They're all corporate executives. They're terrified of making decisions that might blow up in their faces. They haven't said that's what they want to do, but I can read it."

"Would it help if Dray's murder got solved?" I asked. Best to get back on the actual reason I was here today.

"Why? Do you think you can do it?" Mannix thought he was funny. I could tell him stories. Well, one story.

I decided to ignore his refusal to believe in my sleuthing skills, mostly because he was right. "I'm just thinking that if the murderer was found, there would be closure to the story and you'd know how to proceed with the show because you could be sure not to mirror the real events. Like, you wouldn't want to have Dr. Banacek die of an overdose or something." It was sensitive, but I thought I'd slipped in the drug reference skillfully.

Mannix didn't. His face reddened and his back stiffened in his chair. "What does that mean?" he asked a little too loudly. Bagels lifted his head, not threatening but wondering what the heck was going on.

"I'm sorry," I said, although I wasn't sure what to apologize for in this case. "I'd heard that Dray might have been having some problems sticking to sobriety and that might have gotten him into trouble with the wrong people. Maybe I'm wrong in thinking that could have led to what happened with him."

"You're definitely wrong," the producer grumbled, although in a less offended tone. "I know for a fact that Dray was attending meetings and looking for a sponsor to help him through the rough spots. He wasn't about to relapse."

He sounded absolutely sure of his words, but producers are good at that, telling you the next pilot they're producing is groundbreaking and edgy when they know it's just another sitcom. "Maybe it was something else, then," I said. "Do you have any idea who that woman was at the memorial service?"

Mannix didn't have to ask which woman. "The crazy one with the curly hair who was telling me I killed Dray? I've been asking around the crew and nobody knew exactly who she was. You know under normal circumstances I'm not on the set very much. There are other producers who handle the day-to-day stuff. So I'd never seen her before. But they tell me she'd been around Tuesday or Wednesday last week, although nobody here could tell me what her job was or even her name."

"Why would anybody think you'd want to kill your star?" I asked. It's funny what you can get people to say when you play dumb.

"There had been some contract negotiations that weren't resolved yet, and there were stories in the press that we'd had words," Mannix said. "They weren't true, you understand. Dray and I got along famously. But the rumors could lead people to think the wrong thing."

I wondered why the police had been so quick to bring Patty in for questioning when she was hardly the only person who might have had a motive to kill Dray. But I chose — wisely, I think — not to mention that to

Mannix.

"Well," I said, "thanks for keeping me in the loop. If there's a decision on the show, please give me a call." I gave him a business card and got Bagels to stand up and walk away.

I was heading toward the control booth where I had the best shot at finding Heather Alizondo, but was hijacked halfway across the set of the police precinct by Harve, the last person I wanted to be hijacked by, and he was looking unusually nervous even for him.

"You didn't tell anybody what I said, right?" That was Harve's version of a greeting.

Let's see: I had told Jamie and Lo, and I was pretty sure I might have mentioned Harve to Bostwick, so yeah, I might have said just a little regarding him. "Of course not," I said. "I promised, and I never break a promise." This is showbiz language for "You should never trust me because I'll do whatever I have to in order to forward my career," the unspoken law of all things in the biz.

"Well, I think the cops heard something, and you're the only one I told." I didn't care much for Harve's tone: It was hushed and had an edge of menace in it. "I know for a fact that *I* didn't say anything, so that leaves you."

I relied on my stage training — and the stages had all been in resort hotels, not the Royal Shakespeare Company — to look nonchalant, although I was probably more chalant than most. I shrugged. "Somebody must have overheard," I said. "I know I wasn't the one who ratted you out, but if you want my advice, you'd tell the detectives what you know so you don't get into any more trouble. There's no crime in giving Dray Mattone a prop gun to practice with. Is there some other reason you think they'll give you trouble?" I mean, besides the previous conviction and jail time and the fact that Mannix said there would have been no reason for Dray to practice with a gun. Besides those things.

Maybe there was something Harve, not necessarily in the running for a Mensa membership, might say if he was under pressure. We were in a public area, so I wasn't all that concerned he'd do something violent or unpleasant; he wouldn't want to be seen by the crew members walking in and out.

"Nah, there's nothing else." He hadn't been making eye contact before, so there was probably nothing to read into the fact that he continued to look past me, probably to make sure we weren't being overheard *this* time. "You're right. I didn't do anything illegal. You're a lawyer, so you'd know, right?" Actually, Jamie was a lawyer and I was an agent with a law license, so it was likely there were laws being violated I had no idea about, but why bother Harve with that kind of detail?

"To the best of my knowledge and belief, you haven't done anything illegal," I said. It's one of the few legal things I know. It sounds important but doesn't really cover you in any serious way. Harve didn't know that. Best to distract him and disengage from the conversation. "Have you seen Heather?"

This time he did look at me. "She's shooting on location with Ted and Mary," he said. "She's not coming back here until evening, if at all. They have to be done shooting in a couple of days, and then who knows?"

Well, Les Mannix knew, but he wasn't exactly saying, and in any event, it was almost none of my business. It was very little of my business, anyway. I thanked Harve and picked up Bagels's leash. Harve, however, did not believe our conversation was over and took my arm, not hard but authoritatively.

Bagels growled.

Harve let go of my arm but delivered the message he had no doubt intended to do while maintaining contact. "You don't want to be around if I find out you talked to the cops," he said. "Remember, I'm your client and I have a privilege." Around here everybody was theatrical; it was amazing. He turned and walked away, having made his point.

If he was threatening to have me disbarred, he was going in entirely the wrong direction. For one thing, I am obligated to tell the police if I think a client might be intending to do harm to someone. For another, I didn't really care that much if I kept the law license. It was nice to have but hardly essential to my business.

Still, what Harve said had sounded like a threat, and even a lame one like that can have an effect. My stomach fluttered a bit.

I felt the cell phone in my pocket vibrate and reached for it as Bagels and I headed for the exit with not much to report back to Jamie. The phone was showing a text message, and it was from my mother.

Come home, it said.

That couldn't be good, but if it was truly awful, Mom would have called, not texted. Her choice of messaging said "important,

251

not life-threatening." I looked down at my client.

"Come on, Bagels," I said. "Let's get both of us home."

I resisted the temptation to call Mom on the way home. I realized her texting was a way of letting me know there was no serious emergency but that there was at least a situation that required my presence, not just my advice over the phone. If she didn't want to talk to me immediately, that could mean she wasn't able to pick up the phone for a conversation either, and that could mean good things or bad.

Was I overthinking this?

I dropped Bagels off at Miriam's Hell's Kitchen apartment, told her what I knew (which was what I'd already told her on the phone), and took off, saying I was double-parked, which was true. It was something of a miracle my car hadn't been towed when I got to the driver's seat again.

The GPS was on, not for directions but for traffic advisories. I didn't want the trip to take too long. Once I got through the Lincoln Tunnel, I called Consuelo and asked her to set up a conference call with Patty and Jamie because I didn't know how to do that from my car.

Jamie, of course, turned out to be unavailable, so I talked to Consuelo and Patty, mostly about the logistics of getting Barney, who was still in our office, back to Patty's house. Consuelo, like many New Yorkers and certainly a lot in East Harlem, doesn't own a car. Taking Barney on the subway would be, let's say, unwieldy. It was agreed that Patty, feeling better but still under considerable press scrutiny, would drive to the office the next day and Consuelo, who actually liked having Barney around, would keep him in her apartment for another night.

We didn't discuss Patty's legal issues. Patty wasn't interested in rehashing the murder again, Consuelo wasn't involved, and I wasn't qualified. It was a wise move on everyone's part.

Halfway home Jamie called me, no doubt having received Consuelo's message, and I told him what Mannix and Harve had said. He was quiet for a moment, then asked, "Is that it?"

"Yeah. Oddly neither one of them broke down in tears and confessed to the parrot's agent," I said. "What did you expect?"

"I expected to hear you had spoken to Heather Alizondo," he reminded me. "But seriously, you're doing very well." I explained about Heather's absence and Jamie actually asked me to go back the next day to question her.

"Can't I just text?" I pleaded. "Heather doesn't know anything that she hasn't already told the cops and she's on deadline to finish what might be the last show in the series."

Jamie harrumphed a little, said he had hired an investigator to start working on the case, and conceded it would be okay for me to skip the schlepp to Queens the next day if I set up a phone call with Heather, which I thought was magnanimous of him. We hung up.

I pulled into my own driveway with some difficulty; it seemed the level of press coverage around my house had increased again. I guessed Patty's arrest had brought the reporters back around to me, and as I ran the gauntlet to my front door, I lamented my home's lack of a garage. Would have been better if I could have driven in completely without questioning. Next house.

Mom met me at the door and immediately apologized for alarming me. Seated behind her on the sofa was a stunning blond woman a little younger than I am, made up just a little too much, like she'd been expecting bright lights.

Before I got my bearings, she stood up and faced me. "I'm Denise Barnaby," she said. "I understand you're defending the bitch who shot my husband."

Mom sighed a little. "It's been this way all afternoon," she said.

CHAPTER EIGHTEEN

Denise Barnaby sat down again and apologized for her abrupt greeting as my father emerged from the kitchen with what looked suspiciously like one of his signature vodka and tonics. He handed it to Denise, who thanked him. If she was going to be combative, at least she'd now decided not to be unpleasant about it.

She'd flown in from Los Angeles to be with Dray's ashes (he'd been cremated as he'd requested) on the way back to be scattered over the home team bullpen in Chavez Ravine. It wasn't clear whether Dray had been a big Dodgers fan or if the network, which was broadcasting this year's baseball All-Star Game, had thought it would be a good public relations move. Either way, Denise seemed down with it, but she was now on the East Coast to better understand what had happened to her husband.

"First of all, the police have not arrested

or charged my client," I told her as Dad handed me a diet soda with caffeine. I was going to need my wits through this one. "That's important for you to know. They brought her in and questioned her and then they let her leave."

"She did it," Denise said without inflection. "I saw the letter she wrote to Dray. The cops scanned it to me. She's obviously a complete nut job."

Some women don't want to believe their husbands have been unfaithful. But given the state of most marriages in Hollywood, it's difficult to imagine the thought had never crossed Denise's mind. "What makes you say that?" I asked.

"She says she's pregnant with Dray's baby. Right off the top, I've seen pictures of this woman, and come on. He's married to me and he's with her? I don't buy that." She sipped her vodka and left a lipstick imprint on the glass.

"Men are difficult creatures," my father told her. "Sometimes they want what they don't have no matter what. And you were three thousand miles away, after all." If this kept up, I would have to find a good therapist. For me.

"She couldn't be carrying his baby," Denise insisted. "It's not possible."

"Now, dear . . ." my mother began. I think she was trying to let Denise down easy.

"Dray couldn't have kids," Denise said, voice very matter-of-fact. "He was shooting blanks."

There was a stunned silence in the room. For a while, really.

"I beg your pardon?" Mom finally managed.

"Yeah, Dray's little guys weren't good swimmers," Denise said. "We'd been trying for months to get pregnant — although I was really the one who was gonna get pregnant, if you want the truth — and we went to this doctor. Dray couldn't do it. I mean, not that he couldn't *do* it, but . . ."

"We get the idea," Dad said, rescuing all of us.

"He got really depressed about it. I mean, Dray was depressed about half the time and had a shrink who'd do nothing but put him on meds for it. But Dray didn't take his pills when he was shooting because he thought they made him gain weight. Anyway, he got upset about not having kids. I have the records from his doctors. I know he couldn't."

"So if Dray wasn't capable of having a child, who's the father of Patty's baby?" I asked nobody in particular.

"Good question," Denise said. "See, your *client* isn't exactly playing fair with you."

That raised so many issues it was hard to process. First of all, someone wasn't telling the truth. That was a mathematical fact; there were diametrically opposing stories being peddled here, and they couldn't both be true. But if Patty wasn't telling the truth about Dray's parenting her child, did that make her more or less likely to have shot him in a rage when he didn't respond to her letter?

Or was Denise's appearance here just a smoke screen she was trying to set up because *she* had actually, either herself or through a hired hand, killed Dray and wanted to pin it on Patty, the best available fall person? It was perplexing. Then it struck me that this technically was not my problem.

"Hang on," I told Denise. "What you need to understand is that I am not actually Patty's attorney of record. I mean, I *am* her attorney of record, but I'm not a criminal attorney. I'm just her parrot's agent."

Denise stared at me for a moment, no doubt trying to determine if I was trying to eschew responsibility for my client or if I was a raving lunatic. From the look in her eyes, she was tilting about six to five in favor

259

of lunatic.

"What I'm saying," I finally managed, breathing slightly less frantically, "is that you should be talking to her lead attorney. Let me get him on the phone for you."

I reached into my purse to get my phone and was cursing myself for not putting Jamie on speed dial when Denise said, "Hold it. I don't want to talk to two lawyers. I'm just talking to you." Well, me and *Entertainment Tonight,* which was probably why her makeup was a little overdone.

"I'm really not the one you need," I reiterated. "The lawyer handling Patty's case is named James Wallace." I redirected my attention to the phone.

But Denise was not having it; she put her hand over my screen and I looked up into her face. "No," she said, "I'm not here to help in her defense, lady. I'm here to tell you that you should get away from this case because the woman you're representing shot my husband and is lying to her own attorney — attorneys — about it. Don't make a fool of yourself."

I'm an agent for animals, so not making a fool of myself is rarely an option. I learned that as a child, singing and acting in sketches written by my father. So the plea was not as effective with me as it would have been with a normal person.

"Let's sit down for a minute," I said in a soothing tone. "I want to know more about your marriage to Dray."

"What's in it for me?" Denise asked. "I'm not in the business of helping that . . ." — she looked at my mother — "woman get off scot-free. Why should I tell you anything?"

Dad got there before I did but only because he's the person who trained me to begin with. "Because the one thing everybody here definitely wants is for the person who actually killed your husband to get punished for it," he said. "If Kay's client isn't guilty, your giving Kay information that can help in the investigation might enable the police to find the killer and put that person behind bars. Isn't that what you really want?"

Denise narrowed her eyes a little, trying to find the angle in what Dad was saying. "What's the point of talking to her lawyer?" she asked, apparently with sincerity. "If I can help find the killer, why shouldn't I talk to the cops?"

"You should," I said, nodding like an idiot. "You shouldn't keep any information from Sergeant Bostwick and Detective Baker."

"He's the one who doesn't talk?" Denise asked.

"Yes. And you should definitely tell them everything you know. Are they aware that Patty isn't carrying Dray's child?"

It was odd that Denise had shown up without an entourage — not even an assistant or a friend who would ostensibly be here to help the grieving widow through her painful revelations. Her manner was less distraught and more suspicious, and her motive for coming to see the attorney representing the woman she thought killed her husband was at best hazy.

So when she took a moment to answer I couldn't tell whether she was worried she was giving away too much information (which hardly seemed characteristic after everything she'd told us so far) or if she was making decisions about what lie to tell next. It would be so much easier if I could just read minds; I'd have to look into developing that talent when I had less on my plate.

"I talked to the police when they called to tell me what happened and again later on when they had questions about your *client,*" she said. The way she kept emphasizing the word *client* was starting to grate on me, and then I remembered that I really am not a defense attorney. That made me feel better. "When they told me about the letter, I told them what I just told you." Couldn't she

262

have just said yes?

"Then why would they arrest Patty if she can't possibly be pregnant with Dray's baby?" Mom asked.

"Because Patty doesn't know that," Dad told her. And suddenly it felt awful that they were breaking up the act. They worked so well together.

"I just want to make sure you're not operating under the wrong impression," Denise said. "I can give you Dray's medical records if you want proof that what I'm saying is true."

I was sure Jamie would want that, so I asked Denise to email the records to me and I would pass them along. "Rest assured," I said, "we understand that you're going through an impossibly hard time and everybody wants the person who killed Dray to face justice. It's our job — really the other attorney's job — to defend Patty if she's charged, but either way, the truth will come out. Okay?"

Denise seemed torn: She'd come to face the enemy and was not encountering a lot of opposition. "Okay," she said. "But I'm not going to let these stories go around that Dray was sleeping with this *woman*. I have a reputation to uphold."

"How did you meet Dray?" I asked. I was

testing a theory.

"I was working on a commercial a couple of years ago, just background, and he was the spokesman," she said. "We just hit it off."

"So you're a model?" Dad asked.

Denise looked offended. "Actress," she sniffed.

That was exactly what I'd thought. She was concerned about her image now that she was the Widow Mattone. The idea that Dray could be attracted to anyone else, but especially someone as unglamorous as Patty, was abhorrent to her, and in her mind, damaging to her brand. A girl had to look out for herself when her husband was no longer making millions each year as a TV star.

"I'll keep you informed if anything significant comes up, but I bet the police will tell you if they make an arrest even before they tell me," I said.

Denise nodded and stood up. "I've got to get going. I have to make a few stops before I go get the ashes." Not even the hint of a tear — she wasn't acting or she'd at least have put in the effort.

"There are a ton of reporters outside," I said. "Do you want to leave through the back door?" The dogs were sitting in the kitchen, chilling, but Denise did not look in their direction.

"Don't be silly," she said. She shook hands with all of us, stood up straight, checked her face in a hand mirror she took out of her purse, and faced the door. She walked out looking nothing but regal as the horde flocked around her. She kept moving, but slowly, making sure everyone got the shot they needed, until my front door closed.

Well, that was pretty much what I'd expected too.

CHAPTER NINETEEN

My first phone call was to Jamie, who took the information I gave him from my conversation with Denise and did not comment beyond "Uh-*huh.*" He said I'd done good work and promised to get in touch with me in the morning.

This had been at the very least a thirty-eight-hour day. And it wasn't even dark yet.

Dad, seeing how weary I looked, cooked dinner, as my parents had clearly given up their plan to dine out. My mother is a hopeless chef, but Dad has picked up a number of tricks over the decades of living in hotel "suites" (really efficiency apartments in the resorts we were working) and cruise-ship staterooms to make up for his lack of education on the subject. He can scrape together a lovely dinner with little more than salt and inspiration. But he needs the salt.

Tonight he had more than that to work with and made a very lovely chicken Parmesan with rotelle and green peppers. We opened a bottle of red wine that I mostly drank by myself, and by the third glass I was relaxed enough to ask how they had spent their day.

My father's mouth flattened out at the question, which was not the reaction I had been expecting. "I made some phone calls," he said. I took that to mean that he was trying to find a solo booking and had not yet been successful, so I asked no more questions of him.

Mom seemed surprised by the idea that she had done anything at all with the day. She took a bite of her dinner, savored it — she's the biggest fan of Dad's cooking — and chewed thoughtfully. "I've been giving some thought to taking a few college courses, maybe just auditing, once your dad is back on the road," she said. "Art history, things like that. I'd like to be better educated." Mom, who had been stunned when I'd opted for college over the stage, might have been living just a little vicariously through me since. She has always harbored thoughts about what might have been if she'd continued in school. I understood her curiosity.

"Is that expensive?" Dad asked. He put his plate, with a few scraps of chicken left, on the floor next to his chair and the dogs, mostly Eydie, came over to investigate (re: scarf down hastily).

"I haven't gotten that far yet," Mom told him. "I don't know if I'll do it or not."

"If it costs a lot, you might not be able to," Dad told her. "They're not going to pay as much for a single act as they did for both of us." He noted the shining surface of his plate, picked it up, put it in the sink, and walked out of the kitchen toward the guest room where he and Mom slept.

Just to be clear: Dad was not in a good mood.

Mom and I finished our dinner, and each of us made sure one of the male dogs got to lick our plates since Eydie had swooped in on Dad's without asking. Then we put the dishes in the dishwasher and I said I would take the dogs out for a decent walk.

"Would you like some company?" Mom asked. "I could do with a little fresh air." We had the dogs leashed up and out in minutes.

"You haven't said much," Mom said once we were out the back and heading away from the TV trucks (you'd think they'd figure it out by now, but I noticed that all but two had left after Denise swept out and drove away — following a brief press conference).

"I don't have anything to say," I answered. "I'm sorry the woman's husband was killed, but it doesn't have anything to do with me and I don't believe Patty was the shooter. I'm not even really her lawyer."

"That's not what I'm talking about and you know it," my mother said.

We stopped because Steve had found an especially interesting patch of grass to smell and wanted to explore its possibilities. Mom was right; I knew exactly what she'd meant.

"I don't want to say anything about you and Dad breaking up the act because it's none of my business," I blurted out finally. I'd been trying to figure out exactly what I thought about the impending change in their lives, but I didn't want them to make decisions based on my feelings. I thought I needed to respect theirs.

Apparently I was wrong. "It certainly is your business," Mom said with a slight chill in her voice. Eydie nudged Steve out of his nose-induced reverie and we started walking again. "You're part of our family and my being home all the time will affect you the most."

"You know I love having you around," I deflected.

Mom waved a hand. "You haven't actually lived with me since you left for college," she said. "It's nice having company. It's not always great having a roommate."

"What are you saying? You don't want to leave the act?" Bruno, the mop-headed lovable giant of the lot, was getting acquainted with a tree and Steve was watching with what appeared to be admiration for his technique. Eydie was far too much a lady to even sneak a glance.

Mom smiled in a way I couldn't read. "I'm not saying that," she said. "I'm saying I don't want to impose on you."

"You're not imposing." Bruno broke up with the tree and we continued in our alternate route, not heading toward West Roosevelt Avenue but toward the park we couldn't enter once the sun went down, which would be about twenty minutes from now.

"Yes, I am," Mom insisted. "What if you want to bring some guy home one night?"

"Mom!" Eydie turned around and looked at me. I couldn't figure out if she was alarmed or annoyed at my impolite outburst.

"Well, you could," my mother went on, not noticing the neon redness of my cheeks. "Suppose Sam came back with you one night, and —"

"Okay, we're holding it right there," I

interrupted. "There's nothing between me and Sam, and this is a subject I am unquestionably not discussing with my mother. Now, why don't you tell me what's *really* bothering you?"

Mom, who can perform but isn't a great actress, looked away. "Nothing's bothering me. I've made my decision and I'm happy with it."

And that's when I knew. "You want to go back on the road with Dad and you don't know how to back off your stand."

Her eyelids fluttered. Now I couldn't tell whether Mom was trying not to show me what she felt or if she was doing a fairly bad performance of a woman struggling with her feelings. "I don't subscribe to that interpretation at all."

"That's not a denial. I'm pretty sure."

It was just starting to hit twilight and getting harder to see Mom's expression, but I could tell that she shook her head slightly. "Let's talk about something else."

That was the moment my phone vibrated and I saw the email from Denise with Dray's medical records attached, as she had promised. The last thing I wanted to see was Dray's medical records, so I sent Denise a text thanking her and forwarded the email, unread, directly to Jamie.

"Do you think that woman today was telling the truth?" Mom asked. It wasn't the smoothest segue in history, but it did the job.

"I don't think Patty shot Dray, so anything anybody says that makes it look like she did is going to be met with some skepticism," I told her. "But Patty's story is so changeable at this point that I don't know what she's hiding either."

"I believed her," Mom said.

"Who?"

"Dray Mattone's wife."

It took me a moment to absorb that. "You think Patty shot Dray?"

"No, not necessarily. I don't think this Denise knows who shot her husband. But I believe what she said about him not being able to have children and I believe that she doesn't think he was having an affair with Patty. I don't think she was lying."

"No," I said, a little relieved. "But she might be mistaken."

"That's almost always a possibility with people," Mom said. I wondered what that meant.

The phone rang. Mom took the leashes for Steve and Eydie and I hung on to the one for Bruno. I'd like it known that I *could* have handled all three had I been alone.

This was simply a convenience.

Jamie was on the other end, which I had sort of expected. "What do you see?" I asked him.

"The medical stuff seems to be legit," he said. "I'm sending it to a doctor I know just to be sure, but I think so far Denise is telling us the truth."

"So where does that leave you?" I asked, not wishing to be included on the legal team as anything but a bystander.

"It leaves *us* with a client who isn't telling the truth, and that's never good," he answered. Jamie wasn't letting me off the hook. "But that's not what's worrying me."

After all those years in Dad's sketches I know a setup for a straight line when I hear it. "So what *is* worrying you?" I asked.

"This is potentially the biggest case of my career and I don't even know if my client is being charged yet," Jamie said. "But even that's not a big deal; we'll find out what's going to happen soon enough. No, what's bothering me is that I don't know whether Patty is lying or if she's wrong, and I don't want to be the one to break the news to her."

The silence that followed his last sentence was a long one. I knew what Jamie was saying and I specifically did not want to hear it. Mom and I walked half a block with the dogs, and actually had to stop once for Steve.

"I don't know her nearly as well as you do, Kay," Jamie finally said.

"Actually it's pretty close," I answered. "I've known Patty only a little over a month. I like her and I don't think she shot Dray, but it's not like we have a long-standing friendship that's much deeper than an interest in getting work for her parrot. Don't make me go to her house tomorrow and tell her she's not carrying Dray's baby, Jamie. Because that leads to all sorts of questions that I'm not close enough to her to ask."

Mom's lips pursed a little at what she was hearing, but she kept walking the two "original" dogs and I stayed astride with her and Bruno.

"It's better if it comes from another woman," Jamie attempted.

"And that's not the least bit sexist," I said. This was two lawyers talking, mind you. Well, one and a half.

"I'm not saying I'm squeamish about it," he countered. "I've had to say much worse things to clients, believe me. I'm saying I think we'll get better information from our client if she talks to you than if she talks to me. Remember, when she was first detained by the cops, the first person she called was you."

No wonder the man was a good defense attorney; he could argue. "Tell you what," I said. "Patty's coming to my office tomorrow to pick up Barney. Suppose you just happened to be there when she arrived. We could tell her *together.*"

"Nice try, but the whole argument I just made was about Patty trusting you more than me," Jamie said. Mom, the dogs, and I had reached the back gate and were heading back toward the door to go inside. The dogs would take a couple of laps first, but Mom was already climbing the stairs to the back deck. "I'm happy to consult with you after you talk to her. You can record it and send me the file if you want. But my presence in the room is going to hurt more than it's going to help. So what do you say?"

"I'd tell you, but I don't use that kind of language."

Jamie laughed. "I thought you'd see it my way."

"Did I miss the law school class in being a major jerk?" I asked.

"Yeah, but I still have my notes if you want them."

We disconnected the call after I promised Jamie I'd report to him after talking to Patty the next day, a proposition that was already beginning to create uncomfortable feelings in my stomach. Then I called Consuelo at home to confirm the time Patty was coming to pick up Barney and asked her not to let Patty leave before I got there to talk to her. Consuelo, being one of the most efficient people on the planet, did not question my scheduling or my motive; she just said she'd make sure everything worked out.

I searched my incoming emails for a query about representing a cat and found one for a black-and-white female named Oreo, who looked promising. I forwarded it to Consuelo.

I considered asking her to talk to Patty about the baby but decided that was the coward's way out. Then I remembered that I am in fact a coward and considered it again. But unfortunately, what Jamie had said made sense. I was stuck with the job.

Dad was in the living room and in a better mood when I coaxed the dogs inside with the word *treat,* which Eydie knows and the other two will simply follow her anywhere. I gave them some dessert, each in a separate bowl so everybody got what was coming to them, and sat down to relax on the sofa with my parents and a bottle of wine.

There's something wrong with that last clause.

"I think the producer guy killed that actor," Dad said, unsolicited. "I've been thinking about the case, and he was the one whose motive would have been purely financial. It's usually about money when the crime is premeditated."

Since we clearly weren't going to talk about Mom and Dad's professional future tonight — which was actually fine with me in my current state of exhaustion — we were apparently going to solve Dray's murder. As long as I didn't have to do it myself, that was okay. There wasn't anything special on television.

"There are all sorts of things wrong with that theory," I told Dad. "First, we don't know the murder was premeditated. Someone could have walked into the trailer, gotten into an argument with Dray, and shot him in a moment of rage."

"Still fits the producer." Dad is an armchair sleuth who thinks he can do it for real; I am an agent to cats, dogs, parrots, and the occasional ferret.

"Okay, so let's look at the other problem here. Les Mannix is losing money because Dray is dead. His show is in danger of cancellation and he might be out of a job.

That's a terrible motivation to kill some-one."

Mom looked up from her cup of tea. "She has a good point, Jay." Mom listens and absorbs everything and then pretends she's not really involved in anything unpleasant until such time as she can contribute the missing piece.

"You think because the actor is dead the producers lose money?" Dad was ignoring Mom's comment, never a wise tactic. "They take out insurance policies on all those big stars in case something happens. I'll bet they're coming out way ahead on this."

I'll admit that hadn't occurred to me, but I persisted. "There might have been some problems with Dray's last contract negotia-tions, but Mannix said they'd been exagger-ated, and anyway, the contract was signed. There was no upside to killing Dray. If he wanted, Mannix could have just refused a new contract or fired him."

"Your source on that is the suspect." Dad was in full Sam Spade mode now. "You can't rely on information you can't verify."

"When I left the act, I went to college and majored in history," I reminded him. "You're aware I didn't run away and enroll in the police academy?"

"You're her lawyer," he said. "You have to

provide a reasonable alternative to the crime."

"No, I'm the bird's agent," I countered. "Her actual lawyer needs to provide a vigorous defense, not to solve the crime. And since I'm *not* her actual lawyer, the only thing I need to do — other than simply representing the parrot and making sure he's not being cheated by a major television network — is what the lawyer I called in to defend Patty asks me to do."

"It's an interesting question," Dad protested. "Don't you ever think about who really shot this Mattone guy?"

I remembered that one of the things Jamie had asked me to do was contact Heather Alizondo and I had not been able to do that during the day, so I chose that moment (because I was losing the argument) to get out my phone and text Heather with the message *I have a quick question. Do you have time to talk?* I am fully aware many people would have sent *Quik ?: Can U talk?*, but I have a loyalty to the English language. I even know the difference between *you're* and *your.* I am old school.

"What are you doing?" Dad asked.

"Contacting the director." Now I had to think of a reason that Heather and I should talk, since she'd already told me she didn't need Barney again for this episode. We hadn't actually formed much of a bond, so I couldn't pretend to ask for studio gossip about the fate of *Dead City,* especially since the director wouldn't know that much anyway and I'd already gotten much of that from Les Mannix earlier today.

That was earlier today, right? It seemed like a week ago, but a week ago Dray Mattone had still been alive and my biggest concern was whether a Siamese cat would sit still long enough to pose for an Internet ad for litter.

"Why?" Dad asked.

"Stuff." What would an agent for a day player (someone who is not a regular needed on set every time there is filming) who happened to be a parrot want to talk to the episode director about?

Sure. What's up? The reply from Heather was far too prompt. I needed a good lie.

"What stuff?" Dad asked, looking suspicious.

"Dad, Jamie asked me to talk to Heather about Dray's murder and I need an excuse to talk to her. What should I say?" My father, who can be a slight pain at times, it also a softhearted and kind man who can make up a scenario in milliseconds.

"You have a choice," he answered. "Either

tell her you're concerned about Barney's performance and want to see if she needs retakes . . ."

"She'll say no and the conversation is over," I told him. "What's the *or?*"

"Or you can tell her Barney has come down with a bird flu and you want to make sure the rest of the crew wasn't exposed." Dad is great at coming up with melodramatic, unrealistic ideas that end up working when you're sure they won't.

I'm not superstitious by nature. I know showbiz people are supposed to believe in various hexes and curses, and maybe that's one of the reasons I never really identified with the performers onstage even when I was one of them. On the other hand, I do believe in karma, and giving Barney an imaginary disease was not something I wanted responsibility for doing.

"I'm asking her about the retakes," I told my parents. "It gets the conversation going and that's all I really need right now."

"No," Dad answered as I sent Heather the appropriate text. "You're going to need a segue or the conversation will end too quickly."

"So what's the segue?" I asked.

Sure enough, I got a text from Heather reading, *No probs. B did great. No need for retakes.* I didn't see how talking like that was going to help anything.

"You got me," Dad said.

But I've been dealing with showbiz people, especially directors, for a long time. And I know one thing: There is nothing they like better on this planet than talking about themselves, preferably from a position of authority or experience. I texted back to Heather: *Really wanted to talk to you about directing. Would you mind terribly?* In retrospect, I thought the *terribly* was probably selling it too hard, as Dad would say. But it got the proper response: *Sure! Lunch tomorrow?* It would probably be her last day of filming, so that was a really nice gesture. I felt like a heel soliciting it under false pretenses.

That didn't stop me from agreeing, of course.

I told Dad what I'd sent back and the response I'd gotten. He walked over and gave me a warm hug.

"I always knew there was some of me in you," he said.

I went to bed soon after, and it was only nine o'clock. This had been a long day, and tomorrow wasn't looking any shorter.

Just before I turned off the light, I got a

text from Consuelo that simply read: *Thank you!*

CHAPTER TWENTY

Consuelo had already put Barney and Maisie in the same cage when I arrived at my office the next morning. They were getting along famously, probably because they knew they'd have to face Consuelo if they didn't.

She spent five minutes thanking me for the connection to Oreo, whose owner she had already sent an email. Then we got down to business.

"You got a fax from Giant Productions," she told me as I settled in with a cup of coffee, giving her the one I'd bought for her. "They're asking for Bagels's vaccination records, so I'm guessing they want to hire him. Should I send that stuff out to them?"

"Not until I get a deal memo, no," I told her. "They can have what they want when they confirm they're hiring Bagels. I'll call them in a minute."

"No you won't," Consuelo answered.

"Because you got another call from Sergeant Bostwick and he wants you to call him back." She handed me the note that she'd scribbled down on an old coffee receipt as if she thought I didn't believe her.

"Did he say why?" I asked.

"I just take the messages," Consuelo said, sitting at her desk under Maisie's cage. "I don't interfere with the running of the business." This was her subtle way of letting me know she wants more responsibility.

Bostwick sounded distracted when he picked up the phone, like he was looking at something interesting on his computer screen or a member of the Yankees had just walked by his desk. My bet was on the former possibility. "What's going on?" he asked.

"You called me, remember?" I was opening bills with my desk letter opener and was not in a joyful mood. Imagine.

Bostwick's attention seemed to snap into place. "Oh, yeah," he said. I think I heard his government-issued swivel chair squeak as he no doubt leaned forward with his new focus. "I shouldn't be telling you this, but you're the attorney of record and you'd probably find out anyway."

Was Patty about to be charged? I started

285

composing my phone call to Jamie in my head.

"How do you know I haven't found out already?" I asked. It was a way of showing him I was competent, and probably had the opposite effect, since I had no idea what I was talking about.

Bostwick wasn't interested in playing coy, which was probably for the best. "Your client is not what she appears to be," he said.

Oh, boy. He'd found out about the pregnancy and the fact that it wasn't Dray's baby, probably from Denise Barnaby. Wait — wasn't that a good thing? Didn't it mean that Patty had *less* of a motive for killing Dray?

"She's much more," I agreed. "For one thing, she can play the piccolo and has an excellent memory for trivia about the sixties." I had no idea if any of that was true (and I doubted the piccolo thing), but Bostwick didn't know that either.

"Yeah, and she also leased that house she's living in a little over six weeks ago," he responded. "I'm not even sure Patricia Basilico is her real name."

Well, that took the wind out of my wiseass sails! "What do you mean?" I said, although I knew exactly what he meant. It was a device to buy time. "Patty's been living in

286

that house for a couple of years." She'd told me that, or I'd inferred it. It *looked* like she had been living there for a while and besides, she'd once told me she needed the extra money from Barney's career to help pay her mortgage. "That can't be right."

"It's right enough." Bostwick had prepared with every manner of cop cliché and was determined to trot out the lot. "A quick search on the ownership of the property gave us the landlord, a Mr. Elmore Block, and he confirmed the lease. Patricia Basilico is the name on all her IDs and the one she signed on the legal papers, but we haven't been able to verify any history on that name that goes back more than six months."

I was still holding the cup of coffee I'd brought in with me, but I hadn't taken a sip yet. In fact the cup, in my left hand, was halfway from my desk to my mouth and not moving. I made a noise, but I wasn't even trying to be communicative at that moment. My eyes must have bulged out of their sockets.

Consuelo looked up at me, concerned. I was cogent enough to wave her down when she started to rise out of her seat. But she didn't look any less worried. She knew it was about Patty and not me, and that wasn't necessarily helping.

"You're sure?" was the best I could muster.

"Absolutely," Bostwick said. "I don't know what it means, but I wouldn't be surprised if Captain Henderson didn't come in here anytime now and tell me to bring your client back in for more questions. Could lead to charges, probably not. Can you explain it?"

"I'm not the defense attorney," I said, in what I thought was an artful dodge of the question. "Let me call him and one of us will get back to you. Thanks for letting me know, Joe."

"I'm not the ogre you might think," he said, and hung up. That was not a cop cliché and so was especially unexpected.

"What's going on?" Consuelo asked.

"That is an excellent question." I dialed Jamie's number, which I had just started dialing two days ago, from memory on my landline. But his secretary — sorry, assistant — said he was not available at the moment and would call me back at his earliest convenience.

I hung up the phone and walked over to the cage to look at the two birds. "Something weird is going on," I told Consuelo as I picked up one of the larger pieces of chewable wood and held it up so both Maisie and Barney could go for it. Neither of them was interested.

"How unusual for us," Consuelo said. East Harlem wit is a lot like New Jersey wit. It assumes that things are bad, but not to worry — they can always get worse.

"I know. What time is Patty coming in to pick up Barney?" Maisie was pretending to ignore the parrot but was doing a bad job of it.

"Kill Les Mannix!" Barney alerted us all. Maisie was even less impressed than before. She fluttered down off her perch and began combing the floor of the cage for . . . something.

"About two, as it turns out," Consuelo said. "She said something about having errands to run in the morning."

That gave me about four hours. "Good. Let me see what happens when Jamie gets back, but in the meantime I have a lunch with Heather Alizondo and that's all the Patty stuff I'm doing today. Where are you in lining up clients other than Oreo?" Consuelo knows that in order to be even a junior agent in my firm (which consists of me and Consuelo), she has to find clients on her own, not just what I give her. And believe me, I know that's the tricky part.

"How do you feel about fish?" Consuelo asked.

"I'm not making reservations for the lunch. Heather said she'd be in Manhattan and would text me the location as soon as she had one." Bills were piling up. I hadn't been in the office much this week at all.

"I mean as clients," Consuelo said. "I have a man who believes his fish can act."

That took a second to sink in. "His fish? How does a fish act?" Believe it or not, that was a question I had never actually considered before.

"He says it can swim on cue," she answered.

"It's a fish. It pretty much swims all the time. They never stop swimming. So how does he think you can line up work for his mackerel, or whatever?" I opened my email account, which I *had* been monitoring all week, and saw I still had 254 emails to look at. This whole "modern age of communication" thing might have been overhyped.

"It's a flounder," Consuelo said. She didn't sound very convinced herself, which was a reassuring sign that she was sane. "He says it would be perfect for when Disney decides to do a live-action remake of *The Little Mermaid*."

I had steeled myself for her explanation,

and foremost in my mind was the desire not to just repeat back what she'd said out of sheer disbelief. "A live-action remake of *The Little Mermaid*?" I said. I'm sorry, but it just caught me off guard.

"Well, there's a character called Flounder, and he figures once they decide to do that, there'll be a search for flounders who can act. He wants to get ahead of the curve."

If I had worn glasses, I would have taken them off and put them on my desk to signify wisdom and impending advice. "I think maybe you'd better concentrate on dogs and cats for now," I said.

"Yeah," she said. Consuelo never sounds defeated, but this was not her most optimistic tone. "How do I tell him we don't want to represent his flounder?" she asked.

"Tell him we have all the fish we can handle," I said. "Nobody ever told you this was going to be easy. And don't be too anxious on Oreo. Let the owner get back to you."

She nodded and went back behind her desk to work on things other than the acting career of a flounder. It was a shame nipping the fish's acting career in the bud, but now it could concentrate on med school or something practical.

We actually both sat and worked for close

to an hour, which was something of a record at this point. I called Giant Productions about Bagels and got an assurance that we'd be receiving the proper paperwork, a deal memo, by email within a few minutes. We didn't while I was in the office, but that's how these things go sometimes. Consuelo composed an email to the fish trainer letting him down gently, showed it to me, and then sent it.

It went on that way until Jamie called me back and I told him what Bostwick had said to me.

"I was skeptical about Patty to begin with," he said. "My investigator has been on the job less than a day and he says there's nothing he can put his finger on, but there's something about her that's not right."

"I'll be seeing her later today," I reminded him. "What do you want me to tell her?" It seemed pointless to try and get him to show up for the meeting; he'd made it clear he preferred to have me handle any unpleasantness from Patty, although I didn't think there would be any.

"It's not what you tell her; it's what she tells *you*," Jamie said. "Remind her that anything she tells us is in confidence and that anything she lies to us about is only going to hurt her, especially if the police find out otherwise. So far nothing she's told us has held still long enough to be helpful or hurtful in her defense. As soon as she says it, the facts turn out to be something else. That has to stop."

"Yes, Dad," I told him. "But the problem is so far I've believed everything she's said and then found out it wasn't true. What can I do this time to determine if she's really telling the truth?"

He thought for a while. "Who else is in your office?" he asked.

I told him Consuelo would be sitting in on the meeting, mostly because the whole office is one room and there would be nowhere else for her to go. "Okay, don't tell her anything before you see Patty," Jamie said. "See if her impression is the same as yours after Patty leaves, and ask her before you tell her anything about what you think. Is she a good judge of character?"

I looked at Consuelo, who had actually considered representing a flounder because she really wanted to be an agent instead of (or in my mind, in addition to) being an office manager. "The best," I said.

"Good. Get the whole meeting on a voice recorder so I can hear it too. And press her on the idea that she doesn't seem to have any history before six months ago. That's what worries me most."

"Okay, but first I've got a duck who's up for an insurance spot and then I'm going to have lunch with Heather Alizondo." I made up the part about the duck. I like to keep people off-balance on what I do. It's perverse, I suppose, but if they ever heard about an aardvark who can bring an audience to tears, I want to know about it. Dogs and cats aren't the whole business; they're just where Consuelo should begin.

"Good," said Jamie, ignoring the whole duck scenario I'd worked so hard to create. "See if she noticed anything about those people who kept coming in to see Mattone. See if she thinks they're related to some drug use."

It was getting near the time I'd have to leave, so I hung up with Jamie and checked my email. Sure enough, Heather had identified a restaurant in the West Twenties that she thought was convenient to me because it was less than a hundred blocks away and still on the same island. I texted her my acceptance and told Consuelo I'd be back before Patty arrived, but to keep her here if I was late.

On the way out, Barney called after me something about putting down the gun. Barney is nothing if not enigmatic.

294

The trip downtown took about forty minutes, but at least it was unpleasant. The subways are much less awful than they once were, but they're still pretty grim at the right time of day, which is always. People don't look happy. All those YouTube videos where someone launches into an operatic aria on the 6 train and everyone is enthralled? They're all staged. Ever wonder why there's someone who just happens to be filming *before* the aspiring Pavarotti starts tenoring all over the place? Why there are cutaway shots to other subway riders? Why you can actually hear the singer over the noise of the train? Yup. It's fake.

So once I had extricated myself from the train and started walking toward Sloppy Burger (the trend in Manhattan is to sell comfort food, pretend it's chic, and overcharge for it) I was glad just to be breathing regular air again. I was thinking about the lunch with Heather and how to broach the pertinent subjects when Mandy the acting zombie turned the corner of Twenty-Third Street in front of me and looked surprised to see me. I think it was genuine surprise too, though with actors you can never be certain.

"What are you doing here?" I got to ask first.

"We're filming right around the corner," she said, pointing. "I'm breaking for lunch, so I can be out of makeup for a while." Indeed, she did not look nearly as blue as she had when I'd seen her on the slab in Dr. Banacek's morgue.

"I thought you were done for the week," I said.

Mandy shook her head. "We're shooting the exteriors for the teaser today, where I get killed despite being a zombie." We started to walk, although Mandy had originally been going in the opposite direction. "I think it's the last scene on the schedule."

"Have they told you if the show's continuing?" I asked, although I had a pretty good idea of the answer.

"Why tell me? I'm just a guest player. I wouldn't have been back next week anyway."

We dodged a few tourists. You can always tell them; they stare at everything as if they've never seen buildings before and they're not in nearly as much of a hurry as the natives, who always think they're late for the appointment that's going to change their lives. "Can I ask you something?" I said. That was, technically, asking her something, but I figured Mandy would be able to tell the difference. And since I had run into her randomly I might as well make use of the coincidence and see if there was something I could clarify.

"Sure. What's up?" Mandy was walking like an actress; I know the look. She was watching every woman who walked by, trying to see if there was something she could use in a future role. Actors absorb other people. It's kind of like a science fiction thing.

"When we were on the set you said you thought maybe Dray had fallen off the wagon because you saw random people taking him aside to talk to him."

Mandy's face had clouded over when I'd started talking. "That's not a question," she said.

"Okay, but this is: Why do you think those people were talking to Dray about drugs? Did they say anything to you?" I probably should have been subtler about that part, but I don't write the scripts. My father always has.

"You want to know if I'm using cocaine?" Mandy asked. She didn't seem offended so much as curious about my motives.

Maybe I could deflect the insinuation. "I just wanted to see if you had a good connection," I said. "It's always worth knowing where you can pick up decent stuff." Another block to the restaurant.

Mandy looked at me and laughed. "You're not the type," she said.

"I'm not?" I always thought I could pretend to be anything. I was born an actress and became an agent later.

"No, you're not. And for the record, neither am I. I need to keep my body strong and healthy. It's my instrument. Messing it up with that stuff would be bad for my career. And I don't do *anything* that's bad for my career."

"Okay, so why? Why do you think Dray was talking to various people about drugs and not anything else?" We were almost at the door to Sloppy Burger and I'd have to stop in a second.

Mandy shrugged, seeing no reason not to tell me. "I heard a few snips of conversation. About how he couldn't stay sober and how he wasn't even sure he wanted to anymore. Didn't like his wife, didn't like the job. The usual successful TV actor crap. Let them go out and audition for an online commercial for real drugs, like Viagra."

Wait, back up. "He didn't like his wife and he didn't like being on *Dead City*?" I asked.

"That's what I heard, and he said something to me about the wife, but then stars say a lot of things about their wives to young

298

actresses." She shook her hair just a little bit to emphasize what she thought I didn't know she was saying.

"Do you think he was trying to . . . get to you?" I asked.

"Nah, not really. It's a reflex with some of these guys; they don't even know they're doing it half the time." We stood in front of Sloppy Burger and she looked up at the sign. "They're being more careful these days too. You meeting Heather in there? This is her place, apparently." Mandy made a face.

I admitted I had an appointment for lunch with Heather. "Not your thing?" I asked.

Mandy looked at me incredulously. "I'm vegan," she said. "Body is a temple, remember?"

Of course. I thanked her for the information even though she thought it was just gossip and left her to meet Heather Alizondo in a chic hamburger restaurant.

The place was trying its best to be trendy in an ironic way. There were cartoon pictures of cows framed on the walls. French fries with faces grinned at us from the wallpaper. The ketchup bottles on the tables were made to look like they had once held champagne. The paper napkins were of a stronger, more substantial type of fiber than most.

Classy, no?

New Yorkers with incomes in the seven figures stood on line to place an order at a counter whose sign read ALL TOPPINGS, $4. The drink of choice was the milkshake, although some of the recipes (emblazoned on the wall behind the counter) included vodka or rum.

Heather was sitting at a table, a small plastic sign with *42* next to her. "Did you order?" she asked after I sat down. "I would have gotten something for you, but I didn't know what you'd want."

"I'm not hungry," I lied. I had limited time and didn't want to wait on the long line to get a hamburger and fries. I'd pick something up at the deli on the corner opposite my office. "I really wanted to have time to talk to you."

"That's sweet," Heather said. "I'm not sure how much I can help, but I'm happy to offer whatever limited experience I have." Ego is often masked in modesty. "What's on your mind?"

I had concocted this elaborate backstory about how I'd always wanted to be a director and that she might be able to offer her wisdom to me in order to help advance my goals. It's a standard kind of advance that an aspiring showbiz person would use, plus it was only slightly implausible given that I'm an animal agent and not even what the industry would call a "creative." But now I was somewhat pressed for time and had lost my enthusiasm for the false narrative.

A waitperson came by with Heather's order and took the *42* placard away. She looked over the milkshake, burger, and fries and, satisfied, dug in.

"The fact is, I'm trying to find out what exactly happened to Dray," I told Heather. "I know the director isn't a regular on the set and you aren't there every week, but you've done a number of episodes of *Dead City* and I'm willing to bet you knew the company pretty well, so I'm hoping you might be able to answer some questions I have."

Heather's "helpful" face had fallen as soon as I'd gotten the first sentence out of my mouth, and now she was looking somewhat short of hostile but not exactly mentor-like anymore. She wasn't crazy about my mentioning that a TV director isn't one of the most standard fixtures on a set either. So her voice had dropped a few tones when she spoke again.

"Why are you looking into this?" she asked. "Are you one of the security people Dray hired?"

Even in trying not to give me any new facts, Heather had immediately jumped to something I hadn't known before. "Dray had private security?" I said.

Heather shrugged. "Most stars do," she said. "They have a lot of crazy fans and you never know who's dangerous and who's not. Even the most accessible out of the bunch usually has a bodyguard hanging around. The past few weeks Dray had been trying out some new ones, apparently. It was like an open casting call. A different security consultant would show up on the set every day and confer with him between takes. Then that one was never heard from again and a new one would show up the next day."

"How did you know they were security consultants and not, say, publicists or drug dealers?" I tried to slip that last one in there, but I'm as subtle as an anvil.

But Heather didn't blink. "Every one of them was carrying a weapon," she said. "If they were publicists, I think I want to sign on with them. So if you're not private security, who are you?"

"I'm the parrot's agent," I told her.

She squinted. I felt like it had become harder to see me. "So why is the parrot's agent trying to do investigative work on the actor's murder?" she asked.

It was a fair question. "I'm also an attorney. I've been asked to work on the case for the lawyer handling the case of someone who has been questioned by the police but hasn't been charged, and I don't think that person killed Dray, so I'm trying to figure out who did, and why."

Heather took a bite of her burger as a way to avoid talking for a moment. She chewed carefully and took a sip of her milkshake, which might or might not have been one of the "adult" ones listed on the menu. "Is this the crazy woman who said Dray had fathered her child?" she asked.

Swell. Now Patty had a reputation. "I'm not at liberty to say who it might be just yet," I dodged. "Like I said, I'm not really the criminal attorney. I'm not going to represent anybody in court if it comes to that."

"That's a yes," Heather said, sitting back on the high barstool (it had a back) and folding her arms in a gesture of victory. "So then you know who she is."

Okay, that was just a little bit cryptic. No, it was a lot cryptic. "Don't you?" I asked. I could be just as evasive if she wanted to play that game.

"No. No more than the nut at the memorial. As far as I know, nobody on the set knew who she was. We saw her a couple of times and then she stood up and accused Les Mannix of killing Dray. Never saw her since. So why don't you tell me what *you* know?" Directors are just as vicious with their gossip as anyone else. Maybe more. But it at least did tell me that Heather apparently hadn't heard about the suspicion around Patty, or was discounting it. She wanted to know about the mystery woman at the memorial service.

Luckily, I knew nothing about her, which is my comfort zone. I could vamp, which is a lot like lying but technically involves no untrue information.

"I can't say anything about who my client is or isn't," I said. All of which was true, but irrelevant to what Heather was asking. "What I can tell you is there are a lot of possibilities. For example, I heard that Dray was unhappy about his job and his marriage. Did you know that?"

Heather did not miss a beat, although a french fry seemed to fascinate her for a moment as she bit it neatly in two. "I don't know anything about Dray and Denise's marriage," she said, but I noticed she was still staring at her plate as she said it. "As for being unhappy on *Dead City,* he had no reason to sign a new three-year contract for truckloads of money if he wanted out. My guess is that if he was that fed up, he could have left."

"Except he was making a bunch of money," I said. "How about on set? Was he uncooperative? Moody?" I didn't have any food to distract me, but watching Heather eat a hamburger (with arugula, sprouts, organic ketchup, some raw kale, and a multigrain bun, thus making the burger itself irrelevant) was spectacle enough. She was meticulous in her biting and chewing, never a spontaneous move even with the milkshake. How a woman can look thoughtful sipping on a milkshake was something I'd have to ponder for months to come.

"Never," she said. "Dray was a complete pro at every turn, always knew his lines, always took direction well. I never had another actor complain about working with him." That was what any director who wanted to stay employed would say about a star actor, even a dead one. Heather was reacting as if she were being interviewed by an investigative journalist instead of having lunch in the presence of a parrot's agent.

"Okay, you've been diplomatic," I said. "I can tell anyone who asks that you said all the right things. Now tell me what actually happened and I promise I'll keep anything you say to myself."

"I have no reason to lie about Dray," Heather said, looking me steadily in the eye with an expression that was supposed to make me quiver in my boots. Luckily I wasn't wearing boots. "Look, I'm a TV director and he was one of the stars of the show. My interaction with him was all on the set, and he was really good at what he did. He wasn't one of those prima donnas who demand to have an ostrich in their trailers just to see if they can exercise that level of power."

I found myself wondering if I could have gotten an ostrich for Dray's trailer if I'd been called, which was a problem with focus on my part. I shook myself back to the point. "I hear there were some problems after he got back from rehab," I said. "That he might have relapsed, had people on the set who might have been suppliers. You seem to think they were different security agents. Do you know if Dray was using anything that might have gotten him in trouble?"

Heather looked impatient. Here she thought she was going to have her ego stroked for an hour while an aspiring director asked for her wisdom and instead she got interrogated by a crazy amateur detective. I couldn't say I blamed her.

"I go miles out of my way not to know anything about what the actors on a show I'm directing might be doing or not doing when they're not on the set, or even if they are on the set but not in a scene I'm directing." She pursed her lips a little in either contemplation or weary irritation. In retrospect, I'd bet on the latter. "I did not have any interaction with Dray Mattone that indicated to me he was on drugs. But then I'm not great at those things. I'm worried about the whole show, not just one actor, even a star." She looked at her watch. "And that means I've got to get back to my set. We're on location today and the city doesn't like us to go overtime when we have to close whole streets."

Heather stood and pulled her purse from the back of the barstool she'd been sitting on. It opened briefly, and if I hadn't simply happened to be attracted to the style of the bag, I wouldn't have noticed the gun she was carrying inside it, next to the small box of ammunition.

Chapter Twenty-One

"It doesn't mean anything that she had a gun in her purse," Consuelo said. "You know that's not the gun that killed Dray Mattone because the cops have it. She's a woman living in Manhattan and she owns a gun. It's perfectly legal and it doesn't give her a motive."

All that was correct. And I didn't have any reason to think Heather Alizondo had shot and killed Dray. I'm not nuts for guns generally, and seeing it concealed like that was disconcerting. That's what I was telling myself.

But Heather had been on edge during the lunch, she hadn't told me anything helpful, and she had a gun in her purse. She'd also left a meeting to which she'd allotted an hour after only thirty-eight minutes. Something I'd said or done had unnerved her. I couldn't identify what and I couldn't explain why.

And there was no time to think about any of that because my (legal) client Patty Basilico was already on her way up the stairs to my office to pick up her parrot and I had to tell her she was not pregnant with Dray Mattone's baby.

"Yeah, but a guy got shot and she has a gun." It was the lamest possible response but the only one I could process at that moment. "We still don't know where the bullets that shot Dray or the ones in Bostwick's reenactment came from. She had a gun and bullets."

"So does every cop in New York," Consuelo said. "Do you think they all shot Dray Mattone in his trailer?"

"Not all of them," I answered.

There was no further time for hilarious banter because the office door opened and Patty walked in carrying a box and humming to herself. She gave Consuelo and me a sunny hello and set the box on Consuelo's desk.

"It's chocolate chip cookies," she said. "You two have been doing so much for me this week I felt like I had to bake you something special."

My feelings were so conflicted I could easily have declared war on myself. On the one hand, my client had been consistently lying to me, to the point that I had no idea even who she really was.

On the other hand, she'd baked chocolate chip cookies and brought them to my office. You can see my dilemma.

I'd show Patty. I didn't even open the box, although I saw Consuelo eyeing it with a look I wouldn't want to cross. "Come on in," I said as if I didn't wonder if Patty had shot Dray Mattone in the head. "Sit down."

But Patty was already at Barney's cage. Consuelo had separated the two birds so Patty could take Barney home with her, but Maisie was not pleased and was squawking to let us know. Barney was simply sitting on his perch looking inscrutable because he's a parrot and they don't actually ever change facial expression except to open their beaks.

"Barney," Patty cooed into the cage. "How's my Barney?"

"A lot of people want you dead, Dray," Barney said by way of greeting.

Patty looked embarrassed, of all things. "I can't imagine who taught him that one," she said, shaking her head. "I'll have to figure out how to get him to stop saying it." She looked over at me. "I imagine it won't be helpful if there's a trial." She was playing the role of the plucky client who knows she's innocent to the hilt. And she was a good actress; she could easily have auditioned for a role on *Dead City* and gotten it, in my opinion.

"Patty, come over and sit for a minute," I said, pointing to the chair in front of my desk. "I have to ask you about something."

Consuelo clearly decided I was insane and opened the box of cookies. She put some out on a paper plate she got from the storage closet and asked Patty and me if we wanted some coffee. She meant to go to the Dunkin' Donuts on our street, but Jamie and I wanted Consuelo in the room when I talked to Patty, so when our client told her she'd love a cup of coffee, I suggested Consuelo make it from the coffeemaker we have in the office, which we use only a few times a year because . . . did I mention there's a Dunkin' Donuts on our street?

Consuelo frowned a little but must have realized my intentions because she immediately began making coffee, but did it as quietly as possible so she could hear the whole conversation and no doubt quote from it verbatim later.

"Is something wrong?" Patty asked. "Have you heard something else from the police?" Her face was a perfect blend of fear and bewilderment, trying very hard to put a brave face on the circumstances. I wished

311

Mom were here to study her technique. "Well, yes, but not that you're being charged, at least not yet." Maybe I could ease into this. It was a question of prioritization: Which challenge would be the most upsetting so I could build up to that. "See, they've been running some background checks on you, stuff they do routinely in cases like this."

Patty's demeanor did not change. She was still upbeat with a tinge of false hope. "That's not very upsetting. I'd expect them to do that."

"Yeah, but they have questions they can't answer. They say you just rented your house recently and that they can't find any verifiable identification for you."

Not a twinge, even as Consuelo, placing the plate of cookies on my desk, was clearly scrutinizing Patty's face for surprise or anger or . . . something. "Well, that's silly," Patty said. "I have a driver's license and a passport and credit cards and everything."

"There's something else," I said. Might as well jump in with both feet. "You're not carrying Dray Mattone's baby."

That statement evoked the first false note in Patty's performance. Instead of looking stunned, she seemed to be trying for defiance and came up with confusion. "What do you mean? Of course I am."

"No, you're not. Denise Barnaby produced records that the police and Jamie's expert have confirmed. Dray couldn't father a child. And so far you haven't produced any medical records or even the name of a doctor who can confirm that you're pregnant."

Consuelo sat back down at her desk, but she didn't even pretend to be interested in any paperwork there. She was watching Patty and me intently.

"I don't see why you would believe the word of that woman over me." Patty's voice was lower and had a harder edge on it than before. "Dray and I had an affair that she doesn't want to believe really happened, and I got pregnant. Why would I make that up?"

"I don't know," I said, because I truly didn't.

Patty's eyes darkened a little. "What are you saying?" she asked. "Do you think I shot Dray because he *didn't* get me pregnant? Is that the new version? Whose side are you on, Kay?"

"I really don't think you shot Dray at all. But I honestly can't figure you out, Patty. It seems like everything you've told me hasn't been true and everything you've done looks like it was designed to make people —

313

especially the police — think you *did* kill him. Most people would have acted relieved and glad to get out of police custody; you seemed a little disappointed. I want to believe what you tell me, but so far you haven't given me a reason that I should."

To be fair, that little diatribe went above and beyond the mission statement Jamie had given me for this conversation. But if I knew Patty — and that was certainly in question at this moment — I had to push a few of her buttons, particularly those regarding loyalty, in order to make her more open to laying her cards on the table.

It certainly seemed to have worked on Consuelo. She was staring openmouthed at me and had not even eaten the second cookie she'd taken off the plate. It sat in her hand unbitten.

Patty leaned back in her chair as if she'd been pushed. She let out her breath and looked at me for a long moment. "Wow," she said.

I felt like agreeing but kept my feelings unspoken. It was best to let her speak when she was ready.

"Put down the gun," Barney said.

"Enough, Barney," Patty said to him. "I'm sorry I taught you that one."

Consuelo dropped the cookie.

"Wait," I said when I could control my voice again. "You taught Barney to say, 'Put down the gun'?"

Patty closed her eyes and sighed again. "Yeah. And the one about how everybody wanted Dray dead, I taught him that. He really is a very fast learner. That part is true."

My instincts were apparently in opposition to Consuelo's: I immediately picked up one of the larger cookies on the plate and took a huge bite. When I could talk without being disgusting, I said, "Are there any other parts of what you've told me that are true?" My voice sounded weak and a little frightened. I had clearly lost whatever authority I had once possessed in this conversation.

Patty didn't even open her eyes. "Not much," she said.

I saw Consuelo reach into the drawer at her right hand and pull out a voice recorder, which she turned on and placed on her desk. Consuelo, if she ever becomes a full-time agent, will be impossible to replace as an office manager.

"Why don't you break with tradition and tell me what's really going on?" I said.

"You wouldn't believe me." That was overplaying it, although she did not put the

315

back of her hand to her forehead, and that's when it struck me.

"I probably would even if you kept lying to me," I told Patty. "You're really a very good actress."

She opened her eyes and perked up instantly. "You really think so?" Ah, the ego in showbiz. You can't ever go wrong appealing to it.

"I do, and I used to act, so I know what I'm talking about." If you wanted to call that acting.

"That's so nice!" Patty hadn't exactly reverted to her old persona, which I now realized was a role she was playing, but she was definitely sunnier than she had been a moment earlier. "Thank you!"

"But I don't get what role you were playing," I said, trying to get the conversation back on topic. "You seemed to be the perfect suspect in a murder."

"That's it exactly!" Patty pointed at me as a teacher does a pupil who just got something right for the first time. "I was supposed to be the person who looked like the killer. Well, no. That's not what I was supposed to be. I realize now I was being set up."

Consuelo, literally the voice of reason, cleared her throat. "Why don't you start at the beginning and walk us through it?" she said.

"I could get in a lot of trouble," Patty told her earnestly.

"You think you're not now?" Consuelo asked.

Patty's eyes welled up. Actors can go from emotion to emotion literally in the blink of an eye. They have to at auditions, and Patty had obviously been on a great many auditions.

"It's true," she moaned. "I'm in way over my head." The bad dialogue was coming back. I needed to refocus her.

"How did you get involved to start?" I asked.

"I got asked to play a sort of crazy fan stalker. You know, the kind who really thinks she's got some connection to the big star and doesn't realize he has, you know, a wife and everything. So she sends him emails and she gets his phone number and she's all over him on Facebook. Next thing you know she's actually on the set and she thinks they're in this wild love affair when the guy doesn't even know what's going on."

"Who asked you?"

Patty, who had shaken her attempt at crying and was now being very confidential with us, seemed surprised by the question.

"Who asked me what?"

"You said you were asked to play a fan stalker. Who asked you to do that?"

"I knew a guy who knew a guy who knew a guy, you know?" she said.

"What guy did you know? Who was your contact on *Dead City*?"

Patty chewed her bottom lip. "I'm not supposed to say."

"Were they supposed to set you up as a murder suspect? You don't owe anybody anything."

"It's true. The guy I knew on set was Harve Lembeck. You know, the assistant director. I worked with him on an Internet thing once." Ask an actor a question and you'll get a résumé and head shots.

That figured. Harve had been involved in getting the gun into Dray's trailer and was afraid of the police. You had to know he'd be involved if there was something shady going on.

"Did Harve say why they wanted you to do all this?" I asked.

"He didn't even say *who* wanted me to do it," Patty told me. "But he said it could lead to a recurring role on another show, so that was something. All I was supposed to do was stir up some stories about Dray and then recant it all in the end. He gets to look like a hero, I work under an assumed name, and nobody gets seriously hurt."

"Except then Dray Mattone was murdered," Consuelo pointed out. "Why didn't you tell the police what was going on after that?"

"First, I was terrified, but it wasn't that," Patty said after a moment. She looked away, like she was embarrassed. "The fact is, it didn't occur to me that any of this had anything to do with Dray's murder. So I didn't say anything because I wanted the job on that new show and I didn't think I had anything important to tell the police."

"And when they brought you in for questioning?" I asked.

"Well, then I figured I was in all kinds of trouble because they'd found that phony letter I'd written, and it was even in my handwriting." Patty looked over at Barney, who appeared unconcerned with her dilemma, pecking at a piece of stone wedged in the bars near his perch. "If I told them this insane story then, they'd figure they definitely had their killer and that she was completely nuts. I haven't been able to find Harve since before the police came to my door and I doubt he'd back me up anyway." She looked at me and whispered, "He has a record."

"I know," I told her. "Patty, what was the new show they were promising you?"

"Something called *Dead Beat*," she said. "It was going to be a spin-off of *Dead City*, with more of a focus on the cops."

"So another Les Mannix show," I mused aloud. That might cast Les as the man behind Harve's approach to Patty. "But remember now, your best defense is the truth, and you should have at least told Jamie and me before."

"I should have," she agreed. "But I'm telling you now. Can you help me if they decide I'm the one who shot Dray?"

"I wish Jamie were here," I said. "But I'll tell him everything you said and then he'll be the one to get back to you. I'm just . . ."

"The parrot's agent, I know." Patty looked at Barney again and smiled. "I think they chose me because I have the background with birds. The old bird had died and they were looking for a new one. That part was real. But I thought all those phrases I was teaching Barney were supposed to be just to scare Dray, not to cover up his murder by framing me." She closed her eyes again and put her head in her hands. "I have been so stupid."

Even I was going to have trouble arguing with that, but I patted her on the shoulder and said, "We'll work it out. In the mean-time, don't ever lie to me or Jamie again, and definitely don't lie to the police. They hate that. Okay?"

Patty's shoulders quivered a little, but she nodded. "I promise." She stood up and walked over to the cage. "Do you think it's okay for me to take Barney?"

I looked at Consuelo, my moral compass, and she shook her head negatively. "I think now that we know he's not really your parrot we should hang on to him a little while longer," I said. "Who supplied Barney?"

"Harve was my contact. He was the only one I ever talked to. I don't think Barney is his bird, but he never told me where they found Barney. And that's the truth." She looked into the cage. "You take care, Barney. I'm going to miss you."

"Patty," I said as she shuffled toward the door, her bearing far different from when she had entered. "Who do you think killed Dray?"

She stopped and regarded me carefully. "I honestly have no idea." She continued on toward the door.

But Patty stopped again when Consuelo asked, "By the way, what's your real name?"

Patty moved her lips back and forth on

her teeth like she was trying to clean them. "I promised not to lie to you, so for right now, I think we'll leave it at Patty, okay?"

That didn't bode well. "I'd really prefer we know who you are," I said.

She thought that over and nodded. "Patrice Columbo," she said and walked out the door.

"Nice to meet you," Consuelo said.

CHAPTER TWENTY-TWO

It took a *long* time to relay all that had happened to Jamie. I was sort of sorry we hadn't planned the conversation as a Face-Time chat because I'm sure his expression was priceless. But I have to admit the whole story was starting to give me serious butterflies in my stomach. Which is not nearly as nice a sensation as it sounds like it should be.

"That's a lot to deal with," he said finally. "It opens up more questions than it answers. I mean, it establishes a certain rationale behind Patty's — Patrice's — behavior, but it's so loony I'm not sure that helps."

"I don't make the news, I just report it," I told him. "So can I quit now? I'd like to go back to my day job and let you do the criminal stuff if that's all right with you."

"Sure. I'll call you if anything comes up. I just have one question for you."

I braced myself. Consuelo, watching me

like a hawk, looked concerned. Barney, watching me like a parrot, seemed impassive. "What?" I asked Jamie.

"Do you believe her?"

Wow. "Honestly, I don't know," I said. "Les Mannix might have had a reason to kill Dray, but it looks like Denise Barnaby didn't."

"Denise doesn't appear to know that."

I saw where that was going. "Feel free to tell her whenever you like," I said. "Patty — and I'm going to keep calling her Patty — didn't swear me to secrecy."

"I'm not asking you for anything else yet," Jamie assured me. I wasn't crazy about the *yet,* but I got over it. "I'm just saying that Denise didn't know her husband wasn't having an affair with Patty because Patty was apparently being paid to pretend she was a deluded fan."

Hearing it out loud from someone other than Patty made it sound even crazier. "I also saw a gun in Heather Alizondo's purse," I said.

"So what? There's a gun in my glove compartment. I drive in some sketchy areas and I have a perfectly legal permit." I was starting to think everybody had a gun except me. Maybe I was meant to live in Belgium.

"Fine, be that way," I told Jamie. "Go off and prepare a defense. I have a dog getting ready for his breakthrough role." We ended the call and I checked my email for the paperwork on Bagels's part, but it wasn't there. I asked Consuelo to call Giant again and she said she would.

She sat behind her desk not doing that, though. Instead she was chewing the end of a pen and twitching her mouth back and forth as if auditioning for the role of Samantha in a revival of *Bewitched.* "Here's what bothers me," she said finally.

I was back at my desk dealing with an orange calico cat who wanted to be the voice of an animated character. It's a living. For a cat. "What?" I asked.

"Why would Patty make up a nutty story like that? Couldn't she come up with a more plausible lie?" Consuelo was thinking hard and she is very smart, so it was worth considering.

"We're the parrot's agents," I said.

"I know, but aren't you curious? Don't you want to figure out who killed Dray Mattone?"

"Not especially. That's what the police are for." But I did find myself over the next hour or so wandering to the topic in my head. When I finally looked over at Consuelo again, it was like we'd never paused. "So you're saying you believe Patty?" I asked.

"I'm saying it would have been easier to get us to believe her if she'd said she was blackmailing Dray or that she really did think he was the father of her child. Is she even really pregnant?"

I shrugged. "I don't think so. I think that was part of the role. Later on I imagine she would have revealed that she wasn't really having a baby, maybe after there was some tabloid coverage, and they'd send her in for rehab or something. The thing that I don't understand is who would have thought that was a good idea. Who wanted to stir up a fake scandal about Dray so soon after he'd gone through his own rehab for drugs?"

"Well, you said the producer guy had some problems with Dray when they were negotiating his new contract," Consuelo pointed out. "Maybe he thought it would be good to make Dray look bad in the paper, lower his value or something."

"That doesn't really make sense. The last thing a showrunner needs is to have his star less popular to the viewing public, even if it will make his price lower." I stood up so I could pace, which is how I do my best thinking. "No, if we believe Patty, someone put together a really elaborate plan to discredit Dray. Or did they?" I stopped pacing.

Consuelo's eyes narrowed. "What?" she asked.

"Maybe the idea was to make Dray look *sympathetic.* This crazy fan was harassing him, claiming he was the father of her unborn child when he wasn't, making trouble for him. When it was discovered at the end — or even all the way along, if Patty played the part big enough — the public would feel like poor Dray had been victimized and he'd been even more popular than ever. That's the backstory, anyway. That's how they'd sell it to Patty. The real motive was to provide an easy mark once Dray had been shot, someone who could be blamed, tried, and convicted as a distraction from the person who really shot Dray. It's sort of genius."

Consuelo took a moment to absorb that brilliant observation, then sat back and laughed once. "That's insane," she said.

"Yeah, but it's showbiz, Consuelo. Publicists can talk actors into anything. Look, someone talked Patty into essentially becoming a target of the tabloids and TV by convincing her there was a part in it for her down the road. If you're going to be an agent, you have to understand that nobody in this business can see past their own career."

"So what does that mean?" Consuelo asked. "That someone wanted to kill Dray and they set Patty up as the fall guy? Who had the motive to do that?"

I sighed. "It's a good question. I'll have to ask Harve Lembeck."

I spent the night with my parents talking about everything except the Dray Mattone murder because I was murder-ed out. And throughout the conversation even as we put on *The Sunshine Boys* for Dad to get ideas, I kept getting the impression that my mother had no burning desire to leave their dual act but that she somehow expected my father to know that.

Dad doesn't like to walk the dogs far — he has had a knee replacement and it gets cranky on him, especially since he's leery of getting the procedure done on the other knee — so it was hard to get him alone for a significant period of time. But luckily Mom likes to go to bed early, so as soon as the movie was done, she said her goodnights and went into their bedroom. I pretended to be cleaning up the kitchen from dinner, although we'd done that already. Really all I was doing was getting ready to run the dishwasher. But I asked Dad to keep me company, so he came in and sat at the kitchen table.

"How's the market for a solo act going?" I asked.

Dad grimaced. I'd gotten the impression he was having trouble marketing himself alone. In recent years it had been tougher even with Mom in the act, but they had a reputation and could always bank on it, and in performance they were always terrific because they're pros and they love each other, which came across onstage. Don't underestimate the idea that audiences want to believe in the illusion they are being shown. If it happens to be real, that's even better.

"I'll find something," he said. "I haven't hit the right hook with the act yet, so I haven't really been able to pitch it as new and different. The usual bookings on cruise ships and some of the smaller casinos aren't coming across because they don't know me just by myself yet. Don't you worry, Kay, it'll happen."

I walked over and put a hand on his shoulder. "I know. I was just asking." I gave Dad a hug and he looked less grumpy. "How are you changing the act besides taking Mom out of it? It's hard to do sketches when you're by yourself."

He held up a hand. "Oh, it can be done, trust me. But I'm thinking it's more in the area of monologues, maybe reminiscences about the stars I've worked with over the years. I don't really want to get nostalgic about your mother because then people will think there's another reason she's not there and I'll get emotional onstage. Last thing you want." He did not want audiences to mistakenly believe he was mourning his wife when she was at home giving piano lessons and relaxing by the pool. Which is over at the Holiday Inn a couple of miles from here. But you can pay them by the season for access.

"You want to show me what you've got in mind?" I asked. Dad had always acted out the scenes and given Mom and me an idea of the songs he had in mind when he was concocting a new act. I gestured toward the living room where he'd have more space to work.

"Oh, I don't want to make noise and keep your mom awake," Dad said, shaking his head.

That was unusual. Dad is a natural performer; he'd almost never give up the opportunity to show off to any audience, even if it was just me. And Mom could sleep through an attack by the Saracens if they happen to drop by, so he was dodging the chance to show off his act.

"You don't have an act yet, do you?" I asked.

Dad looked away. "Not technically."

I sat down at the table next to him and looked him in the eye. "Dad, you really don't want to go out and work without Mom anymore, do you?"

He continued to stare at Bruno, who was fast asleep in a corner of the kitchen floor. Eydie, not quite as unconscious, was eyeing Bruno, whom she still saw as an interloper, if a benign one. Dad coughed theatrically (what other way is there?) into his hand.

"It's not my first choice," he said.

This was the time to make my play. "Well, guess what," I said. "If I'm reading Mom right, it's not her first choice either."

Dad looked up, startled. "What makes you think that?"

"Just the way she's been acting. I think maybe she's a little tired of the cruise ships, more than you are anyway, but I don't think she wants to retire and she's definitely not looking forward to spending all that time away from you."

My father shook his head. "No, that's not

what she told me. Said she's had it with being in front of an audience and having to be onstage every night. She doesn't like mingling with the audience all day and then doing the act at night. We're old, she's tired, I get that. But we never planned all that great for retirement, so we need the money, and besides, I like to get out there. You know how I am, honey. If I stay off the stage too long I get antsy. Mom's not like that."

"I think it's something else," I told him. This was tricky; I wanted to lead Dad to a conclusion without saying it myself simply because it wouldn't work if he didn't make the mental connection himself. Not to mention that people don't really like to be told something; they want to think their own thought processes were what brought them to this conclusion. They look upon the outcome more fondly and consider it more satisfactory. "I think maybe Mom is just feeling a little insecure and needs to be convinced she shouldn't be."

"Insecure?" Dad looked genuinely lost. "What has your mom got to be insecure about? She's the best singer out of the three of us. She's funny and audiences absolutely love her. If it was *Mom* who was going out on her own, there wouldn't be much of a problem getting *her* gigs."

"Well, she doesn't see it that way," I said. "Maybe she really is tired and she just doesn't feel like someone who sings well and can be entertaining. Because she herself doesn't feel all that confident anymore."

A switch flipped in my father's eyes. "She needs to be wooed," he said. "She needs someone to tell her how good she is and how necessary she is to the act. That would get her back into the mood, don't you think?"

Inwardly I was smiling from ear to ear; Dad had gotten the message in his own process. "I definitely do," I told him.

"Yeah." Dad stood up and started rubbing his hands together, not in a sinister way but to indicate he was thinking fast now. "She needs to hear it from someone she respects, someone whose opinion means something to her." He was on his way in his head and had to walk through it to get to the end. He turned. "You."

Huh? "Me, what?" I asked.

"You. You should talk to your mother about coming back to the act. She knows you love and respect her, and she loves you and respects your opinion. She'll listen to you." Dad's face was lighting up like a jack-o'-lantern, but not one of the scary ones.

I had to nip this in the bud quickly. "No,

no," I said. "Mom knows I love her, but if I suggest to her that she give up this retirement thing, she'll think I see her as an imposition and don't want her living here. No, it can't be me." And they said I couldn't improvise onstage.

Dad stopped pacing and put his hand to his chin. It was a calculated move — I'd seen him do it thousands of times when he was supposed to be thinking in a sketch — but it conveyed the proper message. He had indeed heard and absorbed what I'd said.

"Yeah, you're right," he said finally. "Maybe I'll call your aunt Irene. Mom will listen to her sister."

Subtlety clearly was not going to work like a charm in this situation. Dad knew what had to happen and he knew who had to make it happen. But he doesn't like confrontation and he especially doesn't want to do anything that might make my mother uncomfortable or irritable. They've been married a long time; he's learned how to avoid difficult situations and Mom has been serene and happy a long time.

I had to be direct, which was exactly what I didn't want to be. I came by my non-confrontational traits genetically.

"Dad." I sighed. "You can't call Aunt Irene. You need to talk to Mom yourself."

He had the nerve to look surprised. Or the person he was playing did. Sometimes it's hard to tell. "Really? You think she'd listen to me?"

"Now you're laying it on too thick. Of course she'll listen to you. There's nothing Mom likes more than being needed. No, there is one thing she likes more. She likes *you* more. So if you need her and you show her that you value her in the act, I think she'll be back in no time and you can book yourselves anywhere you like, as long as you don't start with a cruise ship. You might want to give that a little rest."

Before he could answer my phone buzzed and I saw Lo Toscadero's name on the caller ID. I hit the accept button quickly to avoid my father's arguing against his talking to my mother. Which was just weird.

"So did you solve the murder yet?" Lo asked.

"Nope. Haven't quite managed to tie up the loose ends. What have you got?" If I knew Lo — and I did — she'd spent as much of the day as she could *not* tending bar at L'Chaim! and instead surfing the web for background on Dray Mattone's murder. I hadn't asked her to do that, but then you never really ask Lo for anything. She just does.

"Not much," she answered. "The director Heather Alizondo once got a restraining order against the producer Les Mannix, saying he was stalking her."

My eyes might have bulged just a bit. Dad would have noticed, but he was now sitting at the table with a yellow legal pad, making notes on what he might say to Mom to get her to return to the act.

"Whoa, Les was stalking Heather? To the point that she had to go to the cops? How did Sergeant Bostwick not know this?"

"What makes you think he doesn't?" Lo responded. "Just because he doesn't tell you something doesn't mean he's never heard of it."

"No, but Jamie Wallace should. There's no way that could have gotten away from him."

"Not necessarily," Lo said. "The request for a restraining order was dropped, Les and Heather settled privately, and now she's working for him pretty steadily. So something's up, but it never actually made the legal record because a judge never saw it."

"How'd *you* see it?"

"Tabloids, baby. It's where the real dirt is kept."

Did this have any bearing on Dray's murder? If Heather and Les had some private dispute that didn't involve the show or Dray specifically, how did that shed any light? And if Lo had really gotten her information from a tabloid, could we even be sure it was true?

"I'm not sure that has anything to do with Dray," I mused aloud.

"No, but this does — the rumor at the time was that the reason Heather wasn't interested in this Mannix guy is that she had something going on with Dray Mattone."

"Man! If this guy spent as much time running around as they're giving him credit for, he never would have gotten one scene shot." Now I was pacing. "So that brings Denise into play and it also might have something to do with Heather if she heard about the fake letter about Patty's fake pregnancy."

"The pregnancy was fake?" Lo asked.

I filled her in on the day's developments, which was enough to make me want to crawl into bed and stay there until the following April. "Woooowwww," Lo said after I was done. "And I thought I had a lot of intel."

"You did," I said. "I appreciate it. I owe you a drink."

"I'm a bartender, honey." Lo laughed quietly.

"A soft drink. Maybe a milkshake."

"Hardly seems worth it."

"I'm going to bed, Lo. I'll talk to you tomorrow." I glanced over and saw Dad had a list of *no*es that stretched down the left side of his page and *yes*es that had maybe four items on it. Fatigue was being compounded by . . . more fatigue.

"No, wait. I have one more thing. Apparently Dray Mattone was very seriously antigun and refused to be photographed with one in his hand."

"So Harve's story about Dray wanting to practice was a lie," I said.

"I'm guessing. This is based on an interview Dray gave three years ago. Maybe his stance changed, but I didn't see anything that indicated it had." Lo, once loosed on a topic, is like any of my dogs with a new chew toy. There will be no relenting.

"Keep at it, Lo," I said for no reason. I knew she would.

As soon as we ended the call, Dad looked up from his pad, which had not changed much since I'd checked last. "Lorraine's helping you figure out Dray Mattone's murder?" he said.

"Whether I want her to or not."

He shook his head, put down his pencil — never a pen, or heaven forbid, a computer keyboard for my father — and rubbed his eyes. "I can't figure out how to convince your mother to work with me again."

"By being yourself," I said. "Show her you love and need her and she'll respond like she always does."

Dad's eyes took on a determination I'd seen before when someone told us we couldn't hold a booking or an audience wasn't responding the way he'd anticipated. I'd been waiting for this; it was the perfect indication that he was not going to take Mom's retirement lying down.

He stood up and marched to the door of their bedroom. My mother, who wouldn't consider closing her eyes before reading for an hour, was certainly still awake. With Dad this worked up and Mom relaxed, it was the perfect time to resolve their issue and get my life — their lives, sorry — back to normal. He opened the door and walked in as I heard my mother softly saying, "Jay!" She wasn't expecting Dad this early.

I figured this would take a while but would play out successfully, so I read a few new emails, noted that one from Consuelo indicated we still hadn't heard from Giant Productions about Bagels, which was officially troubling, and sent a text to Sam that read, *Haven't had a good cup of coffee in a while.* I waited for a response.

Instead, I got my father walking out of the bedroom much sooner than I would have expected with a look on his face that could only be described as bewildered.

"She said no," he told me, shaking his head in wonder.

"You want to help me solve a murder tomorrow?" I asked.

Dad's faced immediately perked up. "Sure."

Sam texted me back: *Tomorrow?*

CHAPTER TWENTY-THREE

Getting Dad onto the studio lot was not difficult. For one thing, Gus the guard had seen me enough in the past week to just wave me in. Having Barney's cage (complete with Barney) in the back seat helped. Gus eyed Dad, asked for his driver's license, which Dad had at the ready, and nodded after making a copy. He raised the gate and we were in.

"Your plan," my father said, "is not entirely clear to me."

Dad was still pretty shaken by my mother's refusal to rejoin him in the family business. I hadn't had a chance to question Mom on her reasoning because Dad had been present this morning and Mom had come out of the bedroom too late to go on the morning walk with the dogs. That would have to wait until later.

The fact that my plan was not entirely clear to me either wasn't helping. I'd wanted to get Dad involved to soften the blow of the night before, and now I had to more or less manufacture a role for him to play. I knew what *I* wanted to do: track down Harve Lembeck and ferret out what he knew about Patty's wild story of being hired to play a crazed fan that morphed into Suspect No. 1 in Dray's murder. What Dad was going to do here, especially since the sets had been closed for a day now, was less definite.

"It's simple," I lied. "You're pretending to be Barney's trainer because Patty can't come to the set. If anyone asks you, that's your character. You've been training parrots for twenty years, okay?"

"Okay, I get my character," Dad answered as I pulled the car into a parking spot. "But what am I *really* doing? How am I helping you solve the murder?"

It was a good question. "Ah, that's the interesting part." Sure it was. "Remember I told you about that mysterious woman who got up at the memorial service and accused Les Mannix of killing Dray? Nobody I've talked to can tell me her name or what it was she was doing here." All that was true.

"So? Aren't we assuming that was Patty?" Dad wasn't trying to be difficult; he was trying to understand. And since he knew me well, he was probably coming to the re-alization that I was ad-libbing, which left him somewhat in the lurch.

"Probably, although I didn't think to ask her. So, two things. I want to see if you can at least get a clear description of her and what people saw her do or heard her say. Second, Dray had apparently been meeting on the set, briefly each time, with various people who would show up and then never be seen again. Nobody knows what that was all about, but I've heard it said there was some connection to his drug problem. I want you to find out —"

Dad got out of the car and held up a hand to stop me. He didn't speak loudly despite the fact that nobody in the area seemed ter-ribly interested in what we were doing or saying. "You're saying this guy had a habit, went through rehab, was trying to get back to sober life, and was having these brief meetings with people nobody else knew that didn't last long? And the people never came back again?"

That was pretty much the size of it, and I told Dad so. He had a serious look on his face and drew me closer to speak even less loudly. "Dray was attending meetings and he was looking for a sponsor," he told me.

His comment threw me for a moment; it

seemed to come out of nowhere. "How do you know that?" I asked.

My father fixed me with a look. "I've known more than a couple of people over the years who went through it," he said. "He was trying to get it together. If you could find one of those people, they could tell you his state of mind at the time. But they wouldn't. It's not the way these things are usually done, but with the schedule a TV star keeps, it's not that crazy that they'd all come to the set to talk to him. It's like an audition process. Just seems like he was being picky."

I blinked a couple of times. "Dad, is there something you haven't told me?" In an instant my whole concept of reality was being threatened.

Dad let out a quick breath like a rueful laugh. *"No,"* he said. "Believe me, you would have figured that out by now if it was true. I've just known some people. And you see it enough times, you know what it looks like. I'm willing to bet that's what Dray Mattone was trying to do."

"So the parade of people could be a dead end," I said, my mental state returning to what I laughably consider normal. "Even if we knew who they were, none of them would tell us anything. But Heather said they were all carrying guns."

Dad shrugged. "Not illegal," he said.

"People keep telling me that. How come nobody knew who they were?"

"There's a reason Anonymous is in the title," Dad said.

"So I guess we ignore that. I'm going to look for Harve. Why don't you take Barney here to use for cover and see if you can find out anything about the mysterious curly-haired woman?"

"Who am I gonna ask?" Dad wanted to know. "The show wrapped yesterday. I'll be lucky to find a janitor sweeping up."

I shrugged. "Maybe he knows something."

Dad stood still a moment, then picked up Barney's cage and walked away, muttering about how it had been his understanding that I'd had a plan.

I took the moment without a bird to watch to get back into the car and drive over to Giant Productions. Except that Giant's trailer was no longer parked where it had been the other times I'd been there. I called Consuelo, who reported no word on Bagels's big break from the production company.

"I'm guessing the real name of the unit was Fly by Night Productions," I said, and Consuelo did not argue. It was going to be a joy to report this back to Miriam.

It took only a few minutes to drive back to the *Dead City* sound stages and offices, but there were already changes to the area by the time I got there. The name of the show was no longer on the signs at each door. Those are easily changed out — they're simply printed on cover stock and slid in and out of frames — but the decision to remove them told me more than I wanted to know.

The show had been canceled. Everybody I'd met on the set was now out of work, and that meant Bostwick and Baker were not going to be able to easily interrogate anyone but Patty. Cops work hard, but they tend to come up with a theory of a crime and then try to find the facts that support it. And it was fairly clear who the presumed suspect was in this case.

That was a problem, but my first priority right now was finding my father and a parrot.

The door wasn't locked yet, so I opened it and went inside and saw workmen taking apart the set on which I'd seen Dray Mattone work with Barney the one day I was here with a full crew, the last scene Dray would ever shoot. Standing on the floor, watching them disassemble the fake morgue, was Les Mannix in jeans and a white dress shirt, obligatory baseball cap on his head. At least Les wasn't operating under the delusion that he was a millennial; the cap was not on backward.

I walked over to him and saw the pensive, almost sorrowful look in his eyes. "I'm sorry to see it, Les," I said. And I meant that. People working on a theater or film production like to say they become families; that's a stretch, but they do spend many long hours together in pursuit of a common goal. They get pretty friendly and it's always sad to see that experience come to an end, especially when it's unexpected.

"We'll be back," he insisted. "I've got calls in and people are interested. Something will happen inside a week, you'll see." But he'd given that speech too many times now and it wasn't even clear whether he believed it anymore.

"All this because someone walked into Dray's trailer and shot him." Hey, I wasn't that close to the *Dead City* company. I could use the mood to my advantage. "Why would anybody want to do that?"

There was — and I want to be clear about this — no tear falling from Les Mannix's eye. He was not happy about what was going on, but he wasn't about to break down and let himself be seen as a failure. No, Les was determined to be the strong leader, even if there was no one left to lead.

"There were any number of reasons I can think of," he said with a clipped tone. "The man was coming out of rehab and for all I know had relapsed. He was three thousand miles away from his wife, and who knows how many women were taking her place. He didn't like being on a TV series anymore and told me so to my face, even while he was signing a contract for three more seasons at an amount of money that would set up sixteen families for generations to come. He was always good to work with on the set, I'll grant him that, but away from it, Dray Mattone was a hot mess and he hurt a lot of people. I can think of twenty off the top of my head who are not sad that he's dead."

Wow. You don't often get that big an emotional download all at once. I wondered how much of it was real.

"Were you one of them?" I asked, I thought gently.

Apparently Mannix disagreed with my assessment; he turned and stared, eyes slightly bulging. "I beg your pardon?" he asked. Well, he was polite, anyway.

"I was just wondering. I mean, the way

you talked Dray wasn't the nicest guy anybody ever met. How mad were you at him?" I was still trying for a sort of innocent tone, but there wasn't any way to mask the intent of the question.

"I did not shoot Dray Mattone, if that's what you're asking," he said. "I didn't hate him. I wouldn't even say I disliked him. Business is business. We had our negotiations and his agent took me for all he could. That's her job."

As an agent, I was simultaneously offended and flattered. For my clients, the job is really to find work rather than negotiate cushy terms. If I get a cat's litter box being cleaned out at least once a day written into a contract, I'm on a good run.

"I didn't really mean to ask that way," I said, signifying that I *had* meant to ask that way, but more subtly so Mannix wouldn't have gotten annoyed. Maybe the guy had shot somebody; those are not the circumstances under which it's best to irritate them. "I don't think you had a motive. The contracts were signed and you would have known the impact Dray's death would have on the show. You didn't want to see this happen." I gestured toward the carpenters taking down the set.

"That's right." Mannix nodded. The

baseball cap bobbed a bit and I wondered if he was losing his hair. "I had no reason to want Dray dead. If I'd wanted him gone I wouldn't have renewed the contract."

"Still, I assume the show is insured, right? Wouldn't you be protected if one of your key cast members was no longer able to perform on the set?"

"Up to a point." This was business talk. Mannix reverted to his thoughtful-but-tough persona as if he were being interviewed for an article in *Variety*. "We were insured for any costs incurred if Dray had died while filming something we couldn't complete. Dray finished his work on this episode. But now we're facing cancellation by the network, and while they're *saying* it's because Dray got killed, it's really because they saw our numbers slipping, the show was getting more expensive as cast members got bigger contracts, and they saw a way to cut their losses and run."

"What about Dray?" I asked. "Did he have a big life insurance policy or something?"

Mannix looked at me as if I were prescient. "That's amazing," he said. "You'd think a guy with that kind of money coming in at that age wouldn't be worried about life insurance. But in the midst of the negotiations his agent calls me up and says the studio has to pay for a sixteen-million-dollar policy in Dray's name and that has to be part of the deal. We ended up doing it because it was probably the least expensive part of his contract, but that's not something you usually get asked to do."

That tickled something in the back of my brain, but I didn't know what. "Who was the beneficiary?" I asked.

"His wife. Actors, the things they ask for in contracts." He rolled his eyes. "When we get to cable, we'll have to scale back and make it cheaper to deliver."

"Do you really think you'll be able to do that?" I asked.

Mannix dropped the mask he'd put on and looked weary. "I honestly have no idea," he said. Then he straightened himself, took a breath, and added, "But don't you dare tell anybody I said that."

"Of course. Just one thing: I'm looking for Harve Lembeck. Have you seen him?"

Les Mannix stood silent for a moment. "Who's Harve Lembeck?" he asked.

"The first assistant director." You'd think the showrunner would know that, but it actually wasn't all that unusual that he wouldn't because Les would be so involved with studio and network meetings that he was rarely on the set.

"No idea," he said. Then as if he'd been cued, Mannix turned and walked away before I could ask him who on this empty sound stage might be able to help me.

Given these circumstances, I decided (as I'll admit I had once before) that the only thing left to do was find Dad and drive home. I walked over to a stagehand — one of the few who was not carrying a heavy part of the set, but had a small lamp in his hand — and asked if he'd seen anyone matching the description I gave of my father. He had not.

I texted Dad asking where he was and waited a moment, then headed toward the door to get to the parking lot. Maybe Dad had given up on trying to wring information from the stagehands, who wouldn't have had any, and was back at the car waiting for me. In any event, he didn't answer.

I texted to Sam confirming that I'd be around this evening and he at least responded, saying to disregard the closed sign at Cool Beans and just walk in whenever I wanted to, which is what I always do anyway. Sam doesn't lock up until he goes home.

Hitting the door on the way out and being somewhat blinded by the bright sunshine, I fumbled in my purse for my sunglasses and put them on. But as I headed into the parking lot I started feeling uneasy about Dad's not answering. Dad always responds, so this could only mean his phone had died; he's not great about charging it.

To test my theory, I pulled out my own phone and called his number. It rang for a while and went to voice mail. Sure enough. The battery must have been dead.

Once I got to the car and didn't find Dad and Barney there, I was a little bit concerned. It wasn't like my father to just take off on his own. Well, yes it was, but he'd always let me know he was doing so. He's impulsive but thoughtful. Best guess: He thinks he's onto something and is ignoring the phone because he's talking to someone from the show about what happened to Dray.

I considered calling my mother to see if Dad had gotten in touch with her, but that presented two problems: First, I didn't want to upset Mom by telling her I'd lost her husband, and second, Dad probably wouldn't have told her his exact location on the lot anyway.

It gave me a few minutes to think over everything I'd seen and heard since the day I'd accompanied Barney to the *Dead City* set. And while the whole thing was too large to contemplate all at once, there were nagging loose ends that bothered me. I found myself asking questions and coming up with only speculative answers.

Standing next to my car in the sunshine, I wasn't thinking about the parking lot or the sound stage or Bagels and his apparently missed opportunity. I wasn't thinking about where Dad might be — okay, not too much anyway — and I wasn't thinking about why I was suddenly interested in seeing Sam to the point that I'd ask if I could drop by.

Instead, I concentrated on the part of the Dray Mattone murder that I would know and the police wouldn't: the showbiz aspects. Sure, they had the advantage when it came to bullet trajectories, DNA samples (if they had any), and the physical evidence, not to mention years of experience solving crimes. But I knew how a film set worked and what the motive of everyone in that situation might be.

Dray Mattone was the only person on the *Dead City* set who had expressed any dissatisfaction with being there, and that was only to a privileged few. He'd been charming as all get out to me when he didn't need to be, and according to all the witnesses I'd talked to, he'd been nothing but professional in his work. But apparently his addiction problems had been plaguing him to the point of despair and his marriage to Denise Barnaby had been long-distance, often ignored, and no source of comfort for Dray. What Denise thought when she wasn't seeking the spotlight was anybody's guess.

So Dray had been desperately unhappy according to more than one person in the company. He'd been having short one-off meetings with mysterious figures on the set, who according to Heather Alizondo had all been carrying guns. Of course, Heather was packing heat too, not to mention her shaky history with Les Mannix, and still everybody kept telling me that all the firepower around the set was no big deal. I appeared to be unusually sensitive on the subject.

Then there was the mysterious curly-haired brunette who had accosted Les Mannix at Dray's memorial service. People had seen her around for a few days, but nobody knew who she might be. She was seen going into Dray's trailer but not around the time of the shooting, when apparently nobody was paying attention to Dray's trailer.

And I was sure I'd recognized her voice from somewhere, but when?

The thing that finally did it for me was a comment both Heather and Dad had made when we were discussing the parade of armed figures who had met with Dray on the set recently. Independently, each of them had compared the one-a-day meetings in the corner of the sound stage as being similar to an audition process for a role in a film or TV show. And that was when I realized where I had heard the curly-haired woman's voice before.

It had come from Barney.

There wasn't time to think about that because I was shaken — almost literally — from my reverie. From where I was standing I could see the corner of what had been Dray Mattone's trailer. I could only assume it hadn't been hauled away for some serious renovation by the company that had rented it to *Dead City* because it was still considered a crime scene, although there was no yellow tape around it that I could see.

What was especially alarming at this moment was that someone was walking toward the trailer's side entrance, not exactly slowly but in a somewhat jerky, awkward fashion. I almost yelled out because heading toward the trailer was my father, carrying Barney's cage in his left hand. That was unusual. Dad is right handed.

I stopped because he was being followed closely — very closely — by a woman. That proximity was significant. I could tell even from this distance that the woman was guiding Dad toward the trailer and holding him with her left hand on his left hip. I couldn't see Dad's face, but it didn't look like a happy scene and I wanted to cry out.

The woman was the curly-haired brunette from the memorial service. She was almost holding Dad in a hug from behind because her right hand was completely obscured in his right side.

I'm no expert, but I was willing to bet she was holding a gun.

CHAPTER TWENTY-FOUR

I'm not an idiot. The first thing I did was to call Bostwick.

"You see the gun?" he asked as soon as I ran breathlessly through my plea.

"I can't say I saw it exactly, but the way they were walking and the fact that my father is headed into Dray Mattone's trailer with a mysterious woman — yeah, there was a gun," I said.

"You don't have any proof yet, but I'm alerting the studio security and I'll send a car there right now. Whatever you do, don't follow him inside." Bostwick hung up.

He was right, of course. I hadn't actually confirmed the presence of a gun in my father's ribs. I didn't know the woman was forcing him inside. The best thing to do was to wait for the studio cops and then the NYPD cruiser to show up. It wasn't going to help Dad at all for me to come bursting into the trailer and upsetting the curly-haired woman.

I ran for the trailer. He's my dad.

Luckily the trailers here were not surrounded, as many in the Los Angeles industry are, with gravel to make it seem more "homey." So my feet didn't make a ton of noise when I arrived at the steps to the trailer entrance. In the distance, maybe half a mile away, I could see the studio security car, flashers not operating, sirens not sounding, on its way to me. It didn't seem to be in that much of a hurry. But I was.

I was careful to step lightly on the three stairs up to the trailer door, which I was hoping desperately was not locked. If the curly-haired woman had decided to keep Dad and Barney inside and been careful, I'd only be alerting her to the presence of someone outside without actually achieving anything toward the goal, which was getting Dad out safe. And Barney.

The key — no pun intended — here was stealth, which is something I'm not great at. When I was eight I tripped over a slipper backstage at one of the Catskills hotels, which led to me knocking over a tray of water glasses, which led to my making my entrance onstage soaking wet and bleeding from the left foot. And that wasn't even my worst performance that month.

Now I reached for the doorknob and silently attempted to turn it. It moved, which was an excellent sign but not the whole ball game. Once I'd turned it (so slowly the motion could have been adapted into a PBS miniseries), I pushed very gently at the door to open it.

It did not move.

My heart stopped beating for a moment. I closed my eyes and stifled the scream I wanted to let loose. I couldn't get into the trailer, and making a loud sound outside the trailer would only . . . Wait, that was it.

If I created enough commotion out here, the curly-haired woman would have to open the door if she wanted to see what was going on. Sure there were windows in the trailer, but I could duck down low enough to avoid being seen through them. All I had to do was decide on the right kind of ruckus to make. The studio car was still at least three hundred yards away.

The trick was not being obvious in my motives. An electronically generated police siren, for example, was something I could easily download on my phone, but it would sound fake and would alert the woman inside that someone was trying to get her to slip up or at the very least was aware of her presence and her bad intentions.

I fell back on my strength, which is pretending to be something I'm not. I hollered at the top of my lungs like a woman who had just broken her leg in three places. It was possible the memory of that entrance over the broken glasses was fueling my performance. I'm a Method faker.

As soon as I let out my piteous scream I dropped to the ground just next to the stairs and waited only a few seconds. Then I yelled again just to let my quarry know she was not dealing with one isolated incident that would go away, but with someone who could draw attention to this area of the lot for an extended period of time if she didn't act quickly.

Sure enough, the door to the trailer opened. It opened out, and I realized that I could have simply pulled on the door and avoided this whole badly written scenario. But there was no time to ruminate now on my own stupidity because a head was sticking itself out through the doorway to investigate.

It was Dad's, and I was glad to see it, even if the gun behind his head was now clearly in sight. I felt like calling Bostwick back to tell him I'd been right.

Instead I tried to make eye contact with my father, but he didn't react at all when I stuck my face out of the shadows and looked at him. Then he looked down at his feet, which seemed really weird.

That is, it seemed weird until Dad said, "What's this?" and reached down as if he were picking something up off the stairs. That sudden move, which he could justify easily should his captor object, allowed him to get the gun away from his head and pointing into the open air just for a moment.

In that time I launched myself up the stairs and toward the curly-haired woman, who was indeed the person standing behind Dad in the trailer doorway. My father ducked out of the way and I ran past him and, uncontested, into Dray Mattone's trailer. I caught a flash of the gunmetal as I flew into what ended up being one of the leather armchairs in Dray's living room area.

"Hold it!" yelled the woman with the gun. That made no sense. I was the one on the easy chair and she was the one holding the weapon. I turned to look at her and was disappointed to have been right in my assumptions.

"Patty," I said, "I really wish it wasn't you."

My father, who to his credit had tried to run for cover, stopped as Patty Basilico aimed her pistol at him and gestured him back into the trailer. He followed the visual command and stood next to me. Knowing Dad, I realized he was probably figuring that if Patty shot at me he could jump in the path of the bullet. My father is both dear and melodramatic.

Of course we were being held at gunpoint, so maybe *melodramatic* was a bit of a stretch under the circumstances.

Patty reached up and took off the long curly-haired wig. She placed it carefully on the table as if it might break, holding the gun on Dad and me and looking as calm and normal as if she were dropping off another plate of chocolate chip cookies at my office.

"Well, it is me," she said. She pulled a chair away from the table and sat down, leveling the gun the whole time. Not a second of wasted movement, not an opportunity for either of us to rush Patty or the door before being shot. This was not the first time she had held people at gunpoint.

"It is okay for me to be upset about *her* having a gun?" I asked Dad. I'll admit it; I felt a little vindicated.

"I can't say as I'm crazy about it either," he said, and closed ranks just a little bit more on my right side.

Barney, in his cage on a side table nearer to me than to Patty, made sure we knew it was not possible to kill a zombie. It offered little comfort.

"How'd you get involved in this?" I asked my father. "You were supposed to be . . ."

"Looking for the curly-haired brunette from the memorial service for Mattone," Dad said. He gestured toward Patty. "I found her. I take it she's your client?"

I shrugged. "Pretty sure I'll be resigning the case," I said. Then I looked at Patty. "Why'd you come back to the lot? There's so much I don't understand."

"You'll have to get used to it," she said. She seemed to be consulting her phone while keeping the gun trained on us. Her eyes darted back and forth from one plane to the other. "I don't plan on explaining my evil plan to you, Mr. Bond."

"Oh, come on," I tried. "That's not fair. If you're going to shoot us, at least let us know why." Dad tightened at the word *shoot.* He probably thought it was a bad idea to remind Patty of that, although I didn't think she was bound to forget the gun in her hand anytime soon.

"Sorry. But don't worry. I'm not going to shoot you. I have another plan for you two that'll look less obvious." Patty sounded like she was planning the agenda for next month's meeting of the PTA. She still had that homey, cheerful tone to her voice. It was really weird.

This was about keeping this nutty scene going until Bostwick showed up, mostly because I had absolutely no confidence in the studio cops, who had probably been told by the NYPD not to take any action unless they saw an immediate danger. All they'd see was a trailer that was still. Probably they wouldn't even knock on the door until the real cops showed up, and would be happy not to do so.

The best thing studio security does is keep people away from a closed set, and they'd clearly done a bang-up job here. So it was up to me to keep the scene going, but I had a master improviser with me.

"She's not going to tell us," I said to Dad, "but I think I know what happened anyway."

"Really!" My father sounded like I'd offered him the recipe to an especially sinful chocolate cake that I'd just gotten from the pages of *Good Housekeeping.* "You figured it out?"

"I'm not sure, but I have a theory." I took a look at Patty, who appeared less interested in my theory than in whatever was occupying her attention on her smartphone. Probably she'd googled how to tie people up in a luxurious trailer without any actual rope on hand. The key was to engage her. "You were hired to kill Dray Mattone, weren't you, Patty?"

She didn't look up, nor did she answer. Dad would have to carry the load in this performance. "Hired?" he asked. "She wasn't mad at him all on her own?"

"Put down the gun!" Barney shouted. Maybe he was reenacting the crime.

"No, I don't think so," I answered Dad. "See, Dray was depressed. I don't know if he was clinically depressed or not, but he was under the care of a psychiatrist, who certainly wouldn't tell us anything even if we asked, and was on some antidepressant medication. But he'd decided it made him gain weight and had stopped taking it."

Where were those cops, already?

"So how does that lead to your client here being paid to shoot him? The psychiatrist was mad because Dray went off his meds?" Dad, as my mother has often observed, is incapable of not going for the joke.

"No, see if you can follow me," I told him. Patty stood up and backed up to a closet, which she opened with her left hand. Still no clear path to the trailer door. "Patty here is a hired gun. Literally. She kills people for a living. You're not an actress at all, are you, Patty?"

She didn't answer. Instead she rummaged through a shelf of what appeared to be exercise equipment while still training the pistol on Dad and me. She found something I couldn't see and pulled it out. I saw a flash of green. "Oh, look at that," she said.

"See," I said to Dad, "you said Dray's meetings on set were like an audition. Heather Alizondo said the same thing, even though she didn't share your theory about him trying to find a sobriety sponsor. You were wrong about that, Dad, sorry."

"I'll live." Then he looked at Patty. "Well . . ."

I knew I wouldn't hear a siren, but I wasn't hearing *anything* outside, and it was starting to bug me. "Anyway, it got me to thinking. Dray wasn't in a position to audition actors for the show, and even if he was, these people didn't seem to fit the bill. There was a new one every day. They weren't all gorgeous women, so he wasn't just trying to find his next conquest, if what I hear about his preferences is accurate. So what could he have been auditioning people to do?"

"Sit in this chair," Patty said, pointing to

one of the wooden kitchen chairs by the table.

I didn't see any upside in following her orders, so I ignored her entirely. "At first I thought Dray was trying to find some security people because Heather said everyone who came to see him had a gun. But he didn't have to be secretive about that, and these meetings always seemed to be held away from everyone else. Dray never told anyone what they were for."

"I *said,* 'Sit in this chair,' " Patty repeated, perhaps on the assumption that I hadn't heard her. *"Now."*

"I don't think so," I answered, and turned back toward Dad. "I recognized her voice when she spoke at the memorial service, but I couldn't place it. Then I heard Barney say something and I realized he sounded like the woman at the service. And that meant he sounded like Patty, because she trained him."

"Now," Patty repeated. I didn't respond to that either.

"And then I remembered something Dray had asked me the day I was on set that seemed odd. He asked if Barney was the only reason I was there. And he never got to follow up, so I never got an explanation. But I think now that Dray was depressed and suicidal, and was covering up. He'd hired someone to kill him through a third party and they said she was the bird trainer. He was wondering if it was me."

"What do you mean, you don't think so?" Patty demanded. "I'm holding the gun."

"Yeah, and if you wanted to shoot me, you would have done it already," I told her. "You want to tie me to a chair and find a way to dispose of us? I'm not going to help you."

"So Dray Mattone wanted to die," Dad said, picking up my thread and trying to distract Patty, who stepped forward. "What does that have to do with the people on the set?"

"He *was* auditioning them," I answered. "He was trying to find a connection to someone who could supply a hired assassin."

This time Dad looked genuinely surprised. "Why?"

"Do you want to explain, or should I go on?" I asked Patty.

"You should get in the chair," she said, and then pointed the gun at Dad. "Unless you want me to shoot *him.*"

Game, set, and match.

I stood up and walked to the table. But if I kept the conversation going, I might still be able to stall until the New York Police

Department managed to amble their way from the nearest precinct to the trailer door. Where's a cop when you need one?

"Dray didn't like guns and had been adamant about it in the press," I said. "He might not have been the type to do himself in with pills or a rope. Maybe he wanted to make a statement about gun control as his last act. But he was trying to find someone who would shoot him with the gun Harve had gotten him from the set. And somehow he found our pal Patty here."

"Sit," Patty said. Apparently now I was her dog. She nodded in Dad's direction again to reiterate her threat and it was effective.

I sat.

Immediately Patty produced a green exercise band she'd gotten from Dray's closet and pulled my hands behind the back of the chair, where she began to tie them. Tightly. "Hey," I said.

"Don't fight it," she said. That didn't seem very productive. It's like being arrested for resisting arrest. Who *wants* to be arrested? Isn't it natural to resist?

And that was, finally, when I heard a shout from outside.

"NYPD!" It was Bostwick's voice. He wouldn't have just knocked because he'd have gotten a report from the studio security guy that people were being held in the trailer and he didn't want to be right in the doorway if something happened. Cops protect themselves and that makes sense; they should. "Come on out of the trailer!" Bostwick had decided against the bullhorn, which I thought was also a good decision. It added the human touch.

But Patty wasn't buying. She finished tying me up and then looked at Dad. "Now you," she said, and gestured toward another hard kitchen chair with the gun. "Sit."

Dad sat and she began tying his hands to the chair with a blue exercise band I hadn't seen before.

"Police!" Bostwick shouted. "You in the trailer, come on out!"

And that's when I got scared, because Patty's reaction was not what I expected when she heard the cops were outside. She smiled. That couldn't be good.

"Why aren't you answering?" Dad asked her. "What do you expect to gain this way?"

Patty stood up, having completed her task, and put the gun on the sofa across the room because she wouldn't be needing it immediately. Then she turned and answered the first question we'd asked of her since

I'd stupidly launched myself into the trailer. "Leverage," she said, pointing at us.

CHAPTER TWENTY-FIVE

Being threatened at gunpoint is not an experience I would recommend. It's frightening and somehow insulting at the same time. It brings with it the threat of injury or death even as it mocks you for being stupid enough to get into this situation to begin with.

But being a hostage is just a big drag.

Bostwick repeated his order to come out of the trailer three more times before Patty responded. He actually asked to be let inside and she laughed, but not loudly enough that he could have heard her. It wasn't until the phone rang — who knew these trailers still had landlines? — that she sat down at the table between Dad and me, seemed to set herself, and picked up the receiver.

"Hello?" Patty might just as well have been talking to her podiatrist. She listened for a good while. "Oh, I don't think that will be possible." She replaced the receiver and looked at us. "They wanted to talk to you."

"I wouldn't mind," I said. "It's not like I have something better to do."

"You'll talk to them when I want you to talk to them," she answered, and this time I was sure she wasn't going to be baking me cookies anytime soon.

It was like that for an hour. We sat silently for much of the time while there were clear sounds of scurrying police officers outside the trailer, no doubt frustrated with the inability to talk to anyone or see inside to figure out what was going on. Otherwise they might have been just as bored as the rest of us.

When I got tired enough of the quiet, I said, "The part I don't get is why you dropped all those clues, Patty. You were hired to shoot Dray. And you knew you were going to do it. What was with the fake pregnancy letter? How come you wanted to draw attention to yourself? You even signed your name."

Patty sighed a little impatiently and rolled her eyes, but said nothing.

"What makes you think that's even close to being her name?" Dad said. "The cops already know her as Patrice Columbo, and

I'm willing to bet she has three or four more stashed away somewhere."

That had more implications than I had anticipated. I looked back at Patty even as the footsteps outside receded, which meant the cops were planning a move. "You mean somebody set her up? She really wasn't supposed to be known as Patty Basilico and they made her take the name because they could plant those letters and lead the cops to her? You're a professional, Patty. How'd you let that happen?"

She dropped her hands loudly from her chin to the table and used them to push up to a standing position. "I never should have taken the job," she said. "It was way more trouble and risk than it was worth."

"Then why did you?" Dad asked. He can give words the kindest inflection when he really wants someone to talk to him.

Patty made a slight moaning noise and looked around the trailer, but not at Dad or me. "I was a fan," she said quietly.

"Of Dray's?" That seemed . . . a trifle odd.

But she nodded. "I'd seen him in everything he ever did, even the early stuff, even *Doctor Acula.* Now he was in such pain and he so wanted it to be taken away. I never get sentimental about my work; I just can't. But this one time I let my guard down and

375

look what happens." She swept her hand around the trailer as if complaining that I'd forced her into taking Dad and me hostage in a luxurious star's accommodation.

The thing about being a hostage is that after the initial shock and fear wear off, it's just boring. You're not involved in the negotiations taking place (and in this case, there were no negotiations taking place, which made me wonder what Patty's plan might be), you're pretty sure your life isn't in danger until something happens, and if, like us, your hands are tied, you can't even play cards. My arms were pretty numb.

When I'm immobilized like that — to be fair, I'd never been immobilized *like that* before, but if I got sick and needed to stay in bed for a stretch, maybe — my mind goes into overdrive. And it occurred to me that people who take hostages *never* get what they want. Have you ever heard of a hostage taker getting the helicopter to the airport, the fifty million dollars in untraceable bills, and the transport to a tropical island that doesn't extradite? Neither have I, because that doesn't ever happen.

I decided not to mention that to Patty because my hands were still tied and she still had the gun.

"Why the disguise?" Dad asked, now that

Patty seemed to be taking questions. "Everybody on the set knew you as the parrot's owner. Why did you need the wig and makeup, and why accuse Mannix at the memorial service?"

I already thought I knew the answers to those questions. "She put on the disguise to create a separate persona, someone who could have done the murder and was definitely not Patty Basilico," I said. "That was before she realized someone was putting a good deal of effort into proving Patty *had* shot Dray. And I think the scene at the memorial was to get the cops to look more closely at Les Mannix for the killing. Do you think he's the one who left the letters? Did you even *write* the letters?"

"Les Mannix didn't hire me," Patty said. "Dray Mattone hired me. The only way to know who is setting me up is to know who Dray told about our arrangement. Because I sure didn't tell anybody."

When the knock on the trailer door came, it was loud and unsettling. Dad and I both started in our seats at the sound. Patty didn't jump. She turned her head toward the door slowly and smiled.

"Yes?"

"This is Sergeant Joe Bostwick of the NYPD," came the voice.

Patty chuckled. "We've met," she said loudly enough to be heard through the door.

"Suppose I come in so we can talk about what you want," Bostwick said.

"Suppose I shoot the two people in here if you even try to open that door."

"How can we alleviate the hostage situation?"

Patty shook her head with a little smile. "Alleviate," she said in a normal speaking volume. "Two people in here going to die and he wants to alleviate." Then, louder, toward the door: "I want a big truck to come and haul this trailer wherever I want to go."

There was something of a pause. Bostwick's voice sounded a little perplexed when he responded. "You know that's not possible."

"Why not? The thing's on wheels and it has all the amenities. Get a truck. I'll wait." She seemed amused. Clearly she knew what she was requesting was unreasonable. What was she waiting for?

I decided to take matters into my own mouth. "She has the two of us tied to chairs, Joe!" I shouted. "She has a gun!"

"Who's in there besides you, Kay?" Bostwick yelled before Patty could tell me to shut up. Or shoot me. To be honest, she didn't make a move to do either.

"My father!"

"Jay Powell!" Dad yelled. In case Bostwick thought I meant my other father.

"That figures," I heard Bostwick say.

Patty picked up the gun again. She didn't exactly point it at either of us, but the effect was clear and successful. I stopped talking.

Well, I stopped talking to Bostwick, anyway. "I don't get what you're doing," I told Patty. "You can't just walk out. They're not going to go away, but you're not making demands and you're not negotiating. What's your exit strategy?"

It wasn't a huge surprise that she didn't answer me. Instead she checked the tightness of the bands on our arms — which I could have told her was plenty sufficient — and then disappeared into the closet from which she'd previously gotten the exercise bands. She left the door open, but both Dad and I were positioned so we were facing away from the closet. I could hear things jostling but had no idea what was going on in there.

When I heard footsteps coming out of the closet I tried to turn toward the sound, but suddenly there were hands on either side of my head holding it still. "Just a second," Patty said calmly, back to her den-mother voice. "This won't hurt."

Those were the words that scared me the most.

Within seconds there was something — I could only guess duct tape, the current gag of choice — on my mouth and it wasn't coming off. The hands holding my head still were gone and I saw Patty doing the same thing to Dad before he could comprehend what he was seeing and alert the cops.

Patty was wearing an NYPD uniform. It was a little too small for her but she didn't look all that out of place.

"Wasn't it nice of old Dray to leave me something to wear?" she asked. "I guess one of his girlfriends was playing a cop on the show, huh?"

Dad and I couldn't answer but we did grunt a bit, which did no good at all. Patty put the gun she was carrying — one that came from the prop department, meaning it was suitable for a New York cop — in the holster. "Pretty authentic," she said, probably to herself.

From outside I heard Bostwick again, but from farther away. "Plug your phone back in so we can talk, Patrice!" But I knew now that wasn't going to help.

She took her cell phone, which had been lying turned off on the table, and put it on the floor of the trailer. Then she stomped hard on it and smashed it into a large number of pieces.

"It's been nice," she said to us.

Patty looked around the trailer as if deciding after a long sales process whether she wanted to buy it. She walked over to Barney's cage and opened his gate. She stuck her finger in and petted his feathers.

"You really are a nice guy," she said. "Find a way out, okay?"

"Put down the gun!" Barney said.

Patty laughed. "It's in the holster, silly." When she walked away from the cage she actually looked a little sad and she left the cage door open. She went into the small galley kitchen the trailer had for snacks or something and I couldn't see her for a minute. But I could smell something.

Cooking oil. Which can be used as an accelerant.

I tried that thing you see in movies where the person tied to a chair walks the chair to the other person so they can untie each other. But my leg muscles barely responded to my commands and all I could do was raise myself up an inch or two. I tried to tell Dad what I was thinking, but he'd clearly gotten the message himself and was doing exactly what I was doing, with exactly the same degree of success.

Barney flew out of his cage even before Patty reappeared. He flew up to the ceiling and perched finally on a window cutout. I hoped none of the cops would fire in when they saw him, and there was no immediate action from outside. I did hear someone yell, "It's a bird!" I expected, "It's a plane!" to be next, but there was no further conversation I could hear.

Instead I was looking directly at Patty, who did not seem concerned with Dad and me at all, but since I didn't smell smoke I took her indifference as a good sign.

She walked to a spot in the "living space" of the trailer, where I guess Dray had entertained — and I didn't care to think about what that meant — and seemed engrossed with examining the carpet. She finally found a particular spot to the outer side of the trailer, which would translate to the back, and dropped to her knees.

When she ran her hands over the carpet Patty found the mechanism she was looking for and pulled. Sure enough a trapdoor opened and she moved the hatch to one side so she could put herself through. In her NYPD uniform, indistinguishable from the real ones among the many cops outside, she'd be able to slip away completely undetected. And that wasn't even the worst of it.

As she lowered herself down she pulled a lighter from her hand and lit part of the carpet. It caught fire and started almost immediately to spread the flames away from the hatch, which was feeding it with a breeze.

"Goodbye," Patty said, her voice as calm and cheery as if she were selling Mary Kay door to door.

Then she dropped down out of sight and all I could see was her hands reaching up to replace the hatch and keep the spreading flames inside.

"Can't kill a zombie!" Barney said.

CHAPTER TWENTY-SIX

"What's going on in there?" Bostwick sounded frustrated but not alarmed. He hadn't smelled smoke yet. By the time he did, there would be very little chance of getting Dad and me out of the trailer alive.

Barney, clearly upset by the flames (which were moving slowly because I assumed they hadn't hit the cooking oil yet) and the smoke (which was just starting to be visible), began to fly around the small area of the trailer where Dad and I were exchanging panicked glances and trying to communicate with our eyes.

I forced myself to look around the room and consider possibilities. There was no sharp object within reach to cut the exercise bands, and they didn't stretch enough to wriggle out of them. I had tried very hard to push my tongue against the duct tape so I could yell for Bostwick, but that stuff actually lives up to its reputation and would not move. Maybe we can use it to stop terrorism after all. But that wasn't my problem at the moment.

I searched frantically for some tool to use, but there wasn't much in the room and little chance of getting to the next area, especially since that's where the fire was starting. All I could reach with my hands was the back of my chair. All I could reach with my feet was the carpet.

The items on the table — a fragment of Patty's cell phone that had flown up when she stomped it and a small piece of wood the police had left there after it had ricocheted off the windowsill when Dray was shot — didn't seem like much and I couldn't reach them with my hands anyway. Neither could Dad, who was trying to raise his chair by using his hands on the back to lift himself and the seat. He wasn't getting very far, but it was an effort.

"Don't know much about history," Barney said. His agitation was causing him to fall back on phrases he'd learned in his early training.

Wait! Barney. A piece of wood on the table just small enough. Maybe I couldn't reach it with my hands, but my hands weren't necessarily the problem right now.

This was going to take some flexibility,

which has never been my strong suit. But my father, who started his showbiz career as a stand-up comic emceeing for magicians, had learned a thing or two. Sure, it had been almost fifty years, but you take what you can get.

I grunted at him to get his attention, then gestured with my eyes toward the table. Dad looked at the table, then back at me, confused. Then I followed Barney's flight path as he yelled, "A lot of people want you dead, Dray." And I looked back at Dad.

You could see the thought process, and I was hoping it wouldn't take long. The wood . . . Barney . . . the wood . . . Barney . . .

The flames reached the cooking oil at the entrance to the kitchen and I could see the line head toward us, picking up speed and volume. There wasn't much time.

Dad saw it too, took another look at the wood, then at Barney, and his eyes widened.

He'd gotten it.

Positioned closer to the table than I was, he could lean over and get his face close to the table's surface. There was enough play in the duct tape that Dad could manage to open his mouth enough. He lifted, very carefully, the small scrap of wood from the table. He kept it on the duct tape and leaned his head back very carefully. We couldn't afford for him to drop that wood or we were dead. Literally.

Dad sat back, wood on the duct tape. But Barney, freaking out, was not paying attention. And Dad probably knew that trying to shout would cause enough vibration to knock the wood loose. He sat as still as possible, head resting on the seatback.

I tried to yell, "Barney!" but only an incoherent sound emerged from my mouth. Barney did not show any interest.

The thing about a fire is that the flames don't actually kill you. It's the smoke. It fills the space from the bottom up, and that meant Dad and I probably only had a few minutes left before we were unable to breathe at all. I shouted for Barney, louder this time.

And he stopped and perched on the table. That was when I saw my father perform the single most amazing, brave act of his career.

Slowly, deliberately, he lowered his head and kept the wood on the corner of the duct tape holding his mouth. Then he leaned forward to where Barney could see and, more to the point, smell it.

That did the trick. Barney walked over to Dad's face, stared for a moment, and then pecked at the wood. Dad miraculously held on.

Barney clearly liked what he'd tried and pecked at it again. And again. And a few times more. He finally realized Dad wasn't going to let go, so he tried to hook his beak around the back of the wooden chip so he could carry it off. He gave that a few tries, each time inadvertently tearing at the edge of the duct tape.

Sure enough, one time was too many and Barney grabbed the wood out of my father's mouth.

I let out a gasp, the best I could do under the circumstances. But Dad saw that the tape on his mouth had wilted at the end where Barney had been pecking. Dad had a few scratches there too, but he could open his mouth.

"Police!" he screamed. "She got out around the back and set the place on fire! She's out there in an NYPD uniform! GET US OUT OF HERE!"

Bostwick must have been right outside the door because he had pried it open and entered before Dad was finished screaming. Barney took his hard-earned prize to his window perch and sat there gnawing away at it.

The cops rescued us from the trailer in

seconds, literally, and I made sure Barney got out even though his cage did not. They also grabbed a fire extinguisher from the wall of the trailer and put out the flames as quickly as possible. But by that time I was cut out of the chair and standing on solid ground, my legs shaky and my arms fairly useless, breathing in air like it was going out of style. Because for a few moments there, it had been.

Dad hugged me hard, so I guessed his arms were recovering faster than mine. "I don't know what I would have done if something happened to you," he said.

"Me? It was happening to you too."

"I'm used to stuff happening to me. I can deal with that."

"Call Mom," I told him, eyeing some news vans in the distance. "She must have heard by now." Dad took his phone, which amazingly was not melted, out of his pocket and started pushing buttons as he walked away. I exhaled. It felt like it had been a long time since I'd done that.

Before I could do the same and call Consuelo, Bostwick walked over with a face full of reprimand. "Didn't I tell you not to go into the trailer?" he asked.

"My dad was in there and she had a gun. What would you do?"

There were maybe ten uniformed officers surrounding the trailer and another three in cruisers parked nearby. I started scanning each of them suspiciously and Bostwick caught what I was doing. "Don't worry," he said. "We got your pal Patty right after your father called out. The uniforms they give people on the show aren't exactly the same, and hers really didn't fit."

"Those actresses are like a size zero," I said. "I'm surprised it fits any human over the age of eight. You arrested her?"

"No, we bought her a hot cocoa and sent her on her way. The woman took two people hostage in a trailer and tried to burn it down. Not to mention we had enough on her for Dray Mattone's murder to arrest her *before* you got her to confess. Yeah, we took her away. If you're still her lawyer, you have a lot of work to do."

"Thanks, but I think I'm off that case," I said. "It's so awkward when the defense attorney has to testify against her client. Where's Barney?" I hadn't seen what the cops had done with him.

"Officer LaRosa put a coat over him so he wouldn't fly away on the way out. Then we put him in one of the cruisers. Nobody wanted to go back in for a hot birdcage."

"That was the smart thing to do, but I

wouldn't want to have to ride home in that cruiser," I said.

"We put him in the car nobody likes," Bostwick said.

"Did Patty tell you her whole story?" I asked.

"Patty wouldn't tell me the score of the Yankee game if I asked her. Patty has clammed up other than to say she wants her lawyer. The other one." Jamie would be getting the phone call if he hadn't already. I wondered what he would think, but the fact was he was probably on his way to defend his client even now. That's the way our justice system is set up, and it works.

I did my best to fill Bostwick in on what had been said in the trailer. It wouldn't be usable in court because it would be hearsay evidence unless I was the one on the stand, but I figured it would be helpful to Bostwick for building a case. He listened, took a few notes, and asked a couple of questions but mostly just let me talk. If I'd been at all attracted to him, he would have been the perfect man for those few minutes.

When I'd finished, Bostwick chewed over what I'd said. "You're saying that someone framed whatever-her-real-name-is for a crime she really did commit? That's crazy."

"And yet, I think it's true. Patty could easily have gotten away with the murder, or assisted suicide, or whatever you want to call it," I said.

"I want to call it murder. We'll see what the D.A. wants to call it."

The news vans in the distance started getting closer; the cops must have given them the okay. They still wouldn't allow reporters really close to an active crime scene, but they would allow photography. Lo and Sam would be seeing me on television, which had become kind of routine over the past week or so.

"Either way, she could have just left town and become anonymous after she shot Dray," I answered. "Instead she chose to stay in the house she'd rented and keep acting like she was sick so she could send me to the set with Barney every day and scurry around in her curly wig when she wanted to find out who was setting her up. I guess it was personal."

Bostwick shook his head at the sheer nuttiness of the situation. "And she never found out who it was."

"No, but I think I know," I said. "Are you interested in making another arrest?"

I saw Dad get off his phone looking oddly pleased with himself. I imagine it felt good to know how much Mom cared about him, as if that had ever been in question.

"For what?" Bostwick asked. "You can't be held responsible for pointing police to a crime the person really did commit."

"What about fabricating evidence? Knowing in advance the crime was going to take place and doing nothing about it? Lying to investigators? Is there a charge in there anywhere?" I don't know why, but the idea of manipulating the investigation (and in some ways, me) was getting me annoyed.

"Again, that's for the D.A.," the detective said. "But I am curious to see who and why."

"Good," I said. "Come by my office in about two hours." Then I texted Sam and said I'd be late. He immediately answered: *We're always open.*

Chapter Twenty-Seven

"Are you still looking for an agent? I might be interested in a few new clients."

Mandy Baron was sitting in the client's owner chair in front of my desk. She smiled an eager, ingratiating smile I'm sure had gotten her over a number of hurdles in her past. "I sort of figured," she said. "Your text said you might be able to help. But I thought you really didn't work with, you know, people."

Consuelo chuckled quietly behind her desk, pretending to be engrossed in paperwork. Barney, reunited with Maisie in the only birdcage we had now, fluttered his wings a little but otherwise did not comment on the action.

"Well, since we spoke I've been thinking it over," I told her, leaning forward in my chair to appear interested, if not fascinated with Mandy. "A few people who I know are reliable and will work regularly wouldn't be a bad addition to my base. The thing about animals is that if there's a part, they have very little ego about auditioning and that sort of thing. But with you I know from what I've observed that we can get along."

"Oh, I think we can," Mandy agreed.

I'd texted Mandy with the number she'd given me on her business card after checking with Heather Alizondo about Mandy's actual lack of an agent. Heather had pulled the "TV directors don't know anything" card and referred me to Les Mannix, of all people, who said after checking his records that Mandy had been signed with an agent when he'd hired her for the guest spot on *Dead City,* but he had no idea if she'd left the agency since then, a time of about three weeks. He gave me her agent's name and contact information and hung up, saying he was negotiating with a cable network at this moment. So clearly he'd stop to take a call from the bird's agent.

"Great," I said. I pulled a client intake form from my top drawer, stuck it on a clipboard with a pen attached to it, and handed it to Mandy. "Why don't you fill that out and then we can talk?"

Mandy looked over the form and began writing on it as Consuelo and I did our best to look busy. She stopped at one point and looked up at me. "You need the phone number for my old agent?"

"Yes, for the records. I need to confirm with him that you are no longer a client." No reputable theatrical agent will accept a client who is still affiliated with another agency.

"Oh," Mandy said, but she kept writing. After a few minutes of our dramatic "working" pageant, she handed me back the clipboard.

I looked it over. "Okay, great," I said with just the right level of enthusiasm (not very much). "Now I have a couple of questions."

Mandy looked up, audition face on, interested but not desperate. Years of practice had gone into this look. "Shoot," she said. It was only apropos.

"Why did you leave your last agent?" I asked.

"Well, it was sort of a mutual thing, but the truth is, I wasn't getting the kind of roles I was hoping for." Mandy pretended to see something on the back of her hand and brush it off.

"Really. The *Dead City* role was a guest star on a network show. That seems pretty good."

Knowing Mandy couldn't see her, Consuelo looked over at me and gave her head a slight shake. I was overplaying my role.

"Yeah, but it was all about my body," she said. "It's a zombie, so I'm in lot of makeup, but they manage to get me into what amounts to a bikini and it's implied I'm naked under the sheet at the morgue. I'm tired of that. I want to *act.*"

"So you want me to find you roles that are about your talent, not your looks," I said.

"Yeah. Not that I mind them thinking I look good. It's gotten me places before." She smiled with an expression indicating that we girls understand that kind of thing.

Unfortunately for Mandy, I understood it only too well. "Just one more question," I said. "Have you ever framed a colleague for murder?"

If Mandy wanted to convince me she could act, she'd have to do better than the shocked face she put on at that moment. Surprised, sure. She hadn't seen the question coming. But shocked? Not even close. Her eyes told me she had already concocted the response.

Here it came: "What are you talking about?" Original, huh?

"I think you know. You planted the letters that were supposedly written by Patty Basilico saying she was pregnant with Dray Mattone's baby. You told the police she'd

397

been sleeping with Dray. You wanted them to think she had shot him in a rage over their broken love affair. The part that I don't understand is why. What did that get you?"

"I don't know what you're talking about." She was still trotting out the old standards.

"You don't? You've been lying to me the whole time. This isn't even your agent's phone number; I got that number from Les Mannix fifteen minutes ago. You were asking me about representation because you wanted to hear more about the case against Patty and you knew I was working with her. So I'll ask again: Why? Why frame Patty for Dray's murder?"

The expression in Mandy's eyes turned cold and angry. She took a dollar from her purse and laid it on my desk. "I'm retaining you as my lawyer, so anything I say is protected," she said. "Yeah, I framed Patty because she was moving in on Dray at just the time he was going to get me a part in a spin-off of *Dead City*. A regular role!"

"You were sleeping with Dray?" As if I hadn't figured that.

"I don't ever remember sleeping, no." Mandy laughed, but it wasn't with pleasure. "You know how it is for actresses."

I didn't really know how it is for actresses, but that seemed a minor issue at the moment. "So that justified getting her arrested for murder?" I said.

Mandy waved a hand. "It was just to shake her up. I mean, where does the girl who owns the parrot get the nerve to move in when I'm trying to get a full-time job?"

"How'd you get into the trailer?"

Mandy gave me a look indicating my naiveté. "Didn't we just establish that I could get in there whenever I wanted? She wrote out the letter and signed it. I just found it in the trailer and left it out where it could be found. I figured they'd check the handwriting and see it was hers and that would be it."

I knew she hadn't taught Barney all the new phrases he'd seemed to have learned in a fraction of the usual time; Patty herself had set that up and then feigned innocence to indicate someone else had access to the parrot. Me, maybe. Luckily the cops hadn't cared much about that.

"Well, here's the crazy part of it," I told Mandy. "You set up the woman who actually shot Dray Mattone. And even if you didn't know that — and I'm sure you didn't, based on the way your jaw just dropped a foot — it's still a crime to plant false evidence. So I'll be alerting the police to that immediately." I nodded to Consuelo, who picked up her phone and punched in the number I'd given her.

Mandy, having retrieved her jaw from the floor, stood up and looked me in the eye somewhat haughtily. "You can't," she reminded me, pointing at the picture of George Washington lying on my desk. "I retained your services."

Following her lead I stood up too. "First of all, if you think you can buy my work for a dollar, you clearly have a very poor sense of economy. But there's one thing you didn't take into account — I never accepted your offer. I'm not your lawyer, lady." I picked up the dollar bill and stuffed it into her jacket pocket. "Find another. You're going to need one."

She didn't have time to answer because the office door opened and Sergeant Joe Bostwick walked in with two uniformed cops. "You have the confession?" he said.

Mandy saw Consuelo hand him the voice recorder she'd had on her desk during the whole conversation. Bostwick took it and nodded at Consuelo. "Thanks."

"You can't do that!" Mandy tried to protest. "I'm just an actress trying to get work."

I guess Bostwick didn't see the point to handcuffs because when he nodded toward the uniformed officers, they just took Mandy's arms and started her toward the door.

"Mandy Baron, you are under arrest for tampering with evidence and obstructing justice," the cop to her left said. He started reciting her Miranda rights and was up to her ability to pay for an attorney by the time they walked through the office door.

"Well, you were right about that one," Bostwick said to me. "Now if you'd listened to me about the actual shooter, you could have saved us both a whole lot of trouble. I told you not to get involved in that case."

"That's what I like about you, Joe," I said. "You don't rub it in."

He smiled and thanked us, then checked with Barney by tapping on the cage on his way out of the office, which just annoyed Maisie. "Polly want a cracker?" he asked.

That reminded me. "Did you ever find Harve Lembeck?" I asked Bostwick.

He looked over. "Yeah, Baker found him, actually. He had decided that by giving Dray the gun he'd committed some huge crime and was hiding out in the storeroom behind a bar his cousin owns in Jersey City. When we told him we weren't looking to send him back to jail, he relaxed so much I think he'll sleep for a week. After he sobers up."

"Does he know anything that'll help with the case?" Consuelo asked.

"He knows who was coming and going from the trailer. He can identify your pal Patty as the woman in the curly wig, after we showed him a picture of her in it. Funny how he couldn't at the memorial service, huh?"

"It's all context, Joe," I said. "I'm surprised Detective Baker could talk enough to get people to tell him where Harve was; I've never heard the man say a word."

Bostwick stared. "Really? In the precinct you can't ever get him to shut up. Honestly, the man talks all day long. Drives me nuts."

I absorbed that and moved on. "Harve," I reminded Bostwick.

"Harve still doesn't know where the bullets came from, but I'm fairly sure an experienced operator like Patty, or whatever her name really is, probably brings her own. I'm surprised she used the prop gun, but I guess it made it easier for her because the weapon would be traced back to the production company."

"What about the height differential? Forensics said the killer was five-eleven. Patty's nowhere near that."

Bostwick looked sheepish. "She stood on a box. Better angle or something."

He said his goodbyes again and this time actually left. I slumped back in my desk chair and wondered how I could have aged twenty-eight years in the past week. I looked over at the cage with the two birds in it. "We're going to have to find a place for Barney," I said. "This is the second time we've had clients orphaned when their owners got arrested." That was, after all, indirectly how I'd gotten Bruno.

"I think I'll take him home, if that's okay with you," Consuelo said. "We don't know who his real owners are because Patty just got him from somebody as an excuse to be on the set."

"It's okay with me, but we're making this a habit. We need to establish a new rule in the office after this: no adopting clients."

She nodded fervently. "Good rule," she said. "By the way, I did some checking. Giant Productions went out of business two days ago after the principal owner was convicted of fraud. That's why we never heard about Bagels." Welcome to showbiz.

Consuelo seemed awfully cheerful considering all that had gone on, and then I got it. "What's new with Oreo?" I asked.

"I'm going to meet with them tomorrow," she said, grinning widely. "I think it looks good."

■ ■ ■ ■

The news vans were back at my front door. After all this time, it was actually sort of comforting to see them again. I figured I owed the reporters a statement, so I parked the car in the driveway and let them ambush me, answered a few questions about what it was like to be almost fricasseed in Dray Mattone's trailer, and then beat a hasty retreat to my front door to await my inevitable immortalization on all the networks, YouTube, and other means of entertainment disguised as information.

My parents were sitting at the kitchen table when I came in, sharing a bottle of white wine. Dad, who had left directly from the Astoria lot as soon as Bostwick and Baker had released us, was grinning from ear to ear, something I had not seen since they'd arrived back from the Greek tour.

"My phone's been ringing off the hook," he told me as soon as the dog madness which accompanies any return to my home had subsided. I sat down after getting myself a glass to join them in their celebration of whatever this was. "A bunch of my usual bookers saw me on TV almost being roasted, and all of a sudden we're in demand."

It took me a second. I looked at my mother. "We?"

Mom actually blushed. "I might have been a little hasty with the whole retirement thing," she said. "It was lucky that I didn't see the TV until you two were already safe, but just the thought of it . . . Maybe I want to spend a little more time working with my husband, and then come home now and again to see my daughter. You two are precious to me." I got the impression Mom had opened the bottle of wine — or the one I saw sticking out of my recycling bin — before Dad had gotten home.

My father reached over and hugged Mom. "All I could think about in that trailer was you and Kay," he said. The fact that I had also been in the trailer put a weird spin on it, but hey, Dad also had a head start on the wine. They were happy and that was what I cared about.

But the dogs were not, and having been fed by my parents, they needed to be walked by me. Given their current mood and state of inebriation, Mom and Dad could probably do with some time alone in the house for a while, so this seemed an opportune moment to go meet Sam at Cool Beans. With all three leashed up and ready to go, we hit the streets of Scarborough and took

405

off in search of adventure.

Or a cup of coffee and Sam. That sounded good.

Sure enough, after all three dogs had completed their walking tasks, we headed into the coffee shop through the door Sam had indeed left unlocked despite the closed sign in the window. I know he doesn't mind my dogs walking around inside, so I let them all off their leashes and they began exploring as soon as we got there.

Finding Sam was a trifle more difficult than usual, since he was not in the main room where business is usually done. But I could hear voices coming from the office behind the dining room (that's what Sam calls it) and walked in to see what was up.

Sam was sitting with his feet up on the desk, and Lo Toscadero, with whom I had texted feverishly after she'd seen me on CNN, was ensconced in the swivel chair on the other side of the desk. Each of them held a coffee mug, but I had the feeling any coffee they were drinking was of the Irish variety.

"Hey, guys," I said, figuring this was not going to be the time for Sam and me to have a deep personal conversation. "What'd I miss?"

"Not much," Lo said. "We expected you,

like, an hour ago." She giggled. Yep, Irish coffee, okay.

"It takes time to almost get burned up and then catch someone obstructing justice," I explained. There was no third chair in the office and I could hear the dogs rummaging around in the outer room.

Sam saw me looking around the room and stood up. "Let's go out to the dining room," he said. So we did.

He made a cup in my designated mug — I get my own personal mug in the shape of a dog that no one else can use at Cool Beans — and without asking added a shot of Baileys Irish Cream from a bottle he keeps behind the counter. He knew what kind of day I'd had.

We sat at one of the tables and didn't say anything for a while. I think Sam and Lo were wondering how to broach the subject with me, and to be fair, I would have wondered that myself if the tables were turned. We drank our coffees with the extra added attractions in them and let the combination of caffeine and alcohol do its magic.

"I saw on TV that *Dead City* got picked up by one of the cable networks," Lo said. It figured. The extra publicity had finally convinced someone there was still some milk left in the old cow.

"A bunch of people are back at work." I sighed. There was another long silence.

"So someone tried to burn you down today." Lo has the gift of tact. She wasn't employing it now, but she has that gift.

"Yep," I said. I let the warmth radiate out from my stomach to everywhere else. "She sure did."

"I'm glad she didn't," Sam volunteered. His soft tone indicated that if Lo had not ventured by to commiserate, his words might have had a different connotation.

"So am I," I said.

Bruno came over to be patted and was not disappointed. That meant Eydie would follow him, since in her mind she is clearly more deserving. Steve just followed Eydie because that's what he does. Three people, three dogs, no waiting.

"You should offer this as a service," I told Sam. "Customers come in and a dog is immediately assigned to them for petting."

"You know, most bird agents don't end up hanging out with murderers," Lo said, to the point as usual. "What do you think it says about you?"

I looked over at Sam, who was looking back at me. Another night, I guessed. I turned to face Lo again.

"Just lucky, I guess," I said.

ACKNOWLEDGMENTS

I know I'll sound like a broken record (anybody remember broken records? What am I supposed to say now, a malfunctioning streaming feed?) but I just started the process of getting this book to you. Many people have helped since then, and they deserve some credit.

Thank you to David Baldeosingh Rotstein for the lovely jacket design for the original publisher's edition and to all those at St. Martin's Press who shepherded this book and this series through the pipeline. Special thanks to Marcia Markland and Nettie Finn for making it coherent.

I can't begin to imagine how you'd ever have seen this story without the diligent work of Josh Getzler and the gang at HSG Agency, who got me into a room with Marcia to begin with and said, "Tell her your idea." Things went on from there.

I appreciate each and every one of my

readers but can't thank you all by name. Just assume you're thanked and that you never go unnoticed. Without readers I'm some person in a room typing.

Booksellers of all stripes, librarians, bloggers who specialize in the crime fiction area, magazines like *Crimespree* and *Mystery Scene:* Don't ever stop what you're doing. We authors need to reach readers, and you're the ones who make that even vaguely possible. We all love you.

To my family, my friends, and my dog: It's been a rough year, but we're through it now and I can't even imagine how I'd have managed without you (although the dog sometimes made it a tiny bit more difficult, and you know who you are, Gizmo). Thanks for keeping my eyes on the goal and never letting me wallow. Too much. You're the best, each and every one of you.

E. J. Copperman
April 2018

ABOUT THE AUTHOR

E. J. Copperman is someone you could sit down and have a beer with, if that's your thing. Or a hot chocolate. Or a diet soda. Actually, you can have anything you want as long as you don't care what E. J. is drinking.

E. J. is the author of a number of mystery series. The Agent to the Paws series begins with *Dog Dish of Doom.* Other series by this multitalented writer include the Haunted Guesthouse mysteries, Asperger's mysteries, and Mysterious Detective mysteries.